the Weretiger

Stories of the Supernatural

Shaiontoni Bose, Arundhuti Dasgupta,
Bunny Gupta and Nilanjana Gupta

PENGUIN BOOKS

Penguin Books India (P) Ltd., 11 Community Centre, Panchsheel Park, New Delhi
110 017, India
Penguin Books Ltd., 80 Strand, London WC2R 0RL, UK
Penguin Putnam Inc., 375 Hudson Street, New York, NY 10014, USA
Penguin Books Australia Ltd., 250 Camberwell Road, Camberwell, Victoria 3124,
Australia
Penguin Books Canada Ltd., 10 Alcorn Avenue, Suite 300, Toronto, Ontario M4V
3B2, Canada
Penguin Books (NZ) Ltd., Cnr Rosedale & Airborne Roads, Albany, Auckland,
New Zealand

First published by Penguin Books India 2002

For sale in the Indian Subcontinent, Singapore and Malaysia only

Typeset in Sabon by Eleven Arts, New Delhi
Printed at Thomson Press, New Delhi

PENGUIN BOOKS
THE WERETIGER

Shaiontoni Bose is a freelance writer and illustrator who lives with her family in Mumbai.

❖I❖

Arundhuti Dasgupta has a degree in economics, is a journalist and has worked with several leading business newspapers. She lives in Mumbai with her husband and two daughters.

❖I❖

Bunny Gupta is a well-known writer and freelance journalist who co-authored the best-selling *Calcutta Cookbook*. She lives with her family in Kolkata.

❖I❖

Nilanjana Gupta teaches English at Jadavpur University, Kolkata, and her passion is popular culture.

Also includes stories by Easterine Iralu, Pradip Gupta, Kaushik Banerjee, Sugato Chaudhuri, Arabinda Ray, Kashinath Sen Sharma, Louis Herbert Gray, Phoenix and Rohini Chowdhury.

To all our friends who have over the years become family, and
to our families who have become more like friends.
With love and thanks and hope for many,
many more good times.

Contents

Acknowledgements   *ix*
Introduction   *xiii*

ANIMAL AND NATURE SPIRITS
  1. The Weretiger   3
  2. The Pot of Water   8
  3. Ropuilliani   14
  4. The Man Who Became a Bear   20
  5. Ulat Bagh   24
  6. The Song of the Hunter   26
  7. The Third Eye   30
  8. The Old Man   38
  9. The White Boat   41
 10. Fishing in Troubled Waters   48
 11. Yeo Ka?   51
 12. The Helpful Spirit   56
 13. The Legend of the Leaping Dolphins   60
 14. The Temple Spirits   65

HAUNTED HOUSES
 15. From Across the Ages   71
 16. The Gold Mohurs   77
 17. Motihari Bungalow   80
 18. Neel Kuthi   88
 19. The House in Benaras   92
 20. The Well   95

21. Krishnaveni   100
22. The Courtyard   104
23. Room 2   106
24. One Dark Night   113
25. Footsteps in the Dark   117
26. The Poltergeist   122

VILLAGE STORIES
27. Why Women are Witches   129
28. The Lemon Tree   131
29. The Wedding Feast   135
30. Raaghu and the Kudpalbhoota   137
31. One Summer Afternoon   141
32. Silence   146
33. Kosi   148

TALES FROM THE CITY
34. The Legend of Padmasambhava   155
35. The Living Dead   157
36. Aida   163
37. The Auto Ride   165
38. The Dharavi Murder Case   167
39. Shah Mat   170
40. The Piano   172
41. Advice to Motorists   176
42. A Spirituous Interlude   177
43. What's in a Name?   181
44. Ticketless Travellers   185
45. The 11.43 to Nowhere   189

POSSESSION AND REINCARNATION
46. Nikhil   197
47. The Homecoming   207
48. Her Grandfather's Voice   215
49. The Greedy Imp   219
50. The First Wife   222
51. Strong Ties   224

Afterword   230

acknowledgements

This book would not have been possible without help from friends, family and even complete strangers. We have found support and encouragement from places and people we never expected any from, and often doors opened when we thought all had closed.

Firstly we would like to thank the authors who gave us permission to use their stories: Easterine Iralu ('The Weretiger' and 'The Man Who Became a Bear'), Arabinda Ray ('The Gold Mohurs'), Kaushik Banerjee ('Footsteps in the Dark'), Sugato Chaudhuri ('A Spirituous Interlude'), Louis Herbert Gray ('The Legend of Padmasambhava'), Phoenix ('Silence') and Rohini Chowdhury ('Kosi'). 'Kosi' was the runner-up in the New Writer Prose and Poetry Prizes 2001 (www.thenewwriter.com/prizewinners.htm). Easterine Iralu's stories are taken from her collection, *The Windhover Collection* (Steven Halekar, 2001). 'The Legend of Padmasambhava' is taken from *The Mythology of All Races*, edited by Louis Herbert Gray (Boston: Marshall Jones Co, 1917). The remaining stories have not been previously published.

We would also like to thank Kashinath Sen Sharma for allowing us to translate his story 'Krishnaveni' and for telling us the story on which 'Room 2' is based; Pradip Gupta for allowing us to translate his story 'From Across the Ages'; Bijoya Goswami for retelling 'The Living Dead' from the *Kathasaritsagar*; Manabendu

Bandhopadhyay for narrating the story on which 'Fishing in Troubled Waters' is based, Saurabh Chanda for the story on which 'Advice to Motorists' is based; and Anindita De for the story on which 'The Old Man' is based.

Our thanks to D.D. Shetty for being an invaluable source for stories and information. Sudeshna Sen, Partha Ranjan Das, Nandini Das, Nandita Lahiri, Michael James, George Cherian, Indira Balagopalan, Veena Saksena, Dio, Amit Mukherjee, Amitabha Chaudhuri, Vandana, Ram Prasad (RP), Amita Das, Purnima Datta, Mrs Dasgupta and Sharbani Dasgupta, Shomshukhla Das, Krishni Kamath, Chandra Asani, Mr Damu, Mr Tandel, Devamita Sen, Bula Asani, Anagha Patil, Devabrata Nag, Bhaskar Mitter—all told us wonderful tales and anecdotes that we have woven into the book whenever and wherever we could. Their contribution is invaluable and we would not have finished the book without them. Thanks also to Wangchuk Basi for providing much valuable information.

We extend our thanks to Pinaki De for his wonderful cover designs, all of which were brilliant and hard to choose from. We wish we could use them all!

Malini, Gayatri, Hemant Barve, Seeta Chaudhuri, Pronoti Deb, Jaya Chaliha, Nandita Gupta—Thank you for being sounding boards, proofreaders and helping hands whenever we needed you. A special thanks to RDG Systems and Software Pvt Ltd. and to Arundhati Gupta, Sujoy Das and Mihir Ray for patient and practical support at all times, and answering every SOS!

We got invaluable reference material from sources as diverse as Learner's Press and the Indian *Gazettes*, which put us on track for information to research. Other books which we found useful were *The Mythology of All Races*, edited by Louis Herbert Gray, *Folklore of the Santhal Parganas*, translated by Cecil Henry Bompas (London: David Nutt, 1909), and R.E. Enthoven, *The Folklore of Bombay* (Oxford: OUP, 1924).

We would also like to mention Sayoni Basu of Penguin, whose enthusiasm and fortitude in the face of four odds helped bring this book together in its own mad way.

Last but not least, our husbands and children whose pride and enthusiasm were evident at all times.

All of us are also quite sure that there were many unseen forces and spirits at work; encouraging and pushing us along every time we thought of packing away our keyboards and pens. Thank you.

Introduction

'Hello. My name is Kashinath Sen Sharma. My friend, Mr S, tells me that you are writing about ghosts and all ghostly things. Tell me, have you ever seen a ghost?'

These were the opening lines of a telephone call which one of us received. She mumbled a weak 'no' to this voice over the telephone and also felt a vague need to apologize. 'Sorry, I have not. But, have you, sir?' she asked her voice a trifle tremulous at the possibility of turning away a ghost tale on account of her not having seen one.

'Of course, several times!' Mr Sen Sharma answered. 'I can tell you all about it when you come and see me.'

We were curious and apprehensive for there had been a number of times that a promise of a good story had petered out on its actual telling. We were once told of a man having spent a night with a ghost but it turned out that he saw a shadow flit past his door and a tinkle of bells which made him think it was a ghost. And on so thinking what did he do? He turned over on to his other side and said, '*Oye bhoot, chale ja.*' (Hey ghost, go away.) A funny anecdote. Definitely. But a ghost story?

Mr Sen Sharma deserves our apologies for having harboured such doubts about him. He had a bag full of stories, some entertaining, some disturbing and all of them worth a listen if not a write.

Like Mr Sen Sharma, we met several interesting and fascinating people in the course of the book. Most of them had a story, an anecdote or a family folktale and if nothing else at least a theory about all things supernatural and ghostly. Some told us that spirits are like our alter egos; others said that a spirit finds its way into unhappy homes and some said that spirits are always on the lookout for weak bodies to inhabit.

Sometimes these conversations distilled themselves into stories or sparked off a debate that eventually transformed into a story. But at the end of this entire exercise, we are sure that all those late-night chats and long hours spent poring over books or gazing bleary-eyed at our computer screens were very useful. We spoke to hundreds of people, delved into books, gazettes and memories of grandmothers, aunts and uncles of all those who would let us and tried to excavate some local folklore wherever we went. These stories took on shapes and shades as we discovered sociological and cultural issues that shaped the beliefs of the people and their lives during the time that the stories were set. For example, in a story set just after India's independence, we found references to the 1857 War of Independence which was sparked off by Mangal Pande. 'The Motihari Bungalow' recreates the acute oppression of indigo dye workers under the British rule.

Early on in our search for stories, we found that trying to prove the authenticity of the stories was not such a good idea. Fact or fiction was not the issue. In the tales themselves and in the minds of the tellers, the real, the experience and the fears merged, and the best stories were those that preserved or explained old faiths and customs. Several stories are based on fears and superstitions.

All the stories have been extensively researched. When we found little help in libraries or on the Internet, we tapped academicians and acquaintances. Our search often led us into areas of which we had little knowledge. But every time we found ourselves sinking into the debris of information, we found a story or an anecdote to pull us out.

We came across believers, storytellers and people who helped us with our research in the unlikeliest of places. Once, for instance, we heard a chilling tale inside a modern-day infotech office. The storyteller was a young programmer who told us his story without a trace of disbelief or doubt in his voice.

Researching the stories brought in more stories. For example, when digging around for information about Kolis for the story 'Yeo Ka?', we stumbled into another fascinating tale about them that has been told as 'The White Boat'. 'Raghu and the Kudpalbhoota' too evolved after days of researching *churails, shaitans* and *daivas*.

We found that stories sometimes repeat themselves, as with the many versions of the stories that we finally carried as 'The 11.43 to Nowhere' or 'The Gold Mohurs'. Similarly there were innumerable variations on a core group of stories about shape-changing animals, haunted houses, and possessions, as is reflected in this collection. The belief that jungle or nature spirits look after their own is seen in 'The Old Man' and 'The Third Eye'. There were several other stories that held out the same folk theories but, reluctant though we were to keep anything out of this selection, we had to choose.

Some of the stories are family heirlooms. 'The Gold Mohurs', 'The First Wife', 'Neel Kuthi' and several others have been handed down the generations. Some are retellings of popular folktales, like 'The Lemon Tree'. And some we smoked out of dead ruins and dark nights where the storytellers had no face or form!

Spirits or *bhoots* come in a variety of shapes and sizes. To classify them all under one head is not only erroneous but would be extremely disrespectful to their clan. The *Kuttichathan* from Kerala is modelled on a tiny impish character who is mischievous and loves embarrassing people and getting them into trouble. The *bramhadaitya* in 'The Helpful Spirit' is a benign spirit trapped in a large frame. In 'The Lemon Tree' and 'One Summer Afternoon', the supernatural manifests itself in a frightening physical peculiarity. We have tried to keep the flavour of the original telling in all our stories.

As we worked on the book, we found that in the field of the supernatural there is a strange blurring between the 'rural' and the 'urban'; the 'primitive' and the 'modern'. These divides disappear when the imagination is challenged beyond reason. In life, when so many things seem to be beyond the confines of the rational, when coincidences determine the future, when illnesses can strike and wipe out entire regions, when nature's caprice can destroy a whole year's crops, perhaps the only logic that can help man to survive is that of the illogical.

We also found that spirits, djinns, bramhadaityas, bhoots and *prets* are not just the stuff of grandmothers' tales. Customs, behavioural norms and day-to-day life is dictated by belief in the existence of such spirits and their like even today.

Sir Herbert Risley, in his introduction to the *Census of India* (1901), wrote that he found that the rituals of the tribal people of India are addressed to

> the indefinite something which they fear and attempt to propitiate [which is] not a person at all in any sense of the word . . . [but] the shifting and shadowy company of unknown powers or influences making for evil influences rather than for good, which resides in the primeval forest, in the crumbling hills, in the rushing river, in the spreading tree; which gives its spring to the tiger, its venom to the snake, which generates jungle fever and walks abroad in the terrible guise of cholera, small pox or murrain.

This is true even today, in spirit, more than in form.

We hope this book will make a good read and will capture both the variousness and the continuity of the supernatural in India. It is not meant to be a treatise or a representative collection. Some regions are not represented, others may seem to be over-represented; what matters is that the reader glimpses the huge expanse of folktales, fairytales, superstitions and customs which are the thirteen rivers and seven seas of our collective imagination. This vast repository tolerates monsters, princes, sages, peasants, gods and demons, and binds us in one endless shimmering fabric.

✦✛✦

animal and nature Spirits

the Weretiger

While the great correspondence seen between the animal and the human is perceived as an indication of supernatural power, such beliefs increasingly sit uneasily with the emerging Christian values in the Naga community.

He was a half-man, half-spirit, the last in a long line of tigermen. Tsaricho's father and his father before him had carried the spirit of the tiger in their beings. Many in his family thought he would bequeath this strange legacy to his son, who was young but not much younger than Tsaricho himself had been when he became a tigerman. But the lad would have none of it; he attended the mission school and sang the song of the Lamb. It was not long before Tsaricho could tell that the boy did not have it in him to carry the spirit of the tiger. To his credit he refrained from imposing his will on his only son. He checked the elders who would have interfered: Let it be, he has a destiny different from ours.

More and more often these days, Tsaricho found himself remembering his childhood. Had he been seven or eight when his father had called him to his side of the fire and shared portions of chicken liver and fragments of country ginger with him? He could not remember that now but he could certainly recall a time when he had not carried the spirit of the tiger. His life seemed to fall into two sections. That first part was light and unburdened by the knowledge that marred the rest of his life, after he had crossed the boundary and begun to walk in the footprints of his father and his father before him.

If his son had shown any inclination of wanting to carry the tiger, Tsaricho would have been the last man to stop him. But the boy clung to his mother and cringed in fear on those nights when the tiger came up to their compound, treading heavily on the soft soil and making low but unmistakable noises. Some nights the tiger came up so close they could smell him: a thick musky smell that he left behind in the spots where he had rested. But the boy's heart did not leap within him as Tsaricho's still did on those mornings when he came upon the pug marks of the animal or inhaled the musk where the long grass had been pressed down.

Such mornings reminded him of his great-grandfather, a tall lean man who had died when Tsaricho was five and a half. The village people said that Tsaricho was lucky: he had seen his great-grandfather, who was the most powerful tigerman for many villages around. Two men of a neighbouring village had made the mistake of crossing him. It had been a heated argument. One of them had threatened: 'See that your tiger does not come near our village gate. I have yet to see a tiger that is immune to bullets.' As the men turned to go, they glimpsed the old man's face. It was the look that Tsaricho remembered—his countenance darkening like a rapidly gathering storm sky.

The two men never reached their village. They were on the thin path that intersected the woods when they heard the rumble of thunder. They turned this way and that, but all around them trees crashed down uprooted and clawed. The first man turned to shout but words failed to come: in the next moment his blood froze within him as he saw the giant figure of a tiger leap out of the darkness. As the tiger descended upon him, his last thought was that he had never seen a more magnificent animal before, the symmetry of blood and sinew wonderfully displayed in that mid-air leap.

The second man turned and ran back the way they had come. But the fallen trees raised their branches to block his exit; he ran into openings only to be pushed back by the roots of trees and the blackening spirits of dead trees that deceived him into thinking that there were trees where none stood. The forest exploded with unbearable sounds—the wailing of old women, the rapid yodelling of warriors—which were silenced by the insistent growl of the tiger. But though the sound surrounded him, he could not see the tiger and dared not move any further. His heart pounding within him, he waited for the beast to end the terrible suspense with inevitable death. He did not have to wait long. Claws of iron tore into him. Indescribable agony shot through him as one limb was torn off, and another limb followed. Then all feeling left him.

Two days later the clansmen of the two victims came out to kill the tiger and avenge their deaths. From the day the tiger was killed, Tsaricho's great-grandfather began to die. It was not an uncommon event, for the village community had included weretigers before him. But the nexus between tiger and man was still attended by the mystery and the awe that shrouds the supernatural. The old man refused to eat, saying that he found no pleasure in food now. By the fifth day, he was alarmingly weak. A week after the death of the tiger, the old man died.

Tsaricho kept to himself what he had seen in those final moments as his great-grandfather was dying. Across the wall of the old man's room, the shadow of a great tiger appeared and stayed for seconds before life ebbed out of the man. Tsaricho had never told anyone about it. He had been such a child then; would anyone have believed him? One night he began to talk in his sleep. His mother prodded him awake and, still groggy from sleep, he burst out, 'Mother, did you see it too? The shadow of the tiger in great-grandfather's room?' His mother shushed him, 'Hush, son, hush, you mustn't speak of these things.'

Tsaricho did not become a weretiger immediately after he had eaten from his father's plate. In the following month, when he was hunting with his father, a wildcat scurried into the undergrowth. Before its hindquarters were lost from view, Tsaricho had raised his catapult and was readying to let go when his father knocked the weapon out of his hands. 'Father!' he protested. But his father's grim face silenced him. 'Don't be stupid, son, and are you not a child still?' Thus it was that he came to learn that a weretiger progressed from lower forms of life till he attained the final stature of the tiger.

Now that he was a grown man, his tiger was both praised and feared, a great cat almost as big as his great-grandfather's. In the seasons when cows were let loose, neighbouring villages complained that they were steadily losing cattle. What was he to do? Plagues and wars were few and far between, and the village population had grown unchecked so there was little game left for his tiger.

'I'll think of something,' his uncle told him when he confided his fears.

Some time later, he came up with a suggestion: 'There is a man who has been on his own for seven months now. He carries wounds from an ambush. Send your tiger to keep the man company till he grows strong.' So Tsaricho sent out his tiger to the banks of the river where the man was.

When the man first heard the sounds of the tiger he was afraid. 'Elder brother, do me no harm,' he shouted across. But as the days passed, the man was comforted by the evidence that there was game enough to feed the two of them and every night he called out into the darkness: 'It is I, elder brother, may you sleep well.' Game was plentiful and the tiger was no longer hungry and the man was no longer lonely.

The tiger heard him and stayed on, lending his presence to the man. He longed to draw nearer but he knew that the man would retreat. One night while the man was fast asleep in his tree house, the tiger climbed up to him and noiselessly entered the narrow interior of the shelter. Smoked meat hung above the hearth but the tiger had no need of that. His great heart was filled with compassion for the man, outcast from his fellowmen. With no dark thought but an overwhelming rush of brother love for the friendless stranger, he drew near to the sleeping form. But the man was troubled by a dream of a large tiger chasing him and closing upon him. With a muffled scream he awoke and the sound so startled the tiger he turned and sped out of the tree house and made for the safety of the trees.

In later years, Tsaricho's son, burying him next to his father and his father's father, pondered on the desire that led men to become weretigermen. It was the power, of course, but something more than mere power. He had never himself felt the fire to become one with the tiger. Only a few men were destined to carry the spirit of the tiger and his father had been one of those men. Could it be, he wondered, that there was some truth in the story that Man, Spirit and Tiger were once brothers and were some men therefore so driven to recapture their fraternity by the only avenue now open to them? The young man threw some more soil over the mound. No cross for this grave. Unhallowed ground, it would be feared by all who were forced to cross it by night. His answers were buried in that unblest soil with the last of the weretigermen and even then, he doubted that his father had ever known all the answers.

EASTERINE IRALU

the Pot Of Water

In Bengal it is believed that if, a pot of water is poured over a weretiger, it will cause it to change from animal to human in a trice. When a tiger census was being carried out in one area, a group of villagers was asked how many tigers there were. They replied, 'There are nine as far as we know, and ten if you include Haru's pishima; she turns into a tiger from time to time.'

Ma boxed my ears again. She never used to do that. She always used to say I was her *chokher moni*, the jewel of her eye . . . Now she is always angry with me. What can I do?

I can't eat. I can't sleep. Every night I lie awake on my little wooden bed. Sometimes I don't know if my cot is groaning and creaking, or my bones are. I lie stiff. I am cold but I sweat when I hear the snuffle and the padding outside my window. Haru's pishima is going to get me. I don't know what I can do about it. I'm only seven or eight. How do I know what will happen if I tell my parents what I saw?

I always used to do little jobs for Ma. She would send me to the shops for soap and coconut oil or jalebis. Goopi Moira, the sweetmeat maker, makes good jalebis. Sometimes Ma even sends mustard grown in our own fields to the *ghani* to press out the oil. We use the pressed mustard seed cakes for fertilizer and to feed the cows. The oil makes the best *aloo bhaji* I've even eaten. Sometimes she sends our wheat to be ground too.

Now I sit in the room shaking and crying in a corner all day. You would too if you had seen what I have seen.

I was carrying the flour back for Ma after having it ground. Then I saw Sharma, Suku, Shyamal, Kanai and Nitai. They were all het up and excited so I crept up and stood next to Kanai. He is always the most excitable, so he tells you more than the others. He also collects honey from the forest and often gives me a honeycomb to chew if he is in a good mood. Sometimes you have to pick off a limp bee or two drowned in the honey.

A tiger has been visiting our fields, stealing our cattle, goats and sheep. It even stole a little baby. It was only a little girl. No one searched much for her except her father. He cried. Ma told his wife that we were sorry but at least they could now save the money they would have had to spend on her wedding, and that they must hope that their next child would be a son, like me, she said proudly. Now she is not proud of me, and everyone is saying, '*Pagal chhele*, that mad boy.' Some people are sorry for us but some laugh at her and at me. They say she should not have bragged so much about her son.

Everybody was worried that the tiger would steal more animals or attack more people. Nitai said now that it knew it could eat humans it might kill more villagers. He knows about tigers.

They were planning to hunt the tiger down, so they collected lots of bamboo, rope and other things. They were going to make a machaan, and do the goat thing, where they tie the goat up as bait and make a trap and beat drums and chase the tiger into the pit with spears. I helped put up the bamboo and dig the pit, and lay the sticks and leaves over it. I can climb up and down poles faster than you can say my name.

Haru's pishima lives at the edge of the forest. She watched us work. She was very interested. She gave us water, brought rope, food, and even stroked the goat and gave it some grass. She has strange grey-green eyes. She is good-looking and not very old, though she has a grey streak in her hair. I stared at her. As she was patting the goat she licked her lips. I didn't think anything of it then. But I do now. Who can I tell? Who will listen? She is useful in the village. Everyone goes to her for medicine and she helps out when babies are born. Ma is quite friendly with her. In fact she even delivered me. She certainly knows where I live.

I was excited about the chase. Who wouldn't be? Suku cuffed my ears and said, 'Run along home. We have to keep nightwatch.' I begged to stay. I wish I hadn't! Finally Sharma and Suku agreed that perhaps I could take part in some of their activities sometimes. 'Not all,' smirked Shyamal. He is a lout and I don't like him much. He's always standing around our house picking his nose and staring at my sister and Ma when my father goes to the next village.

Sharma, chewing tobacco and mixing something in it, finally said, 'Let the child come. He may be useful. We can send him up and down with supplies.'

We watched for three nights, but nothing came for the goat. Finally everyone decided, 'Maybe we should leave the goat and go. Perhaps the tiger will fall into the trap.'

On the fourth morning the goat had gone, the pit was empty.

'Clever bastard,' said Suku. Ma slaps me for asking the meaning of words like that. 'It must have been watching. As soon as we left just before sunrise, just between that time and our morning tea, after three whole nights keeping awake! What a demon!'

Kanai shuddered. 'It's as if it has human intelligence and planned the whole thing!'

We all made our way to the muddy track home. My head was buzzing. All of them were smoking and gossiping.

Suddenly there was a rustle in the paddy.

Kanai clutched Sharma. 'Did you see that? Did you see? The rice field . . .'

We all stopped in our tracks. There was a great cawing and clucking and rushing and bustling among the small birds and animals in the rippling field.

'We have it, yet we don't,' said Nitai. 'We can do nothing outside the pit. Let's follow and see where it's going. It's going downwind. We can smell it. It can't smell us.'

'I don't think it thought we would come back. It thought we would sleep,' said Kanai. 'But it knows we are here.'

'Shut up. Stop talking as if it's human,' said Sharma. 'You're always making something out of nothing, making mountains out of molehills.'

'Don't make a noise,' said Suku. 'Its hearing must be very keen. Let's just follow it and see where it lives. Then later we can hunt it down.'

The end of the paddy fields came into view. We were blinded by the blood-red morning sun rising over the fields. The coconut palms and the forest beyond were black blots against the sky.

As we crept along, suddenly the creature broke cover. It leapt away past the trees, behind the hut at the edge of the forest. In the strong morning glow, I could hardly see where it went. My eyes were watering so. The others too were rubbing their eyes. '*Shabash*!' said Shyamal. 'Did you see where it went?'

'Somewhere behind the hut into the forest,' said Sharma. 'That's Haru's pishima's hut. Perhaps we can ask her.'

The hut has a little fenced courtyard at the back, near the forest. There are no chickens, no dogs, no cats, no goats, and no cows in that courtyard. Only a well and some *ghotis* or pots full of water, lined up, some sieves to sift rice, a few pots and pans, some baskets and many plants in little mud pots. One of the ghotis was lying on its side. Water was still spilling out of is, slowly.

We went up to the door and shouted 'Anybody there?' There was a shuffling, a scuffling, a clatter, then the door opened. Haru's pishima stuck her head out. She had a white streak on her face. It was shining as if she had just poured water over herself, or maybe she was sweating. She was certainly panting and hot. I see Ma like that sometimes when she's been cooking in the kitchen. Lighting the coals isn't easy.

'Tell us, Pishimoni,' said that smartypants Shyamal, 'could you possibly have been looking out of your window? Did you notice that tiger leap away into the forest? We can't make out whether it has taken cover in the nearby bushes or gone deep into the jungle. It has left hardly any trail, just a pugmark or two near the pit and some blood.'

'I have been busy cutting vegetables, lighting the fire and boiling milk,' said Haru's pishima. 'I hardly have time to breathe in the morning. Where would I be looking out of the window?' But as we left she had time to stand at the door and watch us as we walked away.

'The hunt will have to wait,' said Nitai.

'Spears and stones won't catch this beast. We will have to make a report and get official clearance. They'll bring guns and marksmen,' said Suku.

'She's killing because there is not enough food in the jungle.'

'What a feast we could have had,' said Nitai. He's always telling me how he ate tiger meat when he was young. He used to tell me when I helped him bait fish in the ponds. Nitai will eat anything, even a rat.

While they were chatting I trailed behind. I was thirsty, longing for water, but felt too shy to ask the lady standing at the doorway. I kicked the dust under my feet and turned to look at her. She was leaning, still watching. As I turned around she lifted her arm to chain the door. Her sari fell away off her hand. She quickly replaced it, but I saw it. I can spot a woodpecker between the leaves a mile away, my eyesight is so good.

I saw a large furry white paw with long curved claws hooking the links in the door chain. She saw me turn back. I know she did. She hadn't taken her eyes off me, not once. She knew I had seen it. She knew I knew. All those pots of water, the empty yard . . . Everybody knows when the tiger monster wishes to become human it must pour a pot full of water over itself. If the water misses out even one part of the body . . .

I remembered Kanai telling me just the other day . . .

I ran and ran till I reached home. I dare not leave this room but what can I do?

I heard Ma say she thinks a ghost has got into me in the jungle. She says she will call Haru's pishima, Shanti, to give me medicine to get rid of it. She says Shanti will chase away the spirit. She cannot understand why I am screaming, 'No no no no . . . the water, the water . . .'

I hear Ma say, 'See how terrified the ghost is, Shanti? We must get rid of it.'

I see Shanti smile gently. She moves slowly forward, she says, 'We will, my dear, we will.'

I cannot stop screaming.

SHAIONTONI BOSE

---+---

ropuilliani

This story is adapted from a Pawi tribal legend in Mizoram.

The Council of the Ramhual had ordained that land should be cleared near the dense forest at the edge of the universe. The tribe would burn the scrub at the edge of the forest land, and make provision for their crops. When this *jhum* land had outlived its productiveness, they would move on.

Beyond that forest were the mountains sloping higher and higher upwards forever; or so it seemed to Ropuilliani as she gazed at the mysterious blue haze that rose thousands of miles up till it became one with the sky.

'What lies on the other side, Mother?' she would ask workworn Leplupi as she clacked and whisked her shuttle over the violin-taut strings of their loom.

'The universe? *Pialral? Mithi Khual?* Heaven? Purgatory? Demons? How should I know?' snapped Leplupi. 'That's for the elders to decide.' Then she said more gently, 'Leave the men to think of what lies beyond, my dear. We have too much work to do. The thatch must be mended before the rains. We have to collect enough leaves of *thilthek* and *laisna* to cover the roof.'

Ropuilliani sighed as she placed her basket strap on her head, her black eyes flashing, though lowered as if in submission. She would never give up asking questions.

That song her grandmother used to sing rang in her ears. It told of worlds and countries other than hers, of forefathers who came—man, woman and child—over those mountains, across raging rivers and deep jungles, across gorges and ravines, stark and merciless. It told of terrible famine, of vast rocky deserts, and fierce wild animals. Of monsters horrible and strange, of unearthly fairy lights, that they all had to brave as they struggled through to tame the new land, clearing the thorn and scrub for cultivation as the tribe pressed on in search of land to grow their grain and raise their livestock until the Ramhual, who advised the chief, ordained they should move again.

It was not an easy life. The men brought home tales of hunting and skirmishes with other tribes. She had lost a brother only last year to an enemy arrow. It was just that she looked for something beyond this state of survival for its own sake. She did not believe that it was the need for mere survival that had impelled her forefathers into pushing on into the mountains the way they did.

'We are of the lost tribe that wanders the world,' sang her mother, following the rhythm to weave the lovely patterns that were all that were left of her imagination.

'Lost from where, Mother?' asked Ropuilliani as she hitched her long woven skirt up to her knees, and lifted her *dao* to check the blade. The weeds must be cut in the field and some of the stalks were tough.

Her mother, her rhythmic trance broken, threw a broken shuttle at her daughter and shouted 'Ten *mithans* will cover ten different jhum before you are ready for work!'

Ropuilliani sighed and slapped the rump of the tranquil mithan that stood grazing dolefully, chewing its cud, the last survivor of the bride price paid for her sister many moons ago.

'You give milk, old one,' she muttered as she looked at its liquid bovine eyes, 'or you will end on the platter, tough though you may be.' She scratched its forehead and looked into its gentle eyes.

She stepped out of the bamboo gate and began going up the forest path, collecting twigs as she went. Most of the women foraged systematically. If one was looking for honey, that was all she would collect. Another might look only for edible mushrooms. Ropuilliani would toss her head and pick up twigs in one bundle, leaves in another, gather mushrooms and always a bunch of sweet grass for her friend, the mithan. Earlier her mother might have cuffed her ears because they would not have large bundles of anything, but now she was resigned and perhaps secretly a little grateful that she could leave it to Ropuilliani to make sure there was a little wood for the fire, a little food for the mithan and some leaves for the thatch.

When the season was bad, it was difficult to subsist. The paddy and the livestock the family had was barely enough to survive on, let alone pay the *fathang* due to the chief. Since her brother had died it was harder to maintain the paddy and chop the trees. Boys from the *zawlbuk* did come to help, her brothers' friends, but they were rowdy sometimes and many of them eyed Ropuilliani's delicate beauty in a way that was not always comfortable. Most of them showed off, bragged that they had bested this tiger or that leopard, or that they were admired by no less than the *lasi*, the beautiful spirits whose blessings made great hunters of those they favoured!

Deep in her thoughts, Ropuilliani had not noticed light footsteps following her track. Suddenly she realized someone was padding beside her. He was taller than most of the other boys she knew, and his tawny golden skin shone with health, his face was tattooed with bold black stripes. She started and looked full into his face, afraid.

'I do not wish you any harm,' he said gently. 'I have been watching over you and your mother for some days now. You are very beautiful.'

He stood smiling, looking at her.

Ropuilliani was strangely disturbed. She had never really bothered with the young men who tried to catch her attention, but this one was different somehow.

'Who are you?' she said. 'I have not seen you before.'

'I am new to the village. I have come with news of salt mines. It is not far, it will take a mithan less time than sunrise to sundown to cover the ground to reach it. The chief has honoured me in return for a small service. I saved his life. I am now part of this tribe. I have become part of the *zalen* (the honoured member of the tribe). I need pay no fathang.'

'You are *vai*,' said Ropuilliani. 'You are an outsider. I do not know you.' She picked up her basket and walked on.

'I am Zakapa,' he said proudly. 'I have a name. Your chief has made me one of his own and you call me vai! I will leave now because you are afraid, but I will see you again.' With animal grace he strode into the forest, carrying nothing but a small hunting knife around his waist.

From the following morning onwards there was a deer, a pig, a monkey or logs of wood laid outside their holding, prepared and ready for use.

Ropuilliani's mother muttered and her father growled from his alcoholic stupor, but the comfort of having a table laden with steaming bowls of meat stewed with rice was hard to resist! It was quite all right, and traditionally correct. If he wished to marry her he would pay a handsome bride price and they would not go hungry. If the man was as efficient a warrior as he was a hunter, the girl would live well. Besides, he had the chief's favour. Yet somehow the chief seemed to fear him, and so did Ropuilliani's parents.

Zakapa began to come often to the hut. He would tell stories of the mountains and sing songs they had never heard.

The other young men, who slept all together in the zawlbuk, resented this man, especially his exclusion from the dormitory, and his special favour with the chief. They also resented the attention he received from a girl who had shown no interest in any of them. They called him the outsider and feared him for they knew he could best anyone in a challenge. Some whispered he was a sorcerer who could command spirits at will.

Hrinchala, Ropuilliani's brother's closest friend, was the most vociferous. 'He comes from no tribe that we know of,' said Hrinchala. 'Why does he hunt alone? Where does he go at night? The chief will not question him because he is afraid!'

'Be careful, Hrinchala,' hissed Ropuilliani. 'The chief may be angered at what you say.'

'What has happened to you?' Hrinchala looked at her in amazement. 'You used to be so quiet, so happy to see me!'

'You are my friend,' said Ropuilliani, turning her face towards the paddy she was tending. 'I am happy to see you, but I do not like what you say.'

'I waited too long,' muttered Hrinchala angrily. 'I should have married you long ago!'

'Marriage?' Ropuilliani glared at him. 'I did not ever say I wished to marry you!'

Hrinchala got up, picked up his spear and drove it into the ground. 'I do not understand you,' he said. 'Since when have girls begun to have wishes of their own? You have a duty to the family, to the community, to accept the protection offered to you . . .'

'I do not remember you offering much protection before, Hrinchala,' Ropuilliani flashed. 'You want what is not yours to have!'

The young man turned on his heel and stalked off, shaking with rage.

As time went by however, Ropuilliani began to grow uneasy. Zakapa would disappear alone at night without a word, and stay out till dawn when the moon was waxing. The men in her tribe did not hunt alone and Ropuilliani always wondered how Zakapa could be so fearless. The next day there would always be a sumptuous feast as either sambhar or chital or a nice fat boar would be strung up waiting to be skinned.

What disturbed Ropuilliani was that they never had any spear or arrow marks upon them, but large weals like claw marks on their backs and, more often than not, punctures beneath their throats. She had not believed Hrinchala but could it be that what he said was true? She had been angry with him—angry because she had been afraid?

She began to watch Zakapa closely. One day they went together to the forest as usual, to collect roots and tubers. The light had not yet faded though the evening chill had descended. The mountains rose blue in the near horizon, and the glow of the moon began to wash over the sky. A deer barked in the distance. At once Zakapa stood up, taut with excitement, and was very still for a minute, quivering and sniffing the air. Then he was off, with a leap and a bound over the shrubs and thorns which impeded even seasoned hunters.

Ropuilliani gazed after him in amazement. It was not long before he returned, as silently as he had disappeared. He was licking his lips in a strange, satisfied way and she froze in terror, her heart turning to ice as she looked at him. Blood, raw blood . . . it was not on his hands or clothes as one would find on a hunter, but around his mouth. As he yawned a huge curling yawn, she saw that his teeth were pointed. 'I must go home,' she whispered. 'I forgot to bring my warm shawl, this one won't do.' And she turned and ran.

Zakapa stared at her hasty retreat and trod through the slush to a nearby pool to gaze into the water, wondering what she had seen. As he looked he realized there was blood on his face. His first thought was to go after Ropuilliani, who would warn her family and friends immediately. He was sated after his large meal, but there was no help for it.

Ropuilliani was quite sure that the creature she had loved as Zakapa would come after her. She took off the shawl she was wearing and draped it round her sharp dao, with its blade pointing upwards. She stuck the other end into the ground and arranged the cloth so it looked as if she was sitting huddled on the ground. Zakapa, not pausing to think, sprang forward. As he leapt his form took on the shape of a tiger, snarling and powerful. The dao pierced his heart and he fell to the ground, roaring and groaning with pain, his cries growing weaker as his life ebbed away.

Slowly Ropuilliani backed away from her hiding place and made her way home—perhaps thankful that she had not married a monster, perhaps sad she had lost her lover, perhaps triumphant at having outwitted a sorcerer; who knew but she? And she? She kept her thoughts to herself.

SHAIONTONI BOSE

—+—

the man Who became a bear

In Naga stories, only people who have an inner power can become other beings. What they become depends on the type of force that the individual possesses. He or she may become a tree or a small rabbit or even a small reptile. Only the most powerful become tigers or snakes. One can be different animals at different stages in one's life.

Ridiculous, they said. Go and scare the children with that, they further said. But what of the family who had a loved one go missing never to be traced again? And what of the man who never came back and of whom the seers said: he is alive but he is no longer a man?

When the cicadas were singing their homecoming-time songs, he scraped the mud off his hoe and tipped the tobacco ash out of his pipe and slipped his machete into the holder hung at his back— and did he not set off for home as the rest did? Who can explain the strange voices he heard in the river calling his name sweetly? Or the stranger voices that knew him in the woods and drew him into their depths?

His clansmen led the search, combing the forest and the fields in twos, careful to turn away from the sweet sounds of the river and the soft calls that the woods made, inviting the searchers to tarry a while. A man heard his name whistled twice and, thinking it was one amongst their group, made to turn into the treacherous woods. 'Are you mad?' his companion yelled and halted him. At such times it was necessary to be harsh because that was the only way of shaking a man out of the spell that the creatures of the wood quickly began to weave if you stopped and listened to them.

The search was fruitless. 'Did you not come upon even a piece of clothing?' asked his wife anxiously. But he had disappeared completely, with none of the tell-tale signs that some others left behind—a bit of cloth clinging to some thorny bush, a stub of half-smoked tobacco lying as though it had been suddenly thrown away, a knife dropped in passing, as happened in the case of Vilhou's younger boy who was found after two days. The boy said that he had been playing with a little boy who beckoned to him from behind a gnarled tree, and he was most upset that his father had put an end to his game by finding him.

A woman who had walked out one afternoon to gather edible herbs had never come back. Six months later, a hunter came upon what was left of her: a clump of hair and a weather-worn piece of cloth covering the skeletal remains.

But this was different. The seer said, 'If you don't find him soon, when you do find him he will be no human.' They wondered what the seer meant, but that was all he was allowed to reveal.

The whole village turned out to look for the missing man. By the fourth day of the search, people were exhausted and his relatives did not want to press further. So the search was called off. The funeral was kept in abeyance for the time when some hunters might chance upon his remains or the seer would convey he had entered the valley of the spirits.

He awoke and found himself in a dark place. He felt along the unfamiliar walls for a window but found none. Where was he? He tried to recollect but his surroundings gave no clues. A faint glimmer of light lay to his left. He half-walked half-crawled up to it, careful not to stumble over anything. The last time he had come home late he had knocked two chairs over and that had made such an ungodly racket on their wooden floor that his wife would not give him any peace for the rest of the week. He'd be more careful now. The glimmer seemed to be a window or a door up ahead, but it was the wrong shape—it looked as though somebody in a hurry had bashed it in. His head felt heavy but surely he hadn't slept so long or drunk so much the night before. Where were the children? They were early risers, getting up at the crack of dawn to resume the games halted the previous night.

He reached it finally, the entrance of this odd house. But why were there so many trees? He had cut down all the trees, save two, to clear his front yard. Where was his wife? If the children were up she rarely lingered in bed. Why hadn't she brought his tea? 'Wife, wife!' he called out. What's wrong with his voice? He must be having a sore throat. Serve him right for staying out too long. 'Wife!' Was he really making that noise?

The sky was tinged with the light of dawn. He glanced down at his feet and recoiled at the black fur. My god, when did I grow so hairy? He lifted his hand to his mouth instinctively in a gesture of amazement, but drew it back hurridly when he felt the furriness of it at his lip. He held his hands up against the sunlight and a long scream was torn out of him. They were black paws with sharp claws protruding out at the ends of the fingers. 'What's wrong with me? What? What?' He shrieked as he took in the furry length of his body, and his hands clawed desperately at the fur, trying to wrench off the bearskin.

The pain stopped him finally. He was bleeding where he had scratched himself. If only he could find somebody who could help him. His wife and children were there but would they accept him as he was now? It would have to be somebody who was acquainted with metamorphoses of this nature. It was then that he thought of the seer. Perhaps he could help him. He knew enough magic.

The man felt clumsy in his bear body. He was not familiar with this part of the forest. He traced his way slowly, looking for signs of human habitation. There were no fields but there was a jungle path, an indication that a village was not too far off. He wondered if he should stay on the path or sneak through the forest. Was he to act like a man or a bear, he wondered.

He had not walked above fifteen minutes when he saw two black figures up ahead. They drew closer. He was dismayed to see that it was a she-bear with her cub. Expecting her to charge at any moment he swiftly looked around for a good escape route. To his surprise they walked past amiably with no sign of the hostility that a she-bear would invariably show on encountering a man.

The sun was up now but there were still no men in sight. As he walked on he found a field of maize, the ears of corn ripe and yellow. Involuntarily he began to salivate. He realized that he had probably not eaten for a long time. Surely they wouldn't miss a few ears, he thought. In any case I can always pay them back when I am well again.

He settled himself into the middle of the cornfield and began to eat. He was surprised at how good the corn tasted. It was sweet and sticky and the first cob whetted his appetite for more.

'He's there again! We've caught the rogue this time!'

Ah! People at last, thought the bear-man. I'll explain everything to them and they'll help me. He pulled himself up to his full height, filled with excitement and hope, but just then a bullet pierced his abdomen. He reared back from the pain and roared. Please let me be able to talk to them, reason with them, he prayed. 'Stop! Stop!' He raised his hands and struggled to speak, but only strange bear noises came out of his throat, frightening people even more. Another bullet pierced him, his chest this time, and exploded in his heart.

Only then did his voice come back to him. 'Don't shoot, please don't shoot, I'm a man too.'

The hunters heard his voice clearly above the crack of guns before he fell down dead. 'Could it be the missing man?' they cried out and ran up to check. Pushing aside the fur, they found on his shoulder a long white scar. His relatives, when notifying neighbouring villages about him, had been asked for identifying marks. His wife had remembered the wound he had received from a bayonet in World War I, a scar spreading right across his shoulder like a silver mark.

EASTERINE IRALU

ulat bagh

The fibre of a plant (Bauhinia vahli), beaten out and cooked in mustard oil in a human skull, is said to be a prescription for making an ulat bagh *or weretiger. The* Gazette *even upto the twentieth century records that villagers would be acquitted of murder if they could convince the judges that they had killed a person because he or she was actually a tiger.*

There was once a young man who, as a boy, had learnt witchcraft from some girlfriends. His wife knew nothing about this. They lived happily together and often went to visit the wife's parents.

One day, they were on their way together to pay such a visit. As they walked through the grassland at the edge of a jungle they saw a herd of cattle grazing, among which was a very fine fat bull calf. The man stopped, stripped himself to his waistcloth and told his wife to hold his clothes for him while he went and ate the calf. Astonished, his wife asked him how he was going to eat a living animal. He answered that he was going to turn into a tiger and kill the calf. He impressed on her that she must on no account be frightened or run away. Then he handed her a piece of a certain root and instructed her to give it to him to smell when he came back so that he would at once regain his human form.

He retired into the thicket, took off his waistcloth and at once turned into a tiger. He swallowed the waistcloth and thereby grew a fine long tail. Then he sprang upon the calf and knocked it over and began to suck its blood.

At this sight his wife was overwhelmed with terror. Forgetting everything in her fear, she ran right off to her father's house, taking with her his clothes and the magic root. She arrived breathless and told her parents all that had happened.

Meanwhile, her husband, deprived of the means of regaining his own form, was forced to spend the day hiding in the jungle. When night fell he made his way to the village where his father-in-law lived. But when he got there, all the dogs began to bark. When the villagers saw that there was a tiger, they barricaded themselves inside their houses.

The weretiger went prowling around his father-in-law's house. At last his father-in-law plucked up courage and went out and threw the magic root under the tiger's nose. He at once became a man again. Then they brought him into the house and washed his feet, and gave him some hot rice-water to drink. On drinking this he vomited up lumps of clotted blood.

The next morning the father-in-law called all the villagers and showed them this blood and told them all that had happened. He turned to his son-in-law and told him to take himself off, and vowed that his daughter should never go near him again. The weretiger had no answer to make but went back silently and alone to his own home.

NILANJANA GUPTA

the Song of the hunter

Ere Mor the peacock flutters, ere the Monkey People cry,
Ere Chil the kite swoops down a furlong sheer,
Through the jungle very softly flits a shadow and a sigh—
He is Fear, O Little Hunter, he is Fear!
Rudyard Kipling, 'Song of the Little Hunter'

'Saheb, a rogue elephant has been plaguing the villages and destroying the crops. He is reported to be making his way to the tea gardens. The labourers hope you can do something about it, Saheb.'

Tall, fearless, generous and kind, G.M. Hassan was a hero to his own workers and indeed to all the surrounding villages. They were quite sure that if there was something to be done, he could do it.

Hassan sighed as he went to inspect his guns and shooting gear. Everything had to be shipshape before a shikaar. Sometimes he spent hours cleaning the barrels of his guns, and they shone with years of dedicated care.

He was tired. Shikaar often meant long hours of waiting in uncomfortable conditions, and the excitement of a shoot eluded him these days. There was once a time when he bore his trophies home proudly, used them as furniture, rugs and wall ornaments. An elephant leg had been converted into a table, another into an umbrella stand. A silky, luxurious leopard skin lay on the couch.

This was the done thing. It was not something you searched your soul about. Shikaar was a way of life. Not only was it an exciting sport, where you pitted your wits against the animals (who were anything but dumb), it culled the population of each species down to its healthy optimum. It also controlled any kind of menace caused by a maneater or a rogue. There were rules. You did not shoot certain animals or birds at certain seasons, especially the breeding season. And you shot to kill, not to maim.

The Jonga jolted its deliberate way through the dirt tracks to stop for a rest at the edge of the forest. The last bird was protesting in the gloom: 'Make more pekoe, make more pekoe.' Finally, as if tired at its requests being ignored, its insistent cries died down and the crickets shrilled the close of day.

The two men filled water into the radiator, their thick socks and boots protecting them from hopeful leeches. Their khaki camouflage shooting jackets, trousers and caps protected them from head to foot. If they kept reasonably still, they would be hidden from the sharpest eyes. The *machaan*, the bamboo and palm lookout built into a tree, brought only a relative degree of safety from all the various dangers of the forest, but the men thought little or not at all about danger. They had their duty to do and they would fulfil it.

Like a warm fragrant blanket, the night wrapped itself around Hassan and his driver and general factotum, Rai, a Gurkha who had settled his life and loyalties on Assam in general and Hassan in particular.

The night passed uneventfully. The elephant may have been overcome by too much *mohua*, or changed its course and rampaged through a citronella field in some other district. Towards the darkest hour, just before dawn, they decided that nothing would happen and they might as well catch a few hours of precious sleep in the comfort of their beds before the sun rose.

When the downward-dipping trails are dank and drear,
Comes a breathing hard behind thee—snuffle snuffle through the night—
It is Fear, O Little Hunter, it is Fear!

What follows next is best said in Hussain's own words.

'Allah was with us that night. We got back into our Jonga and Rai began to reverse it. As we moved forward, something pale and white moved out of the bushes in front of us. It was certainly not an elephant. It shuffled in the undergrowth, low down on the ground, rounded and huddled. As the Jonga lights shone full on it, I could tell the creature was moving right in our direction. I may be a shikaari, but running over an animal is not my kind of sport, so I ordered Rai to stop. To my horror, he kept moving. "What are you doing?" I asked. "It cannot harm us, we are well protected even if it charges. If it is a pig I cannot shoot it. Don't run it over!"

'Rai is usually extremely obedient but this time his reply made my blood freeze!

'"Saheb, can you not see, that creature is no pig! It had no eyes, there was no glow in the jeep's light. I know not what it is, Saheb, but it is not good!

'Muslims are taught there are no ghosts and evil spirits, it is against our creed to believe in such things. But when you live for years in a place like Assam and deal with people and situations that challenge the mores of the most confirmed sceptic, a healthy respect grows within you. You learn to take good advice when you get it and you learn not to scoff at things you cannot explain. You follow your own religion as truly as you can but you tread carefully upon the beliefs of others.

'I stopped arguing, and left Rai to decide our kismet.

'As our Jonga reversed fully, it stalled for a few moments and I could see the huddled shape, moving slowly but undeterred, till it reached the window next to my seat. I could hear poor Rai gabbling "Shankar Bhagawan" and anything else that came to mind.

'I looked straight at it; its face if it had any, seemed to be covered. The only part of the body that was exposed was what was grasping the side of the open window. Such a sight! It was neither claw nor bone, a withered subhuman thing that seemed to have a grip of iron. I feel ashamed to say it, yet it is true: even today, I cannot look at an old person's hands any more for fear of seeing and feeling what I felt that night!

'I could hear a scrabbling, yet the thing's grip seemed to slacken not at all. It was as if it was trying to heave itself in but, despite the open window, could not. I confess I was almost tempted to open the door and run, but Rai at that very moment lurched forward and shot off like a bat out of hell!

'As the dim line of light began to spread across the sky, Rai said "*Bhagwan ke kripa se aap bahut bachgaya, Saheb*. If we had not been within the steel body of this car, that creature would have claimed you."

'"What was it, Rai?" I asked in a dry whisper.

'"Death, saheb," was Rai's certain reply.

'Now you may tell me, in the broad light of day, that that was just a poor mad leper or a senile old woman wandering the woods but, believe me, no such thoughts crossed my mind then, and I have never forgotten the complete desertion of all rational thought and the terror that took over my mind that night. It is by Allah's grace, that I am alive to tell the tale!'

Now the spates are banked and deep; now the footless boulders leap,
Now the lightning shows each littlest leaf-rib clear,
But thy throat is shut and dried, and thy heart against thy side
Hammers: Fear, O Little Hunter—this is Fear!

SHAIONTONI BOSE

the third eye

In the Himalayan regions it is believed that demons lurk in the forests, waiting to swoop down on the unwary traveller. It is necessary at every bend of the road to propitiate them and call upon the Buddha for protection. If forests and lakes are desecrated, the gods unleash blizzards, earthquakes and all manner of disasters.

The sprawling tea gardens lay on either side of the reserve forest. Meadows carpeted with wild flowers surrounded the lake. The quiet of the forest buzzed and chirped and fluttered. Little busy sounds filled the air, contributing, strangely enough, to the general air of peace and silence.

A jeep drove up, clattering and bumping over the uneven rock-strewn, leaf-carpeted mossy track. Three men got out.

'This is the spot I told you about. Ideal tourist location. Lake. Trees. Animals coming to drink. Even an echo. You try,' said the forest official importantly.

They bellowed. 'H-e-llo!'

'Hellow-o-o!' The echo bounced back, throwing itself back and forth over the lake.

The men laughed and shook plump grasping hands. 'There is of course the small matter of getting permission to clear the forest but we'll manage that,' smiled one, passing a packet of Pan Parag around, baring his stained teeth. Another began to outline plans with great enthusiasm. 'We will have concrete pillars at the gate, with a tiger's head, big teeth showing.' He bared his fangs in demonstration. The others slapped him on the back in approval. Greatly encouraged, he continued. 'We will cover the courtyard fully in concrete. It will be completely first class, no doubt.' He spat out the betel juice from his mouth and scratched his belly. 'There can even be a separate complex—youth hostel—it will be very fine.'

The others nodded their satisfaction. They were all so excited at the prospect of crores to be made that they did not notice the weather changing. The hills can be deceptively cheerful and sunny one minute, and threatening and brooding the next. You must be prepared to go at a moment's notice from dry to damp, from warm to cold, from sunshine to mist. They took various measurements and left, still congratulating one another. The jeep rattled down the bends, honking furiously.

A passer-by, who had to jump out of the way, paused to watch them. He looked up at the skies, shook his head and muttered a silent prayer. *Om Mani Padme Hum*. He picked up a stone and a leaf, a flower and some lichen and placed them at the large rock at the next bend of the road. He knew, as all hill people know, that to disturb the gods of the mountains or insult the peace of the surroundings is to unleash the wrath of the elements upon your head.

The rape of forest land took place with great speed and violence. Saws and drills and huge trucks bearing the carcasses of trees fouled the air with noise and the choking fumes of diesel and its succubus, carbon monoxide. Animals retreated in terror or, driven into nowhere, gradually died for lack of food and shelter. Only those that could thrive as pariahs could survive in this, the last of their undefiled strongholds. The bare hillsides and the stumps of trees—some more than a century old—stood silent witness to man's lust for more than he needs.

Even the crystal waters of the lake did not escape pollution. Toxic building materials were dumped unceremoniously into it. The city labourers hawked and spat and washed themselves and their clothes in the sacred spring in cheerful disregard. They shouted and threw stones at any animal they saw coming to drink, congratulating one another on their bravery. But these brave stalwarts did not ever stay the night in the forest. No amount of shouting and bullying from their foreman could convince them to stay on site after dusk.

Initially tribals and local residents had tried to stop the desecration. But they believed in *ahimsa*, their protests were seen as weak and ineffectual. The multi-crore project continued relentlessly. Concrete wrapped its insidious way around the hillside in shades of pale ice-cream pinks and pistachio greens. Manicured lawns, square box-shaped hedges and a 'rustic' red path made with earth found nowhere in the region replaced the magnificence of the forests.

'Be in touch with Nature, far from the madding crowd,' trilled one brochure. 'When you're done with your tryst with the sublime, come home to a jacuzzi. Or the raw pleasure of a sauna sizzling with heated stones in primitive fashion. Or laze on the rolling lawns beneath colourful umbrellas, soak in the sun and sip the drink of the day. Round off your day with a session at the swimming pool or gym, guided by health experts. The beauteous hills around will echo to your shouts of joy.'

Sharmila, pretty and newly-wed, leant over her husband's shoulder and said, 'Just see—that's exactly what we've been looking for! Let's book the tickets tomorrow. They've okayed my leave.'

Raghav ruffled her hair and agreed. But rooms were hard to get. 'If Gopal hadn't helped we wouldn't have stood a chance,' he reported to his wife the following day. 'It's heavily booked.'

There was a gala opening with much fanfare. The first VIP guests checked in. The management provided party hats and fireworks and a five-star buffet. The fireworks probably frightened away the few remaining animals but the revellers were cheerfully unaware of this.

Raghav and Sharmila decided to trek further into the mountains. Both of them had been fond of climbing and trekking in college and decided to go on the six-day trekking package the hotel offered, complete with tents and ropes and other gear. They decided they would only trek as much as they could both comfortably enjoy and return to the hotel to 'chill out', as Raghav put it, before they returned to the city again.

Param, Sona, Vijit, Ambika, Rina and Monish, a motley crew from the ad world, were hiking through the forest with a tribal guide who showed them a 'black monkey' and a 'honeybee bird'. The tracker said that all the animals had been scared into the interior or had died for lack of food and shelter. Now cattle, goats and dogs ruled the outskirts of the jungle. He showed them elephant droppings and peered at a pugmark or two. He explained that a leopard or a tiger might get hungry enough to help itself to one of these easy meals occasionally, but would not do this often as they were wary of the increased human population. Then he raised his head and sniffed at the air and shook his head. 'Big wind,' he muttered almost to himself. 'Bad time coming. The gods are angry. Throwing *dorje*. Go. Go home.'

'What's a dorje?' asked Ambika.

'A thunderbolt,' said Rina.

'Good god,' said Param. 'He's really freaked out, man.'

By now the guide was invoking the good Buddha in a steady drone to deliver him and rolling the whites of his eyes. He turned suddenly to his troupe and said firmly, 'We go now.'

He disappeared the next day. The manager of the resort was unable to locate him and no one else was willing to take over.

'Big wind coming' was the general consensus and one youngster from the village, a little more fluent in English than the rest, said, 'My grandfather say no stay. Hotel close. Go.'

The guide service had to be closed down. The management explained it away with all kinds of plausible excuses but the ad crowd decided to pack their bags and leave sooner than expected. As one of the group put it, 'Jeez man, the atmosphere is subzero!'

It wasn't that it was terribly cold. In fact the bright sunshine was almost too bright. There was an exaggerated clearness to the day and not too much wind. The air was unnaturally still. Mr Tewari, avid bird-watcher, commented to Mrs Tewari, 'I had hoped to see the scarlet minivets this time but it seems they have bypassed this place.'

By the time Raghav and Sharmila got back to the resort they were already somewhat unnerved. Their sherpa Tshering was cheerful enough at the start of their journey. He had not complained or refused to do anything. But the return journey had been markedly different. Tshering plodded morosely on, his short stocky body making light of his burdens and of the steep, rubble-ridden narrow paths, growing more and more silent.

On the last day the little party had pitched their tent on a little sheltered niche at a turn of the path. Sharmila loved the little flowers growing in the cracks of the inhospitable rock of the mountainside. They were within walking distance of the little village Thing-po that they had bought their provisions from on their way up. They decided to go down to Thing-po and have a bowl of hot noodles cooked over a tiny charcoal fire, and chat with Palden, the owner of the shop and schoolmaster, who could speak some Hindi and English.

When they arrived at the village they found all the little huts bare of all possessions, and not a soul in sight.

Sharmila was rather perturbed. 'They didn't mention a word about everybody going away!' she said. 'They were so chatty! Surely they would have said something.' They asked Tshering what could have happened but he turned pale and sombre and refused to communicate. The only thing that Raghav could follow was something to the effect of 'It has come to pass'.

'Do you remember the legend we heard about the place?' asked Sharmila suddenly. 'Remember Palden telling us how the lake is a holy place and should never be disturbed? He said terrible things happen to people who disturb the lake.'

'Rubbish,' said the practical Raghav—but there was an uneasy feeling in the pit of his stomach. The absolute quiet was not the dreaming silence of the outdoors with the rustling of birds in the bushes, little breezes stirring in the pines or the sudden alarmed chitter of the squirrel. This silence was one that only Death could bring.

As soon as the young couple reached the resort, they paid Tshering for his services and thanked him. He nodded nervously, and when they asked him in to have a cup of tea he shook his head and said, 'I go home. You go home.' He walked off rapidly.

'That's good advice,' said Sharmila as they went through the gates of the resort. The concrete tiger leered horribly after them. Sharmila and Raghav walked close together, needing the warmth and comfort of each other.

'We're leaving tomorrow for Latang-la,' said Raghav, and Sharmila breathed a sigh of relief. So he too had felt it and was heeding the local people's warnings.

The next morning, it was dark when Raghav and Sharmila got up. They had asked for the hotel jeep to take them down. 'Seven hundred rupees.'

'The hotel rates are six hundred,' said Raghav irritably.

'This early morning charge,' said the driver smugly.

Mr and Mrs Tewari had agreed to share the cost and go down too. Without birds to watch Mr Tewari found time hanging heavy.

The manager, Gurung, began to panic at this exodus.

The sun rose like a blood-red eye in the sky which seemed to be swirling with clouds. It spread no light in its wake. The staff buzzed around the hotel doing very little work, talking in little huddles. 'What's the matter?' Gurung asked irritably.

'The villagers were saying that Ma Tara is angry,' said Kanchha, whose name meant 'the youngest one' though he was pushing fifty. 'They are saying it is *Kaal. Mahakaal*! I am of course trying to make them understand that it is no such thing.'

Gurung was quite sure that wily old Kanchha was much more likely trying to get the rest to panic.

'Nonsense,' he said to Kanchha in Nepali. 'Ma Tara indeed. The rest are fools, but I thought you at least had more sense.'

'Oh, I have sense,' said Kanchha. 'I also have an English-educated nephew who does not believe in all this. He also has very good sense! You just ask, I will bring him this instant.'

'You see to it that all this nonsensical talk stops first. Then we will see about your English-educated nephew,' said Gurung, but his words sounded hollow. Somehow he knew that this phenomenon was outside the control of either Kanchha or himself.

As the jeep-load rattled down the hill the four visitors noticed large groups of local people with bundles on their backs making their way down to the valley. They turned every few paces to look in terror at the looming sky obscuring the snowy mountains they worshipped. They no longer muttered prayers or clutched amulets. Their only objective was to reach safety. Suddenly, all of one accord, they fell to the ground, turning their terrified faces to the terrible sky.

There was a strange howl in the air and a low humming moan which rose above the noise of the jeep. The driver stepped on the accelerator. Whether it was the dust raised by the speed of the car or the swirling of the clouds, Sharmila later swore she had seen a hoard of dreadful, screaming savage creatures swarming over the skies, surrounding the brooding lifeless blood-red eye that was the vengeful sun. Raghav rationalized what they had experienced as soon as he reached the prosaic city lights but in his heart of hearts a question remained unanswered.

There was nothing left of the resort or of the surrounding villages for miles round. The national TV news bulletin described what had happened as a freak blizzard brought on by the indiscriminate felling of trees. 'A landslide, the worst in ninety-seven years, has caused the collapse of almost half an entire mountainside the day after the blizzard. The death toll is as yet unknown.'

There were a few heart attacks and a few suicides brought on by the loss of the crores that had been speculated on the whole project. It was a nine-day wonder which the public forgot when the next big media event occurred—but the forest did not forget. The brooding silence which had taken over was never quite broken. The third eye had opened. Fear had come and crouched over the area like a hunter stalking prey. Destruction had tasted blood and found it sweet.

SHAIONTONI BOSE

the Old Man

In the jungles and hills of Nagaland, many believe that jungle spirits exist to protect animals from hunters, who are today mostly young men out for sport.

All the Naga tribes believe in jungle spirits. Though hunting is part of the Naga way of life, the tribal people believe that the animals of the forest are protected from harm by spirits. These spirits can assume animal or human shape; if you shoot them, they make you lose your way—or lose your senses.

My uncle is a veteran hunter. He and his friends regularly camp in the forest, lying in wait for animals to emerge at a waterhole or stream.

On one full moon night when they were camping by a lake, all his friends said they didn't want to go hunting because they were too tired or drunk, but my uncle wanted to hunt wild fowl and wild boar. He sat up in a tree, waiting for his quarry.

Later, he said that somehow that night seemed different from the very beginning. It was very still, no leaves were stirring. He sat there, waiting. It was midnight, ten minutes past midnight, still he sat, waiting for the animals to come. He could hear wild boars somewhere close by. Then he suddenly started feeling very hot and tense. He removed his jacket and continued waiting with his gun ready. But he didn't get anything and decided to give up.

As he was nearing the camp, a solitary old man was cutting wood. It was the middle of the night so he wondered what this old man was doing. As my uncle approached him, the man stopped chopping.

My uncle asked, 'What are you doing? Where are you going? Where do you stay?'

'Right here,' the old man answered.

My uncle decided to move on. He took a slightly circuitous path. After about ten minutes, he saw the old man again, cutting wood.

Startled, my uncle said, 'What are you doing here? I just saw you there, cutting wood.' He wondered how the old man could have reached the spot before him. Moreover, there was a sameness in the scene—the old man was in the same posture, making the same motions, cutting the same trunk. But my uncle didn't make too much of it.

His camp was within view, next to the lake. To his amaument, there was another camp right next to it. In the jungle, the convention is that one camps at a distance from existing camps. He thought he should go and speak to people at the other camp because it was not right. He went towards it but he came across the same man again. He was petrified at seeing the same figure yet again, 'I got so scared, I turned around and started walking.' But again he saw the same man. He said, 'Now something is wrong', so he turned back, but again there was the same man in front of him and so he turned back once more and found the old man in front of him again. In trying to run away from the man, he lost his way, which was surprising as he knew the jungle like the back of his hand.

I believe he went round and round that same area for three or four hours and he saw that same man everywhere. He remembered hearing that people go berserk trying to run in all directions. So he said to himself, let me just sit down. He sat there for a long time. At dawn he stood up and walked back to his camp. Everybody asked him what he had shot and he said nothing. So they asked, 'What have you been doing for so many hours?' He answered, 'I've just been going round and round. Let me explain to you how it was.'

My uncle is convinced the old man was a spirit protecting the wild birds and animals from the hunters on that perfect full moon night.

NILANJANA GUPTA

the White boat

The seven islands of Mumbai were once covered with coconut groves and ruled by the Kolis, a tribe that lived by fishing. They were fearless and skilled in the ways of the sea, and sailed as far as the Gulf of Oman. They wove their nets as naturally as does the spider its web, so much so that they share the name Koli with the spider.

In today's Mumbai, they have been completely marginalized or assimilated. Though they survive in other areas of India's western coastline. This tale is one of a few stories that survive in modern Mumbai, along with names of areas like Worli, Colaba (Kalbhat), Palva Bandar (Apollo Bunder), Mahim and of course the name Mumbai.

Radhabai sat on the rocks chewing her *paan* after a long day at the bazaar. She could hear the sea lashing against the huge stone wall that separated their houses from the beach. The sea calmed her down after the wearying hours of haggling with the *sethanis* who bought fish from her. '*Agga bai*, they wear such expensive saris and come to the market and then for even fifty rupees they do such a lot of *khit-khit*,' she spat out to her friend and partner of twenty years, Nanda tai.

Every morning, the two of them left together with a basket full of fish perched on their heads, the gold in their ears and nostrils glinting in the sun, their glass bangles jangling and their colourful saris tied in a tight knot around them.

Radhabai plucked out her pouch of tobacco from between the folds of her sari and offered some to Nanda tai. Nanda tai took a pinch of tobacco, rubbed it on her palms and pushed it into her mouth, watching her friend search the seas for her son's boat. 'He will come by tomorrow morning. Stop worrying so much.' Radhabai's son had set out to sea almost a week ago.

'I am tired of all this worrying. Now he has a new boat and god willing, we will now find a good girl and get him married. His *baiko* can do the worrying then,' Radhabai said, still searching the seas.

'*Arre*, you will say this now but when his wife turns you out of the house then . . .' Nanda tai shook her head, her eyes brimming with tears as she remembered her fight with her son and his wife a couple of days ago.

The two sat quietly, the sea in front of them and a row of houses with red-tiled roofs and whitewashed walls behind them. They had lived here for as long as they could remember, sewing nets for their husbands and then their sons, selling the fish they brought back home and praying for their return every time the boats went out to sea.

A group of children rushed to them screaming their names. Nanda tai's grandson was among them, and he came and jumped onto his grandmother's back, pulling at her earlobe which hung under the weight of the gold earrings she had worn as a bride, a mother and now a grandmother. '*Aaji*, you have to tell us a story.'

Nanda tai tried to shoo them away, 'We are too tired now. Give us some rest.' But the children persisted.

Radhabai relented. 'All right. I will tell you a story but everyone has to listen quietly and no asking questions in between.' The children nodded vigorously. She stuffed some more tobacco into her mouth.

'What I am about to tell you is a true story. It is as real as the hair on our heads and the skin on our bodies. Remember this when you go to sea and you girls, think of this when your husbands are out in their boats and you are alone at home crying and worrying.

'There was a time when our shores were green with mango trees and the seas laden with fish. And even though we may think it impossible today, the *devas* often came down to visit us simple folk, and sometimes shared our meals, our sorrows and our joys.'

Radhabai crossed her legs, looking at the rapt faces of the children in front of her. She saw that Meena had joined the group of kids. Meena was married to Shiva, a young fisherman who had taken his boat out to sea a month ago. There had been no news of him since then.

Radhabai continued, 'A long long time ago when Mumbai was a mere drop in the ocean and our ancestors ruled the island, in a *kholi,* there lived a family of five. Aai, Baba, their two sons and a daughter. This was a very happy family. Baba had a small boat and Aai had a lot of gold. The children were happy and carefree without any fear or want in the world and, like all of you here, they spent their days and nights playing and doing nothing else.

'One morning the sea looked bright and beautiful, shining with the pride of a newly-wed bride as the sun danced off its waters. The skies were glowing with the warmth of the morning sun and the heavens seemed to be smiling on all those who lived on earth. Baba said to Aai, "Is my net ready?"

'"Have I ever been late in all these years of our marriage? If it had not been for me, who would have kept your boat ready and the net sewn in time for your trips all these years? Here, this net has the blessings of the goddess and will bring you luck. And don't forget to go to the temple before you take the boat out and say your prayer to the sea and . . ."

'Baba hushed Aai, promising to do all that she asked him to and more. He hugged his children goodbye and bent down in prayer to the trees, the earth and the wind. He prayed to the devi, offering her a coconut and some flowers, and then went to take out his blue-and-white boat. The sea looked calm but he knew as well as every fisherman down this coast that it had an unpredictable temper, especially now that the monsoon months were close upon them. The next three months would be difficult as the monsoon would force him to stay home. Without fish to sell, they would have to make do with whatever money his wife had kept aside. Still, she was a sensible woman, and did not spend her money on flowers for her hair and saris everyday. God willing, she would see them through the rains, Baba thought as he drew up the anchor.

'Praying to the sea gods to keep them happy, Baba stepped into the boat with his brother and his uncle. This was the last trip that the three of them were to take together, for after this, his uncle had decided to hand over the net to his son.

'For three days, they were out at sea. The third night was to be their last night away from home, and they sat quietly smoking their *bidis* and stacking their fish on ice. They were glad to be going back, especially Baba, who sensed a change in the mood of the waters and the skies. The sky was giving up its pale blue colour and the sea seemed to be losing its calm as the third day turned into night for the three seafarers.'

Radhabai wiped her mouth and her moist eyes with the end of her sari. Nanda tai held her hand as Radhabai carried on. 'At sea, darkness falls gradually before night does. With a small lantern to guide them through the waters, the three thought they would steer their boat to a safe spot. But by then the waters were doing their dance, rocking all those that went above it and lived under it.' Radhabai paused to look into the eyes of the children who were completely entranced by the story. '*Kay*, all of you, have you heard the sea when it is angry? The whoosh of its waves and the way it rises and falls, *arre*, I have seen you run at the sight of a big wave—but what do you do when you are in the middle of it! Where will you run?'

Radhabai continued. 'So it was, with no moon to guide them through this night, that the three boatmen were tossed up and down and sideways by the sea. The morning scattered the darkness away but the waters were still in a frenzy and by this time the men were at the end of their strength. They had almost given up hope of ever returning home when, far far away, Baba saw a speck on the horizon. A flash of white and suddenly there was a boat in front of them! A sparkling white boat with its sails bright and fluttering in a calm breeze as if the storm was only in the minds of the three people who had been tossed around in it all night. Inside were a group of sanyasis, monks dressed in saffron, with a smile on their lips. One by one, they stepped into the storm-tattered boat as Baba and his uncle and his brother lay there too exhausted to get up.

'Back home, Aai was praying. She had been praying right through the night after she heard the radio warning about the weather. The children were playing but they knew something was wrong. Aai prayed silently, getting up only to give the children their meals and to put them to bed.

'The night went by and so did the next seven days, but there was no news. Baba did not return and Aai grew more and more worried. She had stopped eating and would only sit by the sea clutching at her *mangalsutra* and calling out to the devi to protect her husband. On the morning of the eighth day, the children were sitting outside the house and Aai was plaiting her daughter's hair when two men in saffron walked into their house asking for alms. The boys ran inside to bring some food to put into their bowls. The men looked at Aai's troubled face and said, "Tai, have faith in God. He will take care of your husband."

'Startled, Aai burst into sobs. She fell at their feet and begged for some word about her husband. The men folded their hands, bowed their heads and said, "Out there in the middle of the sea where your husband and many like him take their boats out, God has His men. They look out for boats and men being tormented by the sea. Your husband too has been helped by these men."

'Aai wiped a tear and asked them between sobs, "You mean my husband is alive, he is safe? When will he come back home?" One of the sanyasis replied, "We have said your husband is safe, but we have not said he is coming back home. God has saved him and God will set him his tasks now. He does not belong to you but to all mankind."

'Now, Aai, like us, was an ordinary woman and she could not understand the language of the sanyasis and so she asked again, "Please do not talk in riddles. I am not a very clever woman and, without my husband, I become even more foolish. Please take pity on this tai of yours. Please tell me where he is. And is he well? And is he going to come back home?"

'It was as if the sanyasis spoke in one voice or maybe it was just that Aai and her children thought it was so but here is what they said, "Deep inside the ocean lives the devi. She protects all of you and your menfolk. Her boat picks up all the fishermen who have given up hope of ever coming back home and saves them from being eaten up by the ocean. But all those who are saved thus can never come back to live the life they left behind. They have to do devi's work. So they become sanyasis who go from village to village helping the poor and the needy, or they take on the work of boatmen on devi's boat."

'Two days and two nights, Aai wept at the thought of never seeing her husband again. Her children wept with her, beating their heads and wringing their hands at the tragedy that had come over their happy family. And then came a morning without any light. Aai thought that the end of the world had come. The skies burst into torrential rain and water gushed into every corner of their house. The children shouted and screamed for help as the flood waters carried their home away.

'For Aai and her children, there seemed to be no hope but to flow with the unrelenting waters of the flood. Suddenly, two men waded in through the water with huge baskets in their hands. Into one climbed Aai and in the others sat the children. The men pushed them out onto the safety of high ground. Dressed in orange robes, these men were so much like the sanyasis who had come visiting a few days previously—but they did not speak, not even when Aai asked them their names. They worked quietly with a smile on their faces, setting up a tent and filling it with food and clean clothes. And then just as suddenly as they had come, they went away. One moment they were there and the next moment, they had vanished.

'"Aai, who were they?" her daughter whispered as she clutched at the end of her mother's sari. Aai thought only for a moment and then replied, "Baba's friends." And for the first time in days, Aai spoke to her children without tears in her voice, "I want you to know that whatever others may tell you, your Baba is alive. He may never come here again but that is not because he is dead, or that he does not love us but because God loves him very much. He is God's chosen one and, like these sanyasis who helped us today, Baba helps people in distress. And for all his good work, God blesses you, his children. So go and play and if anyone asks you, tell them, your Baba lives with you, in your minds and your hearts."'

Radhabai wiped the tears off her face as she finished her story. 'So you see, our men who go to sea can never die. They will always live and thereby give their wives the right and pride to wear their mangalsutras, and their mothers hope to live out their old age.'

The children scampered away one by one after the story, but Meena did not stir. She sat until the sky covered the sea in its darkness; she sat clasping her mangalsutra. No, she thought to herself, she was never going to take it off.

ARUNDHUTI DASGUPTA

fishing in troubled Waters

In the Gangetic delta areas before Partition, the land was rich and fertile, but the rivers ran with salt from the sea, so farming was difficult. Tidal waves could suddenly wipe out entire villages; islands rose out of the waters while others were swallowed up. The waters brought life as well as death—the main source of livelihood was fishing.

Gopal and Rakhal had seen Padma suddenly grow up from the little tomboyish figure tripping around the village with mischief in her huge, dark eyes into the sensuous young woman working alongside her mother and aunts to eke out a living from that soft yet harsh soil. There was still mischief in her eyes, which were still huge and dark and bright, but the nature of that mischief had changed. Now she was a woman and she knew that both these wiry young men looked at her and loved her.

As is the way with such tales, Padma chose one and the other was hurt and angry and wrathful. Yet, the fortunes of love cannot stand in the way of the business of working for survival, so when Gopal suggested that he and Rakhal take advantage of the full moon and the tides to go further out into the sea and look for that huge catch of hilsa that would bring them enough money for a month, Rakhal agreed.

On the still, white night with the moonlight gleaming in the dark woods and throwing the still coconut trees into eerie relief, the two of them rowed out into the narrow creek. They carried a huge pot of drinking water, and a bag of dried rice and *gur*. These journeys were always uncertain. They could be out for days on the salt water with nothing to eat or drink except what they carried with them. The only sound was that of their oars gently slapping the dark water, thick and impenetrable as oil.

The strangeness of the night and the unspoken and unacknowledged tension between them kept them both quiet as they rowed further and further into the maze of inlets until Gopal said softly, 'Let us rest on this island for a while.' He guided their little boat safely into a bay in the tiny uninhabited island. He leapt into the thick squelchy mud to secure the boat and extended his hand to Rakhal. Rakhal was a bit taken aback by Gopal's gesture, but accepted it as an unspoken gesture of reconciliation and so gladly clasped the hand. But Gopal's grip became harder as he pushed Rakhal down and hit his face and head with the heavy, sharp handbeaten blade that all fishermen keep tucked into their *lungis*. Looking up at his partner with sadness, Rakhal just slumped into the mud. In the moonlight his blood looked thick and black like the palm syrup that they had both loved to eat together when they were young and friends and the black flashing eyes had not come between them.

Gopal sat there and smoked a bidi. Relieved at the thought of a job well done, he pulled the body into the muddy waters and set off alone into the stark black-and-white night.

At the very first attempt, Gopal caught the biggest hilsa that he had ever seen and, thanking the Lord for his beneficence, he pulled in the fish. It did not seem to put up much of a fight, which was lucky for Gopal as he would have had trouble landing such a large fish single-handedly. It shone in the silver moonlight, gleaming and beautiful. Flushed with triumph and victory, he covered the huge fish with the wet jute cloth and decided to head for home immediately—ready with a story of treacherous currents and rescue attempts.

He heard the chug-chug of the coastguards long before he saw the lights of the regular patrol. Gopal knew most of the men who worked in this area and so when one of them called to him, 'Alone today? Had any luck?' he wanted to astonish them with his huge catch. He called out, 'Great! I've got the biggest fish in the ocean today. Look, have you ever seen anything like it?'

As the two men leaned over to look with a joke about the fishermen's propensity for tall tales, Gopal flicked aside the jute cloth. And found the bloody body of Rakhal lying there with such a look of sadness in his eyes that it froze Gopal with absolute horror!

NILANJANA GUPTA

Yeo Ka?

This is another story of the Kolis.

Pandurang was the son of Subbutandel and would take over the leadership of the tribe once his father relinquished the reins. He was a vigorous, strong man in his prime, at one with the waves and his boat, and fearing nothing. Like his father, he led his team into the waters with fierce pride, racy wit, the charisma of a leader and the discipline born out of a dangerous way of life. He was used to travelling far and wide, and knew the sea like the back of his hand. This was not a man who would scare easily.

Early one morning, he strode across his hut as the blue glow of dawn was just beginning to touch the misty shores of the coast and sat beside his mother, Lachhmi, who had begun to gather her materials to repair the nets that lay drying like huge, hoary spiders' webs across the yard outside their hut—some draped on beached boats, some stretched out across bamboo poles.

Usually he went straight to sleep after a wash and a light meal, but now he sat on a rock beside his mother, the familiar pungent smell of drying Bombay duck stealing over him like a warm cloak. He watched her skillful hands weave the web that earned their livelihood.

Sushila, his wife, came out with an enamel mug of tea in one hand, wielding a neem stick in the other with which she vigorously scrubbed her teeth. Wordlessly she handed him the mug of tea. She knew he had been visiting that woman Seeta again. She lived a few islands away, but Sushila bore him no resentment. She accepted it as his right. It was no secret. Pandurang was a man and as son of the chief, he had to maintain his status. She knew the woman, but she herself was Pandurang's wife and proud of his position in the tribe. Anyway, she was much too busy to brood over his lifestyle or to question it too closely.

Each day she hoisted her basket of fish which Pandurang's sisters and married nieces had sorted out on the beach. Today she had a fairly large haul which had to be delivered to the next village, about ten miles to the east. She must arrive early enough to be in time to deliver the fish for the family to cook for their big puja.

The family were farmers who tilled their fields and ploughed their furrows with their buffaloes. They would pay her once a year with one *mudi* of rice, as they did every year whether she was able to supply them with large quantities fish or not. She of course kept her part of the bargain as best she could, as did they. She could see Pandurang was perturbed, but she would have to ask him about that later. She had problems of her own. That short fellow, she had heard, had been selling fish on her territory . . . just wait till she caught him. She would beat him black and blue . . . poaching on her ground!

'Humph!' she tossed her head, hitched up the cloth that she had wound round her waist, flashed her eyes at Pandurang and went in to dish out the simple meal of boiled rice soaked overnight they would all eat before they went about their various duties.

Parvati had cut the green chillies and coriander before she went to help her grandmother with the nets. Parvati would wash the clothes and dishes and bathe the younger children. Now she crouched close to her grandmother, hoping to hear what her father had to say as he murmured to Lachhmi, sipping his strong, sweet, milky tea. Sushila could see Subbutandel still out on the beach with his men, tugging at the ropes that controlled the boats and hauling in the nets. It was not like Pandurang to come away from this labour.

He sat with his head bowed thoughtfully, concern on his face.

'What is the matter, son?' asked Lachhmi as she tugged the yarn that bit into her calloused fingers. Her face bore the traces of the ravages of being a fisherman's daughter and wife. She had lost her father to the sea many many years ago, when she was a little girl. The years of fear and uncertainty could not be ignored: would she see her husband and sons home safe? Every day the prayers and the waiting—they were bound to line her face, but there was also a serene acceptance born out of the years of suffering. Fate would bring what it would, what would be, would be. She must simply watch and wait and keep the fires burning.

'I don't know what the matter is,' said Pandurang, shaking his head. 'Early every morning when I go out into the sea, it is so dark I can't see past my fingers. I have always known the dark and the waters below—these I do not fear.'

'Then what is it that you fear?' asked his mother.

Pandurang shook his head. He raised his black eyes to her face. 'Fear itself perhaps, Mother! Every night I hear it on our way back home at that hour that is the darkest before dawn. Little Krishna falls asleep. I keep rowing, but however much oil I put in the lamp, Mother, it goes out. Even on a moonlit night suddenly I can see no moon and no stars. It is dark, Mother. Darker than the night, and I feel it calling to me, every night. I hear it a little louder every night.'

'And what does it say, my son?' Only a slight tremble in her voice betrayed her fear.

'It says "*Yeo ka?*" Shall I come? Every night a little louder, till my blood runs thin and my bones freeze to ice! I do not fear anything that I know, but this I do not know.

'How can I fight it? I cannot see it. If I cannot know it, how should I fight it?'

His dark skin was mottled with sweat. His mother feared for him, but she knew it would insult him to offer words of comfort to soothe him. You did not tell Pandurang not to be afraid. You did not tell him to pray for safety. He was a god-fearing man who followed the rituals for his team and his family faithfully. 'Perhaps,' she said slowly, 'you should go to the temple and ask Mumbadevi what to do.'

Pandurang rose. He would go to Mumbadevi today and seek her blessings. Perhaps the priest would be able to advise him. He laid out the net in the sun, washed his face and went in to rest for a while.

The morning sun shimmered over the wet sand as the gulls strutted sideways to withstand the waves and squawked over the fish that were discarded. Here and there a spiky, bloated puffer fish or a thick black rope of moray eel lay staring and rotting on the beach, abandoned even by the pariahs that explored the leavings on the sand. Later at high tide, the sea would come in to claim its own. A little wagtail, racing forward to peck on small mussels, bobbed and dipped and then raced back as the waves came crashing onto its feeding ground. The water lapped intermittently at his toes as Pandurang took long firm strides over the wet foam. The salt lay in soft dried bubbles on the sand and tiny translucent crabs wove intricate patterns as they scuttled to dig their little holes.

At the temple the priest greeted Pandurang and accepted his offerings of flowers and coconut. There was a string of dried fish as a special treat for the priest, who was a friend of Subbutandel's.

'You seem troubled, my son,' said the priest as the young man laid the offerings at the altar.

Pandurang said, 'I must ask the Devi for help, Uncle. Please tell me what to do.'

The priest sat before the goddess for a while; then suddenly he spoke as if in a trance. His voice became as a woman's and he said to Pandurang, 'Go to the waters of the night. Take with you a small bowl of toddy and throw it into the sea. The evil spirit will stop bothering you once its thirst has been quenched.'

A load was lifted from Pandurang at a solution as simple as this. He paid his respects to the goddess and to the priest and returned home singing.

That night he sailed with little Krishna pulling valiantly at the oars, and they sang rhythmically as they rowed and punted and cast their nets wide and checked them where they had floated their lights to attract the fish. By and by Krishna fell asleep and the stars twirled their course about the heavens. Pandurang waited and watched and as he sailed he saw the darkness loom over the horizon as the formless, menacing voice boomed over the deep: 'Yeo ka? Shall I come?'

This time Pandurang was ready and he threw the toddy into the darkness. Without a word, he turned back towards his lamp. He lit the flame that had guttered and flickered out and sailed home, confident again. He was not afraid. He knew what he had to do.

SHAIONTONI BOSE

the helpful Spirit

A bramhadaitya is the spirit of a brahmin that resides in a tree and is considered the most powerful in the hierarchy of the spirit world. Bramhadaityas seem an ancient Shamanistic belief in tree spirits overlaid by a later Hindu interpretation.

The bel tree was beside the house, laden with fruit that looked like cannon balls. The soft orange pulp from its fruit, thick and sticky, was often made into a cooling sherbet. A coppersmith sometimes came to sit on its branches, camouflaged within the green leaves, adding to the dreamy haze of summer with its insistent 'tuk-tuk-tuk'. The sun-dappled shade beneath the tree harboured a wood ant or two, and Prakash shifted his feet to avoid their hurry and scurry. Their jaws were strong and their bites quite vicious. He stood there, gazing at the tree, remembering his mother's story . . .

It was the middle of the night. Saraswati woke up to find little Prakash whimpering in his sleep. He was ready for his nightly ritual. Saraswati shook him gently by the shoulder and made him walk, not far, just to the window. It was an old house, the bathroom was miles away and it was easier for his mother to dispense with his needs quickly in this fashion. He sleepily obliged, his eyes closed, pyjama strings dangling, then shuffled off again, back to the bed. Saraswati got back in and pulled the thin sheet over her son.

As she dozed off once more, it seemed to her that the bright moonlight streaming through the window suddenly darkened as a huge shadowy shape loomed in front of her. She could just see a massive presence and feel, rather than hear, the voice breathing into her soul: 'Why do you insult me like this?'

'Insult? Have . . . have I insulted you?'

'You should be placing offerings at the foot of my tree every morning. You should be praying to it, to me. Instead, every night you choose to make your son soil my sanctuary. I will curse you. May you be born again as a . . .'

'No, no,' said poor Saraswati hastily. 'I will make amends. I am truly sorry, I did not know, I did not realize . . . I will do puja to you every day from this morning onwards. You'll see. Please, please forgive me!'

Perhaps mollified by the sincerity in her voice, the bramhadaitya graciously conceded her request and returned to his tree.

After that, every morning, as soon as she woke up Saraswati prayed at the foot of the tree. She would light a few incense sticks, place a few sugar balls at the base of the trunk, and bow low holding her hands in a deep namaskar before it, murmuring as she had been taught: 'Om, shanti, shanti, shanti.' Then she would blow the conch shell and begin her daily chores.

Some time later, when Saraswati's puja had been perfectly integrated into the family routine, she had a dream in which the apparition appeared to her once again.

This time his voice was rich and warm with pleasure as he praised her efforts. 'You have pleased me,' he said. 'I have come to you to grant you a boon. If ever you need help, come to me. You have but to ask.'

Many months went by. Saraswati forgot the spirit's promise, though she continued to pray religiously every day.

One day, as she was putting away the clothes and dusting the furniture, her husband burst in, extremely agitated. His hair was tousled, his shirt was askew, his face was crumpled in worry. He threw open his cupboard, rummaged through his clothes, pulled out the drawers and thumbed through all the papers he could find.

He even pulled out a file which had all their investments carefully noted and documented in it.

It was a time of political unrest and in almost every family there was someone who was a member of some secret society and participated in demonstrations, marches and satyagraha. There had to be just a suggestion of underground activities, one rumour, and the authorities came bearing down, demanding proof. 'Where were you on this day, at this time? What were you doing? State your present occupation. Prove it!' It went on and on. If you were not able to put forward a sufficiently confident reply, you might be clapped into jail and dubbed in the police records as *Ek Number ka Badmash*, a Rascal of the First Order.

'What is the matter?' asked Saraswati.

Her husband looked despairingly up at her and said, 'I don't know where it is. That slip of paper I kept here: it proves I was at Raniganj on 3 April. If I don't show it, I don't know what will happen to me!'

He described the paper to her and both searched desperately, but neither could found it.

'They will come tomorrow. I don't know what to tell them.'

Saraswati lay down to sleep that night with those despairing words ringing in her ears. Her eyes were open, or so she thought, and sleep just did not seem to come. As she lay staring at the ceiling, once more she saw the vast shape loom up before her.

'You are troubled,' he said. 'Yet you didn't think to come to me. I can help you. What is the matter?'

Saraswati told him that they had looked high and low for a slip of paper, but could not find it. The spirit listened, and then he said, 'Look in the left-hand corner at the back of the cupboard. The paper has slipped between the cracks. You will find it there tomorrow morning.'

The next morning, Saraswati awoke early. She did not forget to light the incense and blow her conch before she began to look in every crack at the back of the cupboard and there, sure enough, with just the corner sticking out, she found the offending article. She woke her husband up and showed it to him.

From that day onwards, both of them did puja at the bel tree, and little Prakash lit the incense. It isn't everybody's family that has a helpful spirit!

SHAIONTONI BOSE

the legend of the leaping dolphins

The morning was peaceful and the water a calm grey-blue as the *Queen of the Waves* gently chugged through the narrow channels that connected the backwaters to the open sea. Riya hopped first on one leg and then the other until her father sternly told her to sit down.

'Will we *really* see dolphins, Mama, really? Will we?'

Ricardo turned around and smiled at the little girl. 'Yes, little one, you will,' he said. 'You are going out in the *Queen of the Waves*, aren't you? See the saint, how he guides the boat . . .'

'But how can you guarantee it?' Pran, Riya's father, asked the boatman sceptically.

The hilly emerald coastline with its swaying palms and its whitewashed churches fell behind as the waters widened to receive the boat.

There was a short silence, then Ricardo said, 'Well, it's a long story.' He looked reflectively at the little wooden statuette that stood sheltered in the prow of the boat. It was an unusual piece, delicate, with simple, elegantly cut robes and a small carved head and hands that could be made of ivory for all anyone knew. The deep crimson paint was worn dull, and the wood showed through underneath as if each was a part of the other.

'That statuette must be very old,' said Lila, Riya's mother.

'There are many stories about this statue in our family,' Ricardo smiled. 'It is said it was cast ashore by a dolphin one day long ago, when one of my ancestors was lifting his nets out of the sea. He brought it home, and placed it in a hole in the stone wall of our home. The family prospered and grew.'

Riya listened wide-eyed, seeing all the images the story evoked in her head. There was a lot she didn't understand, but that just added to the mystery.

As the generations went by, the family began to take their fortunes for granted, and respect for the family saint began to erode. The sons began to grow careless, their wives neglectful. The altar room was left dark. The candles were not lit.

In the midst of this decay, two brothers were born, Florentio and Agnelo. Florentio grew up the darling of the family, the heir to the family fortunes, spoilt and indulged. He was handsome and fair-skinned, and could sing and dance and charm the birds off the trees and the girls into the bushes. He could also drink. Like a fish.

As he grew older and his drinking increased, he began to sell bits and pieces of the already depleted family treasures, in a curio shop, to sustain his way of life. Tourists had begun to flock to the region in a big way lately, and were always on the lookout for a bargain. He managed to make quite a tidy income, and began to grow fat with alcohol, like a pickled red grape. His fair complexion grew pink, and his mouth slack.

Agnelo, the younger of the two brothers, was more attached to his home and spent a great deal of time dreaming on his own among the stone and wood and plaster of his family home. The lovely curved wrought-iron rails of the balconies and the delicate flower and leaf plaster work on the corners of the pillars, the ornate tiles on the floor, and the sunlit courtyard with the frangipani tree beckoned him to sit with a book or his flute, playing some haunting melody. Agnelo could spend hours watching the wood ants crawling up and down the frangipani. He was quite happy to remain unnoticed so that he could be left in peace to dream as he chose. When he was noticed his ears were cuffed often enough for 'wasting time'.

During the hot summer months he would lie on his carved wooden bed, gazing at the high wooden ceilings which kept the house cool. During the pouring monsoon, so trying for his hot-blooded brother, he would sit at the edge of the balcony to taste and feel the cool drops of rain splash on his thin dark intense face, and on his slim bony hands and trickle down his wrists. He loved the passion of the thunder and the lightning, and the relentless drumming of the rain on the tiles of the roof, and this was the time that his flute took on the rhythms he could hear all around him, and blend and rise with the wind.

He loved the perfect proportions of the house and the beautiful things his family had collected in it over the years. He spent many hours holding them, turning them around in his hands, and longed to create something as perfect himself. But he had no desire to hold them to himself. He felt each belonged to its own place in the house, and there they should stay.

Florentio's complete disregard of them, except as things that would bring more cash to squander, made him angry, but he kept his peace. He did not feel that saying anything would have much effect as his parents indulged his brother.

To Agnelo, the most precious possession in the entire house was the little saint that was kept in the niche in the wall. He would go to it every day, and as soon as he was old enough to strike a match he lit a candle for it regularly.

One day, when he went to the niche as usual, he saw, to his horror, that the little figure was not in its appointed place. All the years of pent-up frustration came out in a long loud howl of despair, as he raced out of the arched door and ran furiously to the curio shop at the back. 'Florentio!' he shouted. 'What have you done?'

Florentio was busy persuading an interested customer to look at all kinds of old and new knick-knacks that crowded the showcases, shelves and tables of the packed curio shop. 'This is a pair of hounds; it is quite old. It's come from one of these old Portuguese homes. Very well worth the . . . What is the matter with you, Agnelo? Get out!'

Agnelo grabbed at Florentio and pulled him by his shirt, yelling, 'What have you done with it?'

The tourist quietly picked up his belongings and made a hasty exit.

'You've lost me a customer, you good-for-nothing idiot!'

'You are selling our birthright, Florentio. What are you thinking of?' sobbed Agnelo.

The cashier and Florentio took Agnelo firmly by the shoulders and pushed him unceremoniously out of the shop. As Florentio returned to the shop, he gave strict orders to secure it with an extra lock. He was not going to risk Agnelo sneaking in to steal the statuette.

From that night onwards things began to go terribly wrong— all kinds of things. Florentio dropped a bottle and a sliver of glass pierced his foot. It began to fester, and he fell ill. When he was finally able to go back to the shop, he found that the ceiling had leaked and destroyed some of the more valuable scrolls and paintings he had stocked. The cashier ran off with the month's savings, and he could get no one else to work for him because people began to report strange flickering lights and said that the shop was haunted.

The curios began to gather dust. Florentio was unable to look after the shop all on his own. He began to grow bitter and angry. It was all Agnelo's fault. Why couldn't the fool do a proper day's work instead of going off in his fishing boat and playing that flute? One night, in a drunken rage, he went up to Agnelo's room and yelled at him. Then he went out into the night with a lantern and stumbled to the shop, where he had hidden an extra cache of his favourite liquor. Agnelo watched him go, then as he looked out he saw there was already a strange light flickering in the shop.

'Fire!' he yelled, and ran downstairs after his brother. 'Florentio, wait, fire! Your shop is on fire!'

The two brothers rushed into the shop. It was silent and dark. There was no sound, no movement, but a strange glow from a dark corner. They edged round the curios and round the shelves, and there was the little figure glowing softly in the dark. As the brothers stood looking, amazed, one spark of light detached itself and moved slowly to the open door. Florentio fell to the ground, sobbing and whimpering, 'Forgive me Father, for I have sinned.' Agnelo hauled him up, and the two brothers followed the light which seemed to wait for them as it moved forward up the path.

The path began to get rocky and sandy, as the will-o'-the-wisp took them down to the sea and up the promontory that overlooked the island of St Peter's where the little family church lay forlorn and neglected.

The next morning a weeping and chastened Florentio and a determined Agnelo took their boat out into the water together for the first time in years. Agnelo placed the little figurine at the head of the boat.

'He will guide us through rain and storm,' murmured Agnelo, and Florentio said not a word.

The two brothers rowed to the island, and began to set their little church to rights. They enlisted all the help they could get, kept them well plied with liquor from Florentio's store, and did much of the work themselves. At the end of it all, the church was restored, shining white in the sun, serene and beautiful.

The day the church was completed, Agnelo and Florentio stood gazing out at it in pride, and as they gazed, a school of dolphins leaped and twirled joyously into the air, at one with the grey-blue sea and the sky, in harmony with the world and themselves.

'From that day on to this,' said Ricardo, 'the dolphins have never failed to leap when the *Queen of the Waves* goes out to sea.'

'And you of course are Agnelo's son,' said Pran, smiling at him.

'No, sir,' Ricardo smiled back, 'I'm Florentio's son.'

SHAIONTONI BOSE

the temple Spirits

The Santhals, one of the original tribes of India now pushed further and further back by invaders, hold sacred the spirits of the trees and earth, of air and water.

David Rosser stood outside his bungalow and watched the jeep being loaded. Forty years in India were over and he was going back to Wales, his birthplace, as alien to him now as India had been when he first came out, a callow lad of twenty-two, fresh out of engineering college. He specialized in mining engineering and had been recruited by an agency house with its head office in London, to help look after their interests in the coal mines on the Bengal-Bihar border.

Brought up on Kipling and Forster, Rosser had had some fantastic notions of the country which was to be his home for the length of his working life. A land of princes and ascetics, of elephants and tigers, of jungles and rivers and mountains. A land of such contradictions where superstition and logic held equal sway, where Job-like patience could give way if disturbed to murderous mutiny.

The part of India where he had spent his years, he mused, was not very different from his native Wales. Both were lands of legends, superstition and other worlds—that of Celts and this of the Santhals.

Each household has its own Orabonga, its tutelary god, which is adored with secret ritual, jealously guarded from even members of the family other than the head. Before he dies, the head of each household whispers the name of this deity into the ear of his eldest son. Their sacred tree is the sal. To propitiate its spirit, and to protect the clan from dreaded disease and calamity, red cocks, chickens and goats are sacrificed after men and women have danced around the tree to the beat of drums, chanting songs in veneration of the chief or of the founder of the clan.

Besides this, there are ghouls and ghosts: the Abgi, the ghost who eats humans; the Pargana Bonga or parish deity; the Daddi Bonga, the well demon; Buru Bonga, the mountain demon; and the Bir Bonga, the forest gods. Chando, the sun god, is generally held to rule supreme.

Rosser quickly grew to love this country, learnt a smattering of the language and often on a Sunday walked in the sal and mahua forests, listening to the calls of birds and rustle of leaves, with no other sound to disturb his tranquillity.

His office and mines were on one bank of the river Damodar, Sanctoria, in Dishegarh, the corrupted name for Dihi Sher Ghar— the town of Sher Shah's fort, built so many centuries ago.

Across the river was the realm of the rajas of Panchkote, a ruined fortress on a forested hill. The twentieth-century rajas had left this fortress for their mansion nearby, as there had been no need to defend it from marauders once the British became the supreme rulers.

In the forests of Panchkote had occured the incident which had changed Rosser's relationship with the country forever. It was soon after the War. Rosser had just returned to his job in India. It was Christmas, the weather was perfect for picnics, and he was very lonely. He decided to drive over to Panchkote and spend the day in the forest, and ramble among the ruins, thinking of past battles that perhaps never were.

Just before sunset, he came upon what must have been a temple. There was nothing left of its structure but the ground around was strewn with terracotta figures, peculiar to that part of the world. He tripped over what he thought was a stone, but suddenly realized was a small, beautifully crafted figure in perfect condition. He picked it up and was studying its beauty when as if from nowhere a gnome-like figure appeared, a Santhal with a bundle of sticks on his head. '*Sheta chhui na saheb, sheta Bonga,*' he warned. Don't touch that, it is a Bonga. But some devil got into Rosser and he paid no heed to the man. He took the figure, put it in his car and driven home.

He called for his servants to unload the car. Sombari and Pahar, his valet and bearer, hurried out, but when they saw the figure they shrank back in fear. 'Take it back, saheb, to the forest where it belongs,' they said. No amount of cajoling or threatening would persuade them to touch it. Eventually Rosser took it out himself and put it on his desk in the study where he could see it while he worked.

Somehow, he felt rather uneasy—not delighted as he had been when he first saw the little figure. He put it down to the superstitious behaviour of his servants and to the strange warning of the woodman. He had a couple of stiff drinks, ate his dinner and went to bed.

That night he was terribly disturbed by unknown fears and snatchy intangible nightmare visions of things he couldn't quite see and yet could almost feel. It was as if all the stories of goblins and giants and eerie spirits which had so terrified him in childhood had come back now, even more fearful, even darker. He tried to put on the light, but couldn't find the switch; he tried to call for help, but no sound would come out. And so he lay, clutching his blanket over himself, until morning.

A hot bath, he thought, and a steaming bowl of porridge would cure the ills of the night. After breakfast he went to the study and found the figure not as he had placed it, but turned to face the east. The servants, he knew, had no hand in this. Even so, he warned them that no one was to change his arrangements. They just looked at each other in fear and said nothing.

Nothing happened for a few days and Rosser went on with his work as normal. He was sitting in his office on a Tuesday morning when he was handed a letter from home. It was from his mother-in-law to say that his wife was suddenly taken very ill and had to be rushed to hospital. Apart from the shock of the news, Rosser had an uncomfortable feeling, a sort of premonition of worse to come.

Rosser went to bed, still worrying about his wife, and again, after a disturbed night, went into his study, to find the *murti* facing east again. This time he saw it had a triumphant look on its face and somehow this made him determined not to be shaken by it. He put it back where he wished it to be and left for the office. At the end of the day he received a cable to say that his eldest son had been injured in a car accident.

Rosser made a trunk call to Calcutta to ask if he could take leave and go home on the newly introduced BOAC flight. While he waited for the official sanction of his leave, he took a decision. He went into his study, took the murti and placed it in his car. He drove eastward to Panchkote and defying the cold, the dark, the deep forest and its unseen dangers, walked to where he had found the idol and reverently, very reverently, put it down on the ground. He then said a prayer over it and went back home.

In a couple of days there were cables from home to say that his wife was out of danger and recovering, and that his son was not as seriously injured as had been thought. Rosser cancelled his leave, reserving it for a happier time.

The last box had been loaded. Sombari and his wife, Lakhia, Pahar and Sukro all stood with tears in their eyes. Their saheb was going away. Rosser looked back and thought of the unmeasured, immeasurable country he was leaving. He sighed and drove off.

BUNNY GUPTA

haunted houses

from across the ages

Legend has it that Sultan Bajbahadur, who was famous for his songs of love, was later known by another name in the Mughal capital of Delhi where noblemen and common people gathered to hear the unforgettable strains of his music reaching the heavens in search of his beloved: Baiju Baura!

Memories of a past life—or the fantasies of an impressionable young romantic? Even after so many years, I still don't know whether it really happened. Did I really see something out of the past, or was it just the effect of the surroundings on my imagination?

It happened more than thirty years ago. I had just graduated and had begun teaching in a college. I had come to Madhya Pradesh with a large group of friends—about thirty in all—during the Durga puja vacations. After visiting the typical tourist spots like Jabalpur and the Marble Rocks, we reached Dhar, the capital of Raja Bhoj of the famous 'Thirty-two Throne' stories.

We could see the ruins of an ancient fort on top of the hill. When we expressed our desire to explore the ruins, a local Bengali gentleman said to us, 'Why do you want to go up there? If you want to see ruins, why don't you go to Mandu, the ancient capital of Malav? Right at the edge of the Vindhya hills are the ruins of a wonderful ancient abandoned city, walled in for an area of nearly forty square miles. It's about four hours by bus. If you set out early in the morning, you can spend the whole day there and return by evening. There are no arrangements there for staying overnight.'

Today, thanks to the enterprise of MP Tourism, almost everyone has heard of Mandu, and it has several hotels. But when we went there, sometime in the 1960s, not many people had heard of it.

Anyway, we took the bus the next day and reached Mandu at around ten in the morning. It really was wonderful. On the hill top were the palaces, masjid, darbar hall and many smaller mahals but, most beautiful of all, sitting on the highest point, was Roopmati's Mahal. This was built by the Sultan Bajbahadur, a contemporary of Akbar, for his Hindu wife, Roopmati. As he showed us around, the guide told us the tragic tale of these two lovers of music, Bajbahadur and Roopmati, which is still sung of by the local bards. The young Sultan Bajbahadur was not only a true connoisseur of music, he was a good singer as well. One day as he was travelling in the jungles near the foothills of Mandu, he was entranced by the sweet, melodious voice of a young girl. The beautiful young girl too was captivated by Bajbahadur and his songs. They fell deeply in love at their first meeting. Bajbahadur came to know that she was the daughter of a Hindu feudal lord whose estates were just outside Mandu and that her name was Roopmati. The two of them met and sang together, and with each meeting, their love grew deeper and deeper. The difference in religion was forgotten in their shared passion for music. Soon, Roopmati was welcomed to Mandu as queen. A new palace was built for her: Roopmati's Mahal.

The next few years passed in happiness. But there was a dark cloud gathering on the horizon of the little hill state. From Delhi, Akbar sent a company of Mughal soldiers under the leadership of Aadam Khan to capture Mandu. The young Bajbahadur took up the sword in place of his taanpura, and he rode with his army to defend his kingdom.

In the battle, Bajbahadur was defeated but he managed to escape with his life. Aadam Khan entered Mandu and spread the rumour that Bajbahadur had died in battle. Greedy and cunning, he proposed marriage to the grieving Roopmati. However, none of the enticements he offered could make Roopmati consent. Finally he threatened her—if she did not agree within the month, he would force her into marriage. Roopmati's belief that Bajbahadur had not died was unshakeable. She waited for him to return triumphantly and rescue her. As each day was succeeded by the next, the bright flame of belief and hope grew dim. The alotted month passed. There was no news of Bajbahadur.

On the appointed day, Roopmati sent word to Aadam Khan that she was ready to marry him and that he should make the necessary preparations. It was a still night. Aadam Khan sat in the wedding pandal awaiting the appearance of the beautiful queen. Finally, Roopmati arrived, dressed from head to foot in royal finery, singing her last song for her beloved Sultan. The strains of her tragic song still lingered in the air as she stopped in front of Aadam Khan and kissed the ring that held the drop of poison that released her from the pain of losing her beloved.

Meanwhile, Bajbahadur had no idea of what was happening in Mandu. He had escaped to one of the smaller border kingdoms and, with the help of the neighbouring kings, began to muster an army to regain his kingdom. A few months later he rode into Mandu and drove out the Mughals. However, it was too late by then.

Bajbahadur could not bear to live in Mandu without his beloved Roopmati, so one night he left his kingdom, never to return. The guide told us that on a still dark night, the sad strains of music could still be heard from Roopmati's Mahal as she sang sweetly and sadly of her separation from her lover.

This tale captured my heart, as it did of my closest friend too. We were young and both of us were born romantics. Though we were students of chemistry, we were fascinated by tales from the glorious past, of rajas and sultans and their heroic wars and romantic loves. Even as we listened to the guide's story, we decided that to really savour the atmosphere, we had to return at night when everything would be deserted.

We had noticed a dharamshala at the foot of the hills a few miles away. That would do! The two of us pretended that we were feeling ill and didn't want to travel back that night. Accordingly, we booked rooms in the dharamshala. Mahapatra, another friend,

also joined us in our plan. The three of us decided to wait till all
the others were asleep and then steal out.

Tired out by the exertions of the day, everyone went to bed quite
early. We waited till eleven o'clock. Then the three of us quietly
climbed out of the large windows.

It must have been close to the Laxmi Purnima; everything was
flooded with silvery moonlight. Above us stood the stark black and
silver form of Roopmati's Mahal, overlooking the mysterious
stillness of the city of Mandu. We walked in silence along the road
for about half an hour, drawn by the silhouettes of the ruins above
us, to reach the gates of the fort. From here the road began winding
up the steep slope, and in and around the ruined buildings.

That morning we had noticed a small office belonging to the
Archaeological Department with a chowkidar's hut alongside. By
this time, all three of us were quite jittery. What had seemed like a
great plan by daylight seemed terrifying by night. It's not that we
were scared of ghosts. Everything that we had seen in dazzling
sunlight in the company of boisterous friends looked strange and
mysterious in the bone-white moonlight. Solid forms seemed
transformed into strange shadows looming around us. We decided
that it would be safer to have the chowkidar accompany us as we
entered the walled city. After much calling and banging, a sleepy-
eyed watchman emerged with a dim lantern. Hearing our plan, he
pleaded with us not to go: '*Mat jao*! The spirits emerge at night
there!' Neither coaxing nor bribes could shake his resolve, so
eventually the three of us went on into the city towards Roopmati's
Mahal.

As we climbed up in the stark white light of the moon, we passed
Hindola Mahal, Ship Mahal and many other palaces until we
reached the masjid. Here, about halfway up, stood a huge two-
storeyed palace, with a flight of stairs that led straight to the terrace
from the street. The terrace, paved with stone, was as big as a
football field. The pillars that held up the roof that covered a part
of it were elaborately carved. The guide had told us that soirees
were held here and the Sultan himself would sit in the covered
part with his begums. Beautiful dancers would sway to the sweet,

melodious voices of the singers. Goblets of gold and rubies brought from Persia would be raised to the sound of the anklets marking time to the complicated taals.

Something made me turn to my companions and say, 'Let's not bother to go up to Roopmati's Mahal. For tonight let's just sit here and be sultans for the night. Let's sit under the roof and bring back one of those nights from five hundred years ago.'

We climbed softly up the stairs and went to sit under the carved stone canopy. We sat facing the huge floor which once rang with melody and passion, and looked at the walls far away which encompassed the wondrous ruins of this beautiful stone city.

I cannot begin to describe the splendour of the moonlit scene in front of me on that calm, still night. The magic of those ancient stone buildings overwhelmed us and we were drunk with delight and anticipation as we leant back waiting for those graceful dancers to cross the centuries and stand before us. I was no longer Pradip Gupta, a newly appointed college lecturer from Behala: I belonged here. Not today, but many many years ago, I too had sat here and waited for the show to begin. These stones, these shadows were familiar to me. The palace, the hills, the buildings, I knew them all so well. How many times had I galloped through those gates on my favourite horse with my turban on my head and my sword by my side. On such a moonlit night had I first seen my beloved as she stepped out onto the roof to dance and weave her web of magic. Where was she now? Why wasn't she coming out with her accompanists to begin that dance of indescribable beauty? I was torn by a sense of anticipation and melancholy.

Unable to bear it any longer, I stood up and hurried down the stairs to the streets of this city of mine in search of those old days so many years ago. I don't know how long we roamed the streets in search of the familiar past. We wandered the shadowy streets of the abandoned, silent city caught in a web of maya. Did I actually see anything? Did I really hear any music? I don't know. But I know that that moonlit night in Mandu brought back memories of a similar night from some past. I could sense the presence of dancers and singers and soldiers and noblemen and the beautiful queen long vanished. I could feel a deep longing for my long-lost love as I roamed the shadowy streets in search of her.

I don't know how we came out of the city. When I returned to my senses, I found it was morning. The three of us were lying in a room with a doctor bending over us. Apparently he had found us unconscious in front of the gates of the ruined city as he went for his morning constitutional. He demanded to know what had happened the previous night. On hearing our stories, he frowned and said that everyone knew that restless souls from the past roamed the streets of the stone city at night. It was they who had caused us to become delirious and roam the streets in search of what was long gone. It was only our great good fortune which we must have carried over from our earlier births that had managed to take us out of the precincts of the city. Otherwise we would have been found dead in one of the palaces the this morning.

I still wonder what happened on that moonlit night so many years ago, when I had become a sultan for a while.

PRADIP GUPTA
Translated from the Bengali by NILANJANA GUPTA

the gold mohurs

Lucknow: Its crumbling palaces and bustling baraars are soaked in history. The memories of ancient loves and hates, jealousies and passions, permeate the winding gullies and lurk behind the wooden shutters of barred windows.

Dr Majumdar and his family had come to Lucknow at the start of his career as a physician. Over the years he had built up a large practice which extended beyond Lucknow, to Kanpur and Allahabad. A kind, generous and conscientious man, the doctor was highly respected by his patients from all walks of life, from aristocratic nawabs to humble tongawalas.

One winter night at the beginning of the twentieth century, the doctor was about to retire for the night when there was a desperate knocking on his door. Taking an oil lamp in his hand, for the house was in darkness, the good doctor went downstairs and opened the door. The two men standing outside were dressed in the elaborate dress of zamindari retainers, holding lanterns which dimly lit the dark around them. The doctor, although he knew most of the local gentry, did not recognize them, but their courteous salutation and air of concern left him in no doubt that their request for him to accompany them to see a patient was genuine. And so he called for his faithful bearer Ayadin to help him dress and carry his bag down to the waiting carriage.

Through the freezing darkness, the carriage went in and out the lanes of the old city, a few flickering flames in high-up windows and the carriage lamps the only light and the clip-clop of the horses' hooves the only sound, for it was winter and Lucknow slept. At last in the small alleyway in Hazratbagh they stopped before a huge studded door which, as one of the men pushed it, creaked open. An old man with a long beard, dressed in fine white clothes—quite inadequate for the weather, the doctor thought— came silently down the stairs and led him up to a large bare room, striking matches all the way, for there was no other light.

In this cavernous space with thirty-foot ceilings, there were no drapes, no floor coverings, no curtains. The wooden shutters were closed and in the centre of the room was a cot in which was a figure covered in a sheet. The doctor was led up to this. His patient was a woman; he had to carry out his investigations under cover, for that was the custom of the time. She was frail, mere skin and bone, breathing in short shallow breaths. He felt for the pulse. His few questions were answered in chaste and courteous Urdu by the old man. The doctor then wrote his prescription and left it by the bed. He was seen home in the same carriage and, as he got off at his front door, two coins were slipped into his hand. Too exhausted by this visit to even look at what he held, the doctor put them in his pocket and forgot about them.

The next day, when he had completed his morning rounds, the doctor made a special effort to go to Hazratbagh and seek out the house of the last night. He found to his surprise that the great door had a padlock on it and the shopkeepers and local passers-by, who recognized the well-known doctor, assured him that it had been locked for many years. Suspecting foul play, the doctor informed the police who came forth in full force and broke open the heavy door.

There was not a soul in sight. A musty smell of forlorn decay met them, and a belfry full of bats, disturbed by the light, flew about. The doctor saw just his own footprints on the dust that lay thick on the ground. What of the other three people who had walked there last night?

They climbed up the stairs and into the room where an empty

cot lay with the prescription by it. Burnt matchsticks littered the floor. The house was scoured from top to bottom, but the only inhabitants to emerge were a reluctant spider and an irate bat or two, the rest having gone back to hanging from the ceiling beams. A completely nonplussed doctor and bemused police force left Hazratbagh.

That evening, the doctor sat in his study and mused over the events of the past twenty-four hours. Strange, he thought, strange that there was not a trace of anyone but he being in that house in the night. Who were these people and where could they now be? Then he remembered. The coins, the coins! He sent Ayadin for his jacket and put his hand in the pocket. There they were, two seventeenth-century Moghul gold mohurs.

For many years they were in the Majumdar puja room and could only be touched after hands had been washed in *Gangajal*. The doctor's grandson felt they would be safer in a bank and there they are today, in a vault.

ARABINDA RAY

motihari bungalow

The unhappy story of indigo in Bengal and Bihar begins at the end of the eighteenth century. In 1788 some ten European planters were invited by the East India Company to experiment with indigo in this part of the world. However, until 1829 they were not allowed to lease or to buy land. They would therefore coerce the local farmers to grow indigo on their own land instead of rice, their staple crop. Protests fell on deaf ears for indigo was the new wonder commodity and fetched a high price.

The European planters, who were expert at the cultivation of high quality indigo, were few in number, their plantation areas large and their private residences and factories bounded by walls enclosing hundreds of acres of land. This isolation and distance from authority made them autocratic to the point of despotism.

There was an indigo plantation in Ghorasarai, in Motihari district, which in 1840 included five villages. One hundred acres of land were walled in to enclose the house of the manager, his outhouses, the main factory and the three other factories, the houses of the assistants, a small hospital, a school for the children of the workers, stables, a farm and a slaughterhouse. While the farmers lived in the outlying villages, the management and staff of the plantation lived within the walled area.

The manager of Ghorasarai, a Scotsman called Fothergill, was a hard worker, a hard drinker and a hard taskmaster. A tall, red-haired, big-built man, he had a violent temper and a contempt for the Indian whom he considered subhuman, born only to be the white man's beast of burden. His extortions from the peasants, his excesses with their families, surpassed the already bad reputation of planters among the ryots. He was widely feared and hated. Reports of his excesses reached the head office in Calcutta and he was advised to go home on a six-month furlough and get married. It was hoped that he might settle down under the calming influence of a wife and family.

He came back with a lovely young wife, much younger than himself, intelligent and eager to learn about and love her new surroundings. Anne Fothergill found herself the mistress of an enormous mansion and a whole army of servants.

The house was built on a high plinth with a flight of steps leading up to an open veranda which went around the rooms, keeping them protected from the extremes of climate common in that part of Bihar. The rooms were large and had high ceilings. There were ten rooms on the ground floor and ten rooms up a winding flight of marble stairs ornamented by a wrought-iron banister which had come all the way from England when the house had been built ten years previously. The reception rooms and offices were in a separate wing and the kitchens detached from the house. Beneath the front steps was the boiler room which supplied hot water for baths. The ground-floor rooms led off a large central hall which was called the ballroom, although when Anne came to Ghorasarai parties and balls were unheard of in the big house.

Upstairs were the bedrooms, a private parlour for the memsaheb to entertain her friends, and a boudoir where she could cultivate her hobbies and write letters home—an important part of the expatriate's life.

Charmed by her new home and quick to understand her responsibilities, Anne began by refurbishing the house. She sent for catalogues from the newly opened Army and Navy department store in Calcutta and ordered bolts of material, sets of furniture for the drawing rooms, bedrooms and dressing rooms; she ordered lamps from De Leemans and saddlery from the best saddlers in Calcutta. She got the tailor who lived in the compound and his two assistants to get to work. They would cut and sew on one end of the veranda all day, while at another end the polishwalas were busy shining the mahogany furniture for the rooms. Soon the heavy wooden louvred doors were open all day, to give glimpses, through the new curtains, of rooms filled with gleaming furniture. The Ghorasarai house took on the look of the burra saheb's house it had hitherto lacked.

Nor was Anne idle herself, for one of the first things she did was to take Hindi lessons from a munshi. She then began to ride out into the villages and talk to the women and children. Sometimes she would bring them home and sing little Scottish songs to them and teach them nursery rhymes and how to draw. She would let them play in the garden and feed the fish in the tank with her.

The work she was most deeply involved in, however, was at the hospital which she visited regularly. Once there was an outbreak of cholera in the district and some of the factory workers were affected with it. Anne Fothergill had been in Edinburgh when her father's friend Dr Robert Grahame had carried out a successful cure during a similar epidemic. She told the local doctor about it, and he experimented with large injections of saline and had a good measure of success. Quite naturally, this was regarded as a miracle and Mrs Fothergill became the patron saint of the hospital.

The wives of the two assistant managers who lived within the compound were much older and more conservative, and after a few attempts at advising her to leave the natives be, they proceeded to treat her with some distance. She did attend their sewing sessions and had them to tea at Ghorasarai House, but only occasionally.

Fothergill looked at his wife's popularity with the locals with thorough distaste—he disapproved of her 'hobnobbing with the natives'. As the months went by, his annoyance grew. If ever he came home to find any of the village women there, he would fly into a rage and have them thrown out.

Gradually the Bengali and Bihari women, fearing for their men's jobs, stopped coming to see the memsaheb. The two Englishwomen too, sensing difficulties, made excuses and the occasional visits stopped.

Anne began to lose her spirit as she had to face her husband's outbursts of temper each time she came home from a ride in the village or from visiting the hospital. She restricted her movements to the lonely limits of the garden and house. Sketching became her favourite pastime. She would sit under the huge shady tamarind tree at one end of the compound and sometimes she would peer down into the deep well which stood by the tree and try to see her face reflected in the water.

The very house she had been thrilled with initially now seemed a large implacable prison, and she wandered about the high, dark rooms wondering what fate had in store for her. When she found that she was pregnant, it was the end of April. She begged her husband to send her home; she wanted to be with her family when the baby was born. But he was adamant. 'Don't the natives you so admire breed like rabbits here? Why should you worry about having your child in Ghorasarai? I'll arrange to get the best help from the new medical school in Calcutta—and I plan to hire an English nurse too. My child will not be handled by native women—I know their dirty habits too well!'

The months passed slowly. Anne tried to be enthusiastic about decorating the nursery, she embroidered tiny garments and thought about names for the child. When the days became long and hot she lay down with the wooden shutters down, with the punkhawalas pulling ceaselessly at the ropes attached to the long wooden frame holding the printed cloth going back and forth, back and forth. Tall glasses of *nimbu pani* came to her room, brought in by her one faithful servant and friend, Abdul the khansama. In the quick turnover of servants frightened off by the saheb's wrath, Abdul had remained staunch. He would bring news of the village to Anne, give her the daily report on the hospital, cool the rooms by watering the khus blinds and do whatever he could to make her comfortable.

With monsoon's stormy entry, the parched earth drank up the water as the rain pelted down. By August the new crop of indigo was to be planted and the farmers agitated for more money for their labour. Fothergill was in a fouler mood than ever for the profits had been lower than expected. He cursed and swore at the house staff and when they left for the night, his wrath would descend on his poor wife.

The monsoon ended and one fine October morning Anne, now eight months pregnant, looked out of the window and saw that the light in the sky had changed and everything outside was calling her to come out, come out. She saddled her favourite horse, Century, and rode with the free fresh wind in her hair. She forgot her sadness as Century galloped and trotted across the vast compound stopping occasionally to admire a flowering tree, or to let Century drink from the large tank of water. The countryside was lush and green after the rains. Anne drank it all in eagerly as she rode up to the tamarind tree and looked, as was her habit, down into the well as if there was some healing magic down there. It was almost dark now and she sped away home before her husband returned.

That night she went into early labour and by the morning she was delivered of a baby girl, assisted by only a Bihari midwife, for the Calcutta help had not yet arrived. Fothergill did nothing to hide his disappointment and rage that the child was not a boy and that a 'dirty native' had assisted in her delivery. He hardly glanced at the child and walked out to the factory. In the weeks that followed, he started drinking very heavily, partly because of his rage about his child and partly because of the growing unrest in the indigo fields.

Quite suddenly, Anne Fothergill and the child were not seen in Ghorasarai any more. It was believed that they had left for home as quietly as they had lived in India.

The following mouth, when Abdul came to collect his pay at the office it was Fothergill, and not the clerk, who was sitting at the desk. He had been drinking. He was violently abusive and accused Abdul of fathering Anne's child. Before Abdul could defend himself, Fothergill shot him through the head. The Company hushed up the matter. Fothergill's contract was terminated and he was sent home. The factory, already in the doldrums, was shut down.

A quarter of a century later, indigo had given way to the new aniline dyes and Ghorasarai House was the circuit house for visiting civil servants on tour in Motihari district. In the winter of 1870, a newly arrived member of the Indian Civil Service, John Sidgwick, was appointed Collector in Motihari. On his first tour of the district, he had planned to stay overnight in the Ghorasarai circuit house. The sub-judge, Chaudhuri, advised him to travel to his next camp, or even stay with him, since the circuit house staff would not spend the night there, as they went home to the village. But Sidgwick was tired and loath to travel in the cold night and decided to stay on. The servants served him his evening meal, lit a fire, locked all the doors and left for the night.

The next morning, when the chowkidar came on duty, he found the door leading to the garden open and no sign of the saheb. Fearing foul play, he made a thorough search of the house and the garden, but could find no sign of Sidgwick. He informed the sub-judge who arrived with a team of men. They went further afield in the compound and by the boundary wall, near a disused well, was the unconscious form of Sidgwick. When he came round, Sidgwick was running a high temperature and quite delirious. He was taken to the local hospital and from there he was sent to Calcutta to take the first available boat home.

While he was waiting for his ship, he wrote to Chaudhuri at Ghorasarai.

> *The United Services Club,*
> *Calcutta*
> *31 January 1870*

My dear Chaudhuri,

I must thank you for all the kindness and concern shown to me during the extraordinary two days I was in your subdivision.

Let me also take this opportunity of recording the events of that horrible night.

When the kitmatgar left after serving me dinner, I chose to sit in the room overlooking the garden on the lower storey of the house. As you know, the ceilings at Ghorasarai are higher than in most homes and the doors are made of heavy wood. The curtains were drawn and the door locked on the inside. A roaring fire blazed in the fireplace and I had a lamp on the table. I thought that since it was still early, I would write the day's report and then retire. As I sat down, I heard footsteps going up the stairs and then a woman's pleading voice, 'Alan, I swear by all that is sacred to me, the child is yours.' Absolutely mystified, for there was no other English person in the whereabouts, I took the lamp and went upstairs. All the doors were padlocked, for only the lower storey has been in use, and the floor was dusty.

I went back to my table and started on my report. I had not worked for long when I felt someone watching me. I looked up and saw an elderly man with a trimmed beard in the liveried uniform of a domestic servant, with 'F' monogrammed on his sash and turban. He did not say a word but I saw in his eyes a most awful pathetic plea as if he had a sad message to deliver. He raised his hand and beckoned me and I could do nothing but follow him. It did not strike me then that the door opened without a touch. I was out in the garden following the man, across the lawn, through the mango grove, beyond the fish tank right to the edge of the compound beside the well. And there what I saw chilled my very soul. A young white woman, her clothes in disarray, her hair unkempt and her eyes wild with some unbearable grief appeared as if through a mist, walking towards the well. In her arms was a tiny baby. She looked into the depths of the well as if searching for some answer and before I could go to her, she leapt into the well. I looked around for the Indian and saw that his turban had come off and that he had a gaping wound on his temple. I do not know what happened after that—the next memory I have is the hospital bed.

I sail for home next week, but I pray you sir, make a thorough enquiry into this matter.

> I remain, with all good wishes,
> Yours very sincerely,
> John Sidgwick

Chaudhuri lost no time in organizing a team of inspectors, but the men were not to be persuaded to go down the now-dry well. After many threats, much cajoling and promises of baksheesh, two men agreed to be let down by a rope. They came up with the skeletons of a woman and an infant.

Anne Fothergill had not gone home after all.

BUNNY GUPTA

◆┼◆

neel kuthi

This story was narrated by a friend who had lived in the house as a small child. He revisited it as an adult, and discovered that a new wing had been built because so many guests had complained of the disturbances in the original building.

He asked to stay in the old wing. 'We spent a perfectly peaceful night with no disturbances at all. I was almost disappointed. The next morning I mentioned that I had experienced nothing at all.

'The old man I was talking to gave me a benign smile and said, "The wing is huge. There is only one section which is closed to the public. If you had stayed in that part, you would have felt the disturbances." So I still don't know for sure. All I can say is that the ceilings must be about twenty feet high and the pillars as tall! And the courtyard was as bare as I remembered.'

My father was the district magistrate, posted in B'pur on the banks of the Ganges in Murshidabad District, when I was a little baby. The house we were allotted was originally a *neel kuthi*, which meant an Englishman must have lived there and managed an indigo plantation. Indigo plantation managers were notorious for their oppression, and it is my guess that this one was no better than the rest of his kind.

A notable point of the house was the paved courtyard around which the house was built. There was neither well nor tree in this courtyard—just bare flagstones, which became unbearably hot in summer. The courtyard still exists, as bare as ever.

When we moved in, we were a small family, with a few retainers and orderlies, and did not require all the rooms of the huge house. Some rooms were used as the treasury for the district and were under heavy security, with guards posted there day and night. It was my father's duty to carry out a random check from time to time on the guards. Some rooms were just kept locked because we couldn't use them all. My mother once opened one of these rooms out of curiosity and discovered that it was fully furnished. One old chest of drawers actually had a bundle of old letters in it. My mother opened the bundle and was somewhat disturbed to find that many of them were letters from women who had been mistresses of the plantation manager and, from the pleading tone in them, had obviously been used and discarded. She put the letters away and thought no more about them.

It all began with my brother who must have been about three or four. He slept in a separate bedroom with my father's mother, *thakurma*, while I slept with my mother on the second floor. My father travelled a lot on work, so usually it was just the four of us. We hadn't been in the house long when my brother began to wake up every night, crying and pointing to the door or screaming at random, 'Tell him to go away.' My father did not believe this was anything beyond childish fancy and refused to worry about it. My brother began to grow thin and pale and very sick. My father decided to summon the doctor.

The doctor, Narottam Ray, was an old-style GP, gentle and sound. There was no disease he was not acquainted with, and his clinical examination was very thorough. 'There's not much wrong with the little chap, Mrs Sen,' he said, 'but his nerves seem badly shaken.' He looked around at the house and shook his head a little.

Soon after, my father went on tour again. Late one night my mother was lying down in her huge bedroom with me near her. Perhaps her own discoveries and my brother's illness were playing

on her mind. She felt that someone was just outside her mosquito
net, standing and looking at her. The moonlight was bright, and
she thought her eyes were playing tricks on her. When she got up
and switched on the light, there was no one there.

Another night she heard a sound. The louvres of the wooden
shutters moved, and moonlight flooded through into the room.
She saw, to her amazement and horror, what looked like a man's
head silhouetted against the brightness outside, looking into the
room—a room on the second floor of a house where the ceilings
were twenty feet tall and there was no balcony outside the
window . . .

Soon after this she heard sounds from the wooden staircase,
slow deliberate steps that climbed up and down and faded away
as she listened. The orderly on duty went to check but could not
see anything. 'It could be mice, memsaheb, or rats,' he said. But
memsaheb was quite convinced that this was no mouse. A mouse
or rat could have made a noise like that going down, but not climbing
up a staircase. She said no more, but she did tell thakurma, who
felt it was about time we asked a few more questions and ended
these disturbances for good, never mind what my father said!

More than one person in the neighbourhood, when questioned,
said they believed there was something inexplicable about the
house. Other people who had lived there had left in a hurry. Many
people my mother and grandmother met felt we should take heed
before it grew too late.

My mother consulted Dr Ray. She wondered if her restless
nights and fervid imagination and her son's nightmares could be
linked to the same cause.

'Could it be the heat, Dr Ray?' my mother asked. 'Those flagstones
in the courtyard make the place very hot and sultry. Perhaps we
could remove the flagstones and have a little garden there?'

'No, no, no, do not think of removing those flagstones!' The
doctor grew very agitated and alarmed.

My mother was surprised. 'Why not?' she asked. 'They aren't
particularly attractive.'

Greatly agitated, the doctor said, 'This house has a very

unsavoury history. I am a man of science, and I should not give credence to these stories, but I have lived in this town a long time, and I cannot completely disregard what I have seen in all these years.

'You have heard of the habits of the indigo planters of old. They were a terrible lot. They tortured the villagers, seduced or raped their women, murdered anyone who dared oppose them and were thoroughly evil. The exact history of this place has been wiped out, but perhaps the planter himself was murdered one night by villagers who could not take the tyranny any more, or perhaps the ghosts of the people he murdered and buried there. Beneath the flagstones are restless spirits that cannot forget.

'No one really knows, and no one really wants to find out, but I do beseech you to have a Satya Narayan puja. Perhaps it will lay some troubled spirits.'

My mother listened and agreed. She told the doctor about the letters and he agreed they should be locked up in the chest of drawers in the unused room once more.

Thakurma and Ma had a Satya Narayan puja without much more ado, and whether they laid the spirits to rest or not, they certainly laid their minds at rest.

My father was transferred soon after and there the matter ended. Many years later we had a visitor, who had lived in the same house. We asked him about it and he said his family too had suffered all kinds of strange experiences in that neel kuthi.

SHAIONTONI BOSE

the house in benares

The wind blows through what were once the walls of a clergyman's home. The house is gravel now, razed to the ground long before its time. Small mounds of earth mark the gate that was always covered with flowering red bougainvillaea. And buried in the dust is the story that drove some of its residents to despair and some to madness.

The clergyman who once lived here came from a part of India that few here knew and almost no one had ever been to. Young, energetic and full of enthusiasm, he bore within him the light of his faith and his Church. He came with his wife and daughter to build a new parish, far, far away from his homeland.

He was Father John Mathai, of the Marthoma Church of Benares. He walked in here with his small round face shining bright. He was young and always smiling. Whispers circulated that he would perhaps become the Church's youngest bishop ever.

He was charmed by the city, its narrow lanes, the muddied Ganga and the din and chatter of the people who poured in from every corner of the country. He had not been enthusiastic when he was first told that he would have to go to Benares. He had serious reservations about moving so far away from his home. But it was God's will, and he accepted.

They first came to this house one warm summer morning. Set in the middle of an army cantonment with rows of neat houses and tree-lined streets, the house drew a ring of calm around itself.

Its stone walls and high ceilings and the garden in full bloom charmed them. They were happy to find a home cut off from the clamour and noise of the rest of the city.

Father John Mathai and his wife made nothing of the cold darkness inside the house. Nor did they hear the voices behind the walls that spoke of times long gone by.

But soon the day slipped into evening, and the quiet of the house was broken. The house was rocked by voices, by a tempestuous volley of threats to tear its inhabitants limb from limb and hurl them out of the house. Father, mother and daughter stood transfixed, clinging to one anohter. A bowl clattered to the ground, and then the clang and clank of metal objects resounded all around. The peace of the charming bungalow was shattered.

The night turned into morning and the house returned to silence. Father John stepped out of the room, his eyes sunken and a prayer on his lips. The previous night was just their imagined fears playing havoc with their minds, for their thoughts had wandered from God. Or so he told himself. He looked at his child, sleeping peacefully. He felt that the worst was behind them and went out to discover his new parish.

His wife's nerves were not as easily calmed. She walked hesitantly through every room, speaking to the walls, asking them what transformed them so at night.

Benares enveloped Father John Mathai. He marvelled at her agelessness, at the temples carved with sculptures so fine, at the maze-like lanes filled with the smell of golden fried *jalebis* and other sweets. He walked through the lanes, he walked past the ghats where fires burned all day and all night, and he rowed across the river that both drew and gave life to the city.

But the nights got increasingly stormy. Father John Mathai and his family were prisoners inside their bedroom that was also their prayer room. Calm and strong in his belief, Father Mathai stood like a rock between his family and the tormented cries outside.

Once he stepped outside into the large living room into the noisy darkness. The house seemed to be tossed from side to side, and he fell down in a heap. Deep moans and groans and shrieks of pain pounded his head all night as he lay there, his arms crossed over his head and his lips moving in the name of God.

Night after night, the walls wailed in pain, and Father Mathai and his wife held their child and the Bible close. Their days were spent trying to sleep and their nights in terrified prayer.

Father Mathai hunted all over Benares for answers. Finally one day, a man who sat hunched up by the river, followed him home. He stood by the gate and smiled grimly.

'The hospital still lives here,' he said. 'Sahebs, white men, were brought here. Beaten up by our sepoys.'

Father Mathai heard the story unfold. 'The year was 1857. Our sepoys rose in mutiny against those British infidels. They wanted us to give up our faith and invite the wrath of our gods to fight their wars. Pigs' meat, cows' meat, who knew what they used for the rifle cartridges.' The old man spat and sat on his haunches.

'Our men refused and killed many sahebs in battle. The wounded sahebs came here. I saw them weep as bullets were torn out of their flesh. I held the white bowls for the nurse sisters and doctor sahebs as they operated and bandaged the wounded white folk. I was the wardboy in this special hospital meant only for the white sahebs.'

That night was noisier than any of the earlier ones. That night soldiers screamed in pain. A bullet fell to the floor and then a kidney bowl. Scalpels, knives and other surgical instruments clattered to the floor as nurses rushed from bed to bed. Doctors in white coats moved from soldier to soldier and the room resounded with the moans and groans of the wounded men. Father John Mathai sat with his wife and child on the bed that rocked all through the night. The fury of the forces that swirled across the house lifted the bed high and shook it like a leaf. They sat holding it down, fighting back with the force of their faith. But they also made themselves a promise. This was going to be their last night in this house.

The house was turned to dust before its time. It had to be.

ARUNDHUTI DASGUPTA

◆-I-◆

the Well

Stepwells or vavs *and* baolis *are found in northern and western India, and were built by both Hindu and Mughal kings. Most stepwells consist of two parts: a vertical shaft from which water is drawn and the elaborately carved subterranean passageways, chambers and steps which provide access to the well.*

Acres and acres of green rolled past. Trees, shrubs, fields—all merged into one as the car sped along the highway. Shreya looked out through her Ray Bans, wishing that this journey would end sooner than it was scheduled to. Her shirt and trousers clung to her in sticky sweat and her delicate skin was getting seriously sunburnt.

Deven sat beside her, taking in the green fields, the mud huts with thatched roofs, and the women with pots on their heads in shimmering red, green and yellow *ghaghras*. 'Ramji, how much longer to the city?' he asked the driver.

'At least seven or eight hours,' he replied into the mirror.

'I think we should stop somewhere,' pleaded Shreya.

Ramji would much rather have driven straight home. Deven would too. He did not mind the heat or the distance. But for Shreya's sake, he knew that a short stop was necessary. Her face had broken out in red patches and she looked as if she was going to be sick.

Ramji stopped the car near a freshly painted house with garish pink walls and a grey roof. It had a few creepers climbing over the walls and in the courtyard there was a small tin shed with red and white plastic chairs and a refrigerator stocked with soft drinks. Shreya made her way gingerly to one of the chairs and collapsed in a pool of sweat and exhaustion.

A young girl looked at them shyly from behind the wall. Her red skirt embroidered with mirrors glittered and shone in the sun. 'Can we have something cold to drink, please?' Deven gestured with his hands to explain what they wanted. She giggled and ran into the house.

Deven stood, absorbing the complete silence of the afternoon. A few mud huts stood by the road. A cow slept in the courtyard of one, while in another a few goats munched dry grass. In the distance, there was a large octagonal courtyard bordered by trees that must have been at least a hundred years old.

'What's that?'

'Baoli,' the girl replied in a timid voice.

'Oh, an old well, one of those stepwells! Let's take a look at it, Shreya.'

'No, you go. I'll just put my feet up.'

Shreya grimaced as she eased her tiny feet out of her shoes. Deven walked towards the well with Ramji following a few steps behind. He climbed over a small gate to an open patch overgrown with shrubs and weeds, and walked towards the flight of steps that peeked out from the end of the courtyard.

A thick black fog covered all that lay below. Deven stumbled down a few steps and blinked several times to adjust to the darkness. A maze of columns and stairs opened out in front of him. He saw several flights of stone steps cascading down to a square well, delicately carved columns and beautifully tiled landings that wandered off into tiny dark chambers. The two men stood transfixed.

The columns were carved with dancing apsaras, gods and goddesses, flowers and animals. And there were empty blackened niches in the columns that once held oil lamps. The well was five flights of stairs down from where Deven stood. To reach the well, he would have to climb down at least two hundred steps and then to climb all the way back—it seemed too much trouble.

'*Chaalo*, it's an old baoli. You won't get to see anything like this in your New York.' One look at Ramji's toothless grin and Deven was reminded of his childhood when the two of them would go off exploring new places. He bounded down the steps with the old man.

The water in the well was covered in green slime. Dead leaves and flowers floated on it, and there was an awful stink. Deven wished that he had not made the journey down. The view from the top had not shown up the state of the well and he would have gone back with his sense of enchantment intact.

'No one comes here any more. But, believe it or not, it used to be a hub of social activity once.' A bespectacled young man who emerged from the shadows where he had been standing looking at the well. He introduced himself as Rajul Mehta, a student with a design institute. He was here to study the architecture and stone carvings, he said.

'This is one of the oldest stepwells in the country. It was probably built around the sixth or the seventh century. The carvings are just priceless—I mean how many of us can even think of getting this kind of symmetry and beauty together on such a scale? Look at the arches, the walls; these ornate designs and these empty brackets in the walls show that people used this place for ceremonies and rituals in the olden days. And here, look at these flowers, the friezes, look at the eye for detail!'

Deven stifled a yawn. 'Yeah, but look at the way it is today. I mean nowhere else in the world do people treat their beautiful heritage this way.'

Rajul said nothing at first, as if he was not sure whether he should respond or not. And then, suddenly, he blurted out, 'You know, don't you, that no one, I mean none of the villagers comes here at all? They won't come near the water because of the Raval legend. They are so afraid that they won't even clean the place. I have been speaking to quite a few of them who believe that this well must be destroyed for their village to regain its old prosperity.'

Deven, who had been getting ready to leave, sat down again.

'Well, you see, this is what people say,' Rajul continued. 'I don't believe in all this, of course, but the people here believe that the spirit of a Raval haunts this place. They don't let the women come here because they believe that the Raval is not going to spare them this time around.'

'What or who the heck is a Raval?' Deven interrupted. Ramji, who was sitting beside him, shuffled his feet and coughed, 'I am a Raval or used to be. Our ancestors were drummers. We played for kings and emperors.'

'That's right,' Rajul took over. 'The Raval tribe were musicians. They performed for kings and queens, and on festivals and weddings. Today there are just a handful who still follow their ancestral profession.

'Anyway, the story goes that once a young newlywed, Devki, came to the well after sunset. She had guests at home and had run out of water. Now in most Indian villages no one is allowed near the well after dark. But she had no choice. When she got there, she saw an old man sitting in one of the arches here but she paid him no attention. He was a Raval, sitting and beating the drums.

'Devki filled two pots and was about to leave when this old man reached out for her with, er, well, his feet. The feet—they grew and grew and stretched across these waters. Devki watched in horror, her mouth dry with terror as she was caught in their grip. The old man's face spread into a toothless smile. "Wash my feet," he croaked. Devki did as she was told. "Wipe my feet." Devki said that she did not have a clean cloth to wipe them with and that if he let her go home, she would come back with one. The old man knew that if he let her go, she would never come back so he said, "Two hours shall I wait here and if I don't see you, I shall come and hunt you down. Tell me where you live and describe your house, or you can't leave." Devki replied that if he had to come looking for her then he should look out for a door that had the print of her hand.'

The stairwell felt damp and cold. Deven wished that he was listening to this story in the hot sun rather than in this dank dimness. Rajul went on, 'Well, Devki turned out to be a clever one. She ran home, dipped her hand in some wet mud and plastered every house in the village. Outwitted, the old Raval raged and screamed out her name all night. The villagers believe that he still does that— and till this day, the village women continue to mark their walls or doors with earthen handprints.'

Rajul said that some of the villagers had even described the old man for him and he showed Deven a sketch of a man with a deeply wrinkled face and calloused hands. Deven stood staring into the still waters of the well until Ramji nudged him and suggested that they leave before it got too dark.

'What's taken you so long?' Shreya shrieked. Deven got into the car without a word. He did not wish to stay another minute in this village. But as they were about to leave, he asked Ramji to stop the car. He went and took one long hard look at the freshly painted pink walls of the house and came back with a grin. 'Just a story; no palm prints there that I could see,' he muttered.

As the car drove off, Deven did not look back. He should have— for then he would have seen the girl in the red skirt dip her hands in wet mud and place them on an old faded imprint of a hand on the wall.

ARUNDHUTI DASGUPTA

Krishnaveni

It's up to you whether you believe this story. It took place around thirty years ago. One's personality changes over a span of so many years. Perhaps if I had noted down the incident while it was still fresh in my mind, it would have had a different flavour. Now I have changed. I must depend on my memory, and my perceptions must have changed too.

A snag had developed in the heat-treatment section of the heavy metals plant in Voltaire. I had to visit the plant to detect the fault and determine how it should be repaired.

Both the township and the plant were absolutely new. The buildings had only recently been constructed, and the place was still almost uninhabited. I deposited my things with Mr Punnyaswami at the office and rushed off to deal with the emergency. He told me later that they had assigned me a brand-new flat for the length of my stay and that he had sent my things there. Though the flat was furnished, there was no one to cook for me, and I had to eat out.

The township looked as if it would be very attractive in a few years. It was very well laid out, saplings had been planted and the existing trees had not been cut. The roads were straight and clean, and the general atmosphere was surprisingly contemporary. Not the sort of place one would expect to meet any kind of ghostly beings at all!

People used to visit Vizag and Voltaire to recuperate and stay for quite a while, but my work was over in a day. The plant began to function smoothly again and the client was pleased. I was entertained at the the Sea and Sand Hotel which was well known for its 'night life'. After drinks and dinner I was dropped at my nice new flat, where the watchman had been ordered to take good care of me. His name was Dandapani. Apart from him there seemed to be no one else in the building at all.

I wasn't sure I liked this arrangement too much. As I went up, I began to feel unsettled and thought, Where have I arrived, in the middle of nowhere with not another soul in sight!

As soon as Dandapani let me into the flat, I opened the steel-framed window opposite my bed and locked the hasp to keep the the window from swinging in the wind. The smell of new paint in a closed room was quite overpowering. Everything was silent and still. I hoped my book would help me banish the loneliness that suddenly engulfed me.

It was a moonlit night. The moonlight poured in through the window. Though I had switched off the light, the room was not at all dark. I lay in that dream state between sleep and waking, thinking about home, when suddenly there was a noise at the door.

I had locked the door. Who could have opened it? How? My eyes were falling out of their sockets! I could see someone slowly moving towards my bedside!

'*Kaun hai*?' I asked nervously in Hindi. No answer.

I tried again in Telugu, '*Aoru, em kawala*?' No reply.

I tried Tamil, '*Eyare? Ennaveno*?'

All these phrases meant the same thing: Who are you? What do you want?

Still no reply.

As the form moved closer I was acutely embarrassed to find it was a woman, in a sparkling white sari! A young, unknown woman . . . in the middle of the night in my room! What had she come here for? Her sari was flung carelessly over her, and barely covered her breasts and thighs. The curves of her young body and her glossy black skin were strangely at variance with the thin muslin of her careless drapery. A younger man may have revelled in the sight, but it seemed to me as if the very cobra that brings the end of the world stood in front of me, stretched tall and ready to strike! A bad name is worse, they say, than a bad man! If anyone saw this, my name would be mud!

As she approached me the expression on her face seemed to mock my fear. My heart seemed to drum in my chest, beating hard at my ribs. Who was this black beauty? Where did she come from? Why was she here?

It was as if a voice in my head boomed out a name: 'Krishnaveni!' I started. I had not asked her name. Where did that name come from? I did not see her speak. As I stared at her, sweating with fright, I suddenly noticed . . .

What was that patch of darkness, that strange space? No feet? She had no feet! Her seemingly solid body did not seem to have any definition between the floor and the careless skirt of her strangely draped garment.

'*Ruko*, stop!' I gabbled. '*Irenge! Unanndu!*' Hindi, Tamil, Telugu . . . whatever I knew.

She seemed to understand.

'Don't come near me,' I shouted. '*Ra-ledu, akda-ledu, byanda, po! po! po! Owellu, owellu* . . . Go, GO! Not interested!' I had exhausted every language I could think of. Now I had no recourse but to name all the gods I knew: 'Hanumanji, Ma Kali, Durga, Ram, Ram, Ram . . .' Was this some dreadful vampire who had come to suck my soul away?

Yet she did not touch me. I closed my eyes tightly and screamed for Dandapani but in my fright I could only shout 'Thanda pani! Thanda pani!' Surely my brain was scrambled in my terror!

I opened my eyes. She had gone, vanished! Where was she? I sat there on my bed, chanting the forty names of Hanuman and the trusted Gayatri mantra! As I chanted, my courage and strength returned. I looked around. Nobody. Where did she go?

The next morning, as I was leaving, I asked Dandapani, 'Have there been any other guests in this flat recently?'

'Oh no, saheb, you are the first . . .' He hesitated a little, then said, 'Why, did you see anyone, sir?'

'Yes, I did,' I said. 'My door was closed. Locked. Yet a woman came in and then disappeared, though that seems impossible.'

He hesitated again. Then he said, 'Yes, she is a ghost, saheb. Her name is Krishnaveni.'

'How do you know her name is Krishnaveni?' I asked, taken aback.

He laughed a little, then he said, 'Oh, she comes every night, and wanders about here. I used to be frightened at first, but she never does any harm, so I've got used to her. Before this building was built, she had a little hut here, with a roof of palm leaves. Her husband was bad-tempered and violent and used to drink heavily. He would drink toddy, then beat her up. They had no children, so she wandered, if you know what I mean. Many babus called her to them. This was the cause of her quarrels with her husband. One day, unable to bear her husband's beatings any more, she hanged herself from that large tree outside your window. Her husband has run off. He doesn't even live here any more. The police didn't bother to search for him since he had left the area.'

Having heard this tragic story, I gave Dandapani fifty rupees, and requested him to do the *kriyakarma* required to lay the spirit and set it free, and made my way home in great relief, safe and sound!

KASHINATH SEN SHARMA
Translated from the Bengali by SHAIONTONI BOSE

the Courtyard

Winter was leaving Jabalpur. The night air had lost its edge and the early morning darkness was quietly growing light. Soon summer would be beating down on the streets and houses. Then it would be quite impossible to stay out on the terrace after ten in the morning as Suma had done today. She stood drying her hair and staring down at the courtyard that lay in the centre of this large house.

Dry leaves and twigs covered the small red tiles of the courtyard. Suma knew that she had to sweep it clean. Her mother was sure to point it out if she did not. But she just could not bring herself to go down into the courtyard. She could hear her mother's voice in her head, 'Suma, you good-for-nothing—always sitting and combing those long tresses of yours! Don't you think it's time to help your old mother?'

Shaking her head to rid it of all such unwanted thoughts, Suma pulled her hair into a loose knot and set out, broom in hand. She stepped into the courtyard and then, before she knew it, she felt herself falling. A large dark vacuum engulfed her and her mind erased itself of all memory of the past and the present.

'Suma, beta, child, wake up!' She heard her mother's voice from a distance. Her face paled at the thought of having to step back into the courtyard. She just covered her face and wept.

Sunlight crept into the courtyard. 'Beta, go get me the clothes from the line,' Suma heard her mother say. The red tiles glared at her, daring her to walk over them. Silly me, Suma thought. She walked slowly but firmly towards the clothesline. But then again, at the same spot as before, she was sucked into a dark bottomless hole. Her head felt like an empty box without a thought or memory inside.

Lying down on the bed, propped up by pillows, Suma saw the doctor bending down to peer into her eyes. 'Doctor saheb, we don't know what is wrong with her. She keeps fainting every now and again,' she heard her mother say. Suma wanted to scream, 'No, not now and again, only there outside, on those red tiles.' But she kept quiet.

'Suma, Suma!' she heard her mother calling. Suma stopped feeding the birds and ran down the stairs. 'Come here, come and touch his feet. This is Bhairo Babaji, a great man who has sent many ghosts and evil spirits away, back to their world. He will get rid of the *buri nazar,* the evil eye. And then your fainting will stop.'

Suma hesitated. She saw the old man walk in a haze of smoke towards the courtyard. He stood at the spot, on those red tiles, and turned to Suma's mother. 'Get some men and have this dug up.' He walked out of the house without look in her direction but Suma felt as if his eyes had never left hers.

Soon six burly men arrived with pickaxes and shovels. They did not have to dig too long or too deep before all but two of them fled shrieking. Suma saw them pull out a skeleton. She crumbled into a small pile.

When she came round, Suma heard the maid tell her mother, 'Bibiji, there was a young girl. She was married to a construction worker. She is said to have fallen to her death in this house while working with her husband.'

Her mother sat, holding her hand. She looked at Suma and Suma looked at the sun shining on the red tiles outside. They did not frighten her any more.

ARUNDHUTI DASGUPTA

✦✦

room 2

This story is set in Brajarajnagar, Orissa. The village lies in the Sambalpur belt and its people speak the local dialect. It has a large tribal population and its people and language are strongly influenced by that of nearby Madhya Pradesh. Brajarajnagar, like the rest of rural Orissa, is green and full of bubbling streams but underdeveloped and poor.

The early morning light slid off the red-tiled roof covering the station platform. Coolies in red shirts were scurrying about while a couple of young boys walked up and down the platform, peering into the windows with steaming cups of tea. I yelled for a cup. 'Coming, saheb,' the boy answered.

I craned my neck to read the rectangular signpost at the end of the platform. Kharagpur. 'Still at least five hours of travel left,' I said to my fellow passenger. I had struck up a conversation with him after boarding the train from Calcutta.

'For you, journey is very difficult, na?' he asked, looking at the white plaster covering my right hand and wrist.

'This is nothing,' I said, sipping my tea. 'You have no idea how difficult it has been for the last three months. There was a time when I thought that I had come to the end of my time in this world.' And then, over the next couple of stations, I told him about it. 'There I was, walking in the middle of a huge room in my factory in Delhi, when—bang, boom, crash!—I found myself several feet below. It was like sinking into the netherworld. I don't remember much until I woke up in hospital. Three full months— it has taken me to get back on my feet,' I said, putting them up in a more comfortable position.

My fellow traveller let out a deep sigh of empathy, stretched his legs out and rolled his eyes heavenwards. 'You have truly suffered. God has His strange ways.' So saying, he turned to a book he had been trying to read for quite some time. A little miffed that he had turned his back on my tragedy, I turned to the trees, fields and wide open spaces rushing by my window.

The train sped past countryside soaked in hues of green. I had been told by Rosy, Mr Feldman's secretary at the Calcutta office who had been brought up in Bhubaneswar, that Orissa was beautiful; full of sal and sheesham forests, streams and rivers. As I looked out of the window of the speeding train, I thought I must tell Rosy what a fool she had been to give up all this for the dirt and grime of Calcutta.

My first glimpse of Brajarajnagar was a small boy wearing a wide grin waiting beside a driver holding up a placard with my name. As I approached them, the boy leaped forward to take my luggage and guide me to the car which was to take me to my destination: B Paper Mill.

The paper mill and its township was the hub of Brajarajnagar. Nestled among hills and forests, the site office was the most picturesque one I have worked in. The guest house was charming, with antique furniture and a long veranda that ran all the way around the house and on to which each room opened. After a sumptuous lunch cooked by the caretaker, Bhagovan, I made my way to the factory to inspect the machinery that my company had supplied.

I was holed up in the factory until quite late in the evening and by the time I was ready to leave, there were only a couple of people left. 'Room 2 for you, sir,' a voice spoke up near my ear. 'Mr Vigerley and his wife are staying in Room 1, sir; just opposite you, sir.' Mr Vigerley was my boss, and the owner of the voice was Mr Mohanty, the chief administration officer at the mill who also looked after the guest house. A small and grim man, I was yet to see a smile cross his face.

'It has an attached bath, I hope?' I asked him. For some time Mohanty stared at me, wondering, I presume, whether my question deserved an answer or whether the room really had one—and then he left without a word.

Too tired to pursue the matter, I left for the guest house soon after. Room 2 was large and airy and it did have an attached bath—but somehow it was markedly unfriendly. I felt a strong urge to pick my bags up and run out of the door. The thought of the ridicule I would thus generate kept me sitting on the huge four-poster bed in the middle of the room.

'Saheb?' A small voice called at the door which led to the hallway within the house. Before I could answer, a boy crept in. 'I have to make your bed, saheb,' he said. I found myself staring into a pair of very familiar twinkling eyes. It was the boy from the station. 'What is your name?' I asked him as he went about making the bed, having displaced me from it.

'Natobar, saheb,' he answered almost as soon as the question had left my lips. He worked even faster than he spoke and within seconds, he had changed the sheets, fluffed up the pillows, strung the moquito net all around my bed, and was ready to leave. 'Saheb, when shall I come with your tea in the morning?'

'Late,' I told him, and then as an afterthought asked, 'Do you sleep in the house?'

'No, I have to go home as the Rojo festival is going on but Bhagovan dada will be there if you need any help at night.' He slipped out of the room.

Not quite sure what assistance I would require during the night, I locked the door and went to sleep. It wasn't very long before I found myself sitting up in bed, soaked in sweat. I could hear a faint sound on the door, not the one I had locked which led the hallway but the one that opened out to the veranda and the hills. It was as if someone was scratching at the door.

I walked up to the small window next to the door and peered outside through the pelting rain and the black night, but I saw no one. Yet the scratching continued. I tried to go back to sleep but the sound would not go away. I covered my head with a pillow, stuffed my fingers into my ears and tried everything else, but nothing could block it.

Eventually I could take it no longer, got up, opened the door to the hallway, and yelled for the caretaker. 'Bhagovaaaan!'

The man staggered in with eyes full of sleep and whatever else he had been taking that night. In the most officious voice that I could manage at that late hour, I ordered him to check who was knocking at the door. He gave me a look that seemed to condemn all city-bred fools like me to hell and then did as he was told. I heard him curse aloud and then there was the sound of a shrill yelp and pitter-patter of feet.

'A dog,' Bhagovan said, slamming the door shut.

'What?' I asked, my ears a burning red.

'There was a dog, but I have sent it away,' he said and a smirk, masked as a smile, crossed his face.

'Achcha, achcha. Now go back to sleep,' I mumbled and went back to an uncomfortable slumber. I was not able to get rid of the feeling of unease, however.

The next day the feeling got worse. I spent the evening reading in the garden until temple bells rang out all over the township, and mosquitoes and a darkening sky sent me back into the room.

Night crawled into Brajarajnagar. With it came the clickety-clack of insects, the hum of mosquitoes, drum beats from the village where I presume Rojo was being celebrated, and my growing dread of the room. Natobar came in to make my bed and I questioned him some more about the room. He was guarded in his answers and refused to divulge anything.

'Saheb is getting bad feeling from room, na?' he asked after I had threatened that I would break his bones if he did not tell me the truth.

'Yes,' I sighed, exhausted by my own questioning.

'But there is no worry, Bhagovan dada is there outside,' and with that Natobar sped away into the night.

It must not have been too long past midnight when I woke

screaming. I was being pushed out of bed and my plastered hand was pinned to my side while the other was being twisted around. I screamed and shrieked but could do nothing as a huge force threw me out of bed. The four posts of the bed came crashing down around me, and I was tangled in the mosquito net. I was sure that my last hour had come—when I was struck by a thought which has helped keep all ghosts at bay ever since.

I clutched at the frayed white sacred thread strung around my neck and torso, chanting the Gayatri mantra. I muttered and tugged at the same time, hoping for a miraculous deliverance from whatever it was that had knocked me flat on the ground. So panicky was I that all that came out from my parched throat was a hoarse whisper.

But it worked! I don't know what it was that turned the evil spirit away, but whatever it was, I was desperately grateful. In as loud a voice as I could muster, I shouted for Bhagovan. Several yells and shrieks later, the man arrived and pounded on the hallway door. It seemed a long time before I could get up and let him in. I asked him whether the room had any ghosts in it but he looked at me as if I were one myself and said nothing. However, I was taking no chances and the rest of the night I spread myself out on the couch outside with mosquitoes and a snoring Bhagovan for company.

In the morning Natobar came back to make the bed and clean the room. I followed him into the room. 'Natobar, there is a ghost in this room, isn't there?' I asked, a little nervous at the thought of the boy reporting our conversation to all his friends at the factory. Natobar smiled. He smiled! He wordlessly went about cleaning the room and feigned complete deafness when I asked him more.

Two bad nights were more than I could take and I had made up my mind to talk to Mr Mohanty about changing my room. When I approached him, I was a little sheepish in bright daylight about talking to so solemn a man about my fears. But one more night in that room I could not spend.

'Er . . . Mr Mohanty, it is about my room,' I sputtered and stopped. I started again resolutely, 'I wondered if you could change my room as I . . .'

To my complete amazement, Mohanty smiled. He said conspiratorially, 'Room 2, *yes* sir.'

Stunned at the realization that Mohanty could actually smile, I made no reply as he checked his register and said, 'One more night. Tomorrow, you can shift to Room 1.'

One more night had to be spent in Room 2, and I was dreading it. Once again, it seemed to me as if the room was extremely reluctant to let me in and I spent the evening wandering around the township. Night dragged me back and I decided to stay up and read a book.

I must have nodded off for I woke with a start. There was someone at the window, knocking hard on the panes. I was sweating in fear and before anything else took place, I decided to chant the Gayatri mantra again. My sacred thread in hand, I kept muttering, but the knocking would not go away; it got fiercer and even acquired a voice.

'Please . . . Please, let me in!'

I panicked. Of ghosts who threw people out of their beds, I had heard but of one who could talk and in English, I had not. The knocking persisted and finally, unable to bear it any more, I opened the door to the hallway and yelled for Bhagovan. I yelled and yelled but he did not appear. I assumed that he had overdone his drinking and could not hear the whisper that my voice had turned into.

After what seemed hours, I finally went to the other door with my umbrella in hand, ready to drive any ghost out with it. The sweat on my brow was running down my face. I opened the door a crack and a pair of red eyes stared back from behind a thick set of glasses.

A ghost who wears spectacles! Now, I thought, I had seen it all. Who would ever think that a ghost would need to wear glasses! *It* entered my room and, struck dumb by *its* presence, I let the umbrella clatter onto the floor. *It* extended its hand, 'My name is Raghavan, from the Bangalore office.'

I think I fell on the bed and checked whether *its* feet were pointing the right way before I took his hand and answered. 'I am

Sen Sharma from Calcutta . . . I am sorry I did not open the door earlier.'

The man probably thought that I was incoherent because I had just woken up, and went on to explain how he had tried to come in through the main entrance to the guest house but it was locked, and although he had knocked and shouted no one had come to the door.

Bhagovan is drunk, I thought to myself. Mr Raghavan went on to say that he had decided to walk all around the house and, on seeing a light in my room, had resolved to take a chance. We shook hands one more time before he left the room to sleep on the couch and I sank into my bed.

I did not dare meet Mr Raghavan's eyes the next morning and nor did I ask him how long he had knocked on the window that night. I was glad to move rooms, and in a couple of days I finished my work and left the complex. Before that, however, I got this story out of Natobar.

'A memsahib lived in this village, saheb. Her husband was doing some work here and, my aunts and my mother tell me, she would come to the village quite often. Her husband was not a nice man and he was very angry with her for mixing with the villagers. This memsaheb died very suddenly. People say she died of malaria but some say she was killed by her husband. We don't know what is true and what is not, but they say that this complex was built on the ruins of their house.' And then as an afterthought, he added, 'Please don't tell Mohanty saheb I told you this or else I will be out of a job.'

ARUNDHUTI DASGUPTA

One dark night

Originally a picturesque hamlet in the hills, Shimla was once called Shyamala, named after the goddess Kali. The story goes that a local priest, looking after the temple in the town, was visited by an Englishman who wanted to build a home at the very spot where the temple stood. The priest tried to dissuade him but the Englishman was adamant. The goddess Kali then unleashed her fury on the Englishman, and frightened him so much that he abandoned his plans. From then on, the town took on the name of the goddess.

It was Shimla's first winter after Independence. The Mall was brimming with people—Indian people in brightly coloured clothes who were just getting used to walking there without the fear of a *lathi* on their backs.

Dr G was a young man. Born and bred in Shimla, he knew every walk, every slope and every corner of this town. He too was soaking in the town's new-found freedom by venturing into areas that had been out of bounds for years.

'Doctor babu, take some vegetables from an old lady. Fresh from my garden,' someone shouted.

Dr G stopped to buy some, 'So, Ma, how is the pain in your knees?' He smiled at the old lady who was one of his patients. She resisted taking any money from him but he pressed a few coins into her hand.

Until a year ago, the Mall would have been out of bounds for women like her. Freedom has changed so much in such a short time, he thought as he walked home with a bag of vegetables.

Dr G was popular in Shimla, especially among the poor because he did not charge them and never hesitated to call on them when they were too ill to come to the clinic. Many people believed that the doctor was far too good and that he would have done better for himself if only he had some sense of self-preservation. But then, Dr G was not about to change his ways because of what other people thought about him.

One night, after a long walk around the Mall, Dr G was getting ready to curl up with a book when there was a loud knock at the door. A young man stood outside, wearing a monkey cap and a muffler. He was out of breath and very agitated.

'Please Doctor babu, you have to come with me. That small boy—Kalicharan Master's son—he is very ill. He is shivering with fever . . .'

'You are from the Piano House, aren't you?' Dr G asked.

'Yes yes, sir. Kalicharan Master lives upstairs and I stay downstairs with two others. You know him, don't you? He comes to your clinic.'

Dr G nodded and said that he would be there in half an hour. He asked the young man to go ahead and gave him some pills for the child to take as soon as he got back.

Piano House was small and broken down. There was an old piano in one of the rooms. I think it is on the first floor—that is where Kalicharan lives with his wife and son, Dr G thought as he packed his bag.

It must have been close to nine o'clock when Dr G set out but it seemed closer to midnight. He had walked some distance when he was halted in his tracks by a strange sight. A young man—he looked like an Englishman—dressed in white stood on top of the hill carrying a strange contraption on his shoulders.

To Dr G, it looked as if the man was carrying what milkmen in Shimla used to carry their wares: a long bamboo pole with two cans tied to both ends with a rope. Strange, thought Dr G, at this time of the night and that too an Englishman who looks like a milkman. He thought that perhaps the darkness was playing tricks on him and quickly made his way to the Piano House.

Kalicharan Master and his wife were in despair. Their son had been suffering from a mild cold, but had suddenly taken a turn for the worse. He had been lying in bed all evening, burning with fever and moaning. Dr G diagnosed pneumonia, gave the boy some pills and an injection, and waited to see if his condition improved. In a short while the boy seemed to get a little better.

Dr G decided to spend the night in the house, with the three young men who lived on the ground floor. I can keep a watch on the child and in any case there is no way I want to walk back at this hour, he thought as he settled down with a cup of tea.

It was around midnight when the parents sent for him again. And then Dr G saw him once more. The same man with the same contraption stood at the foot of the stairs, smiling. Before he could say anything, the man went out of the door, bringing a rush of cold air into the house. Puzzled, Dr G went up to his patient.

He found the child much worse than when he had left him. A stronger dose of the medicine helped and he fell asleep. Dr G retired to get some rest. He must have been asleep for a couple of hours when he was woken up by a loud shriek that rang around the house. Loud wailing and an even louder playing of the piano followed.

The three men and Dr G ran up the stairs. Once again the man was there. This time he was waiting at the head of the stairs, the smile on his face seemed more like a smirk, and he looked back at them with the cans dangling from his bamboo pole before he vanished.

'I don't know if any of you will ever comprehend the terror of what I saw next. Inside, the piano was playing. The keys moved of their own accord. Standing next to the piano were Kalicharan and his wife, their faces white with fear and their mouths open wide. They were screaming but I don't think they even knew that they were. The piano played louder and louder as if to drown the screaming. And on the bed lay the boy. Even before I had walked up to him, I knew I had lost him. I don't know what claimed him— the cold that had gripped his chest or the chill that had wrapped itself around all of us that night,' Dr G told the small group that had gathered in his house that evening.

ARUNDHUTI DASGUPTA

✦‡✦

footsteps in the dark

Calcutta, December 1985. Winter holidays: sheer bliss, I thought, as the plane landed at Dum Dum Airport. One whole month to catch up with old friends and enjoy the city I loved.

Amit was there to collect me. Amit is my closest friend and was to be my host in Calcutta. I used to be at his place practically every weekend during my hostel days but had never actually spent a night there. In school, I never saw him study for his exams, but he always managed a straight first. A commerce student with an amazing flair for electronics, he knew everything about everything. He was also heavily into the paranormal, an avid reader of books on ESP, the supernatural and the like. Amit is an only son, with two sisters, one older and the other younger.

We reached the house at around 9 p.m. A perfectly charming old mansion in Alipore, built sometime in the early 1890s, it stands two storeys high in grounds that cover an area of over two acres. The house itself is vast. It is painted a pristine white, with a driveway leading off from the road to the south and a large manicured garden to the north. The driveway leads up to a covered entrance. Pillars flank the wide marble steps leading to the huge, intricately carved teak doors. The doors open into a large foyer with the antique stairway on the left. A crystal chandelier hangs from the vaulted ceiling. The foyer divides the house into three sections, one in which Amit's parents, sisters and grandparents live, the second where Amit's own living quarters are, and the third, above Amit's section, where some cousins live.

Amit's parents' section was by far the largest, with an enormous living room, dining room, three bedrooms and a glassed-in patio overlooking the garden. The garden was beautiful with several varieties of rare plants and flowers in numerous beds and pots. There was a small pond with colourful fish darting this way and that. Amit's section was at the other end of the house, separated from the rest of the rooms by the foyer and a corridor a good forty feet long. Amit had taken advantage of the high ceilings of the house and split the section in which he lives into two: the upper section was the bedroom and the lower the living area.

The rest of the family had already finished dinner. They were early eaters and strictly followed the policy of early to bed and early to rise. I was very fond of Amit's family, and they were equally fond of me. They have always treated me like a member of the family. Amit's elder sister, whom I also called Didi, was some three years older than he was and we had always been fast friends, though I must admit that I had always been slightly in awe of her. Amit's younger sister was a very shy person, and hardly ever talked. Amit's mother spent most of her time solving jigsaw puzzles, painting and watching movies on the VCR. His father ran a copper wire factory and his sole relaxation was to solve problems in mathematics.

After having spent some time with the family, I showered and joined Amit for dinner. We sat around afterwards, chatting and catching up with each other, and it was about eleven when we decided it was time to turn in. I had taken it for granted that Amit and I were to share his room, which had a spare bed.

I said as much, and that was when he started hemming and hawing, and came up with something quite absurd.

He said, 'Well, I've not been sleeping in my bedroom for some time now. My grandparents have asked me to sleep in their bedroom, and I also felt that I should, in case they require some help or attention at night, so I had an extra bed put into their room.'

This seemed reasonable. However, he added, I felt absurdly, 'I want you to sleep in my grandparents' bedroom too. I have already had another bed put there. I do not want you to sleep upstairs; it's very distant from the rest of the house, and should you need something, it would be difficult for you to find your way to the other section in the dark.'

I assured him that I would be perfectly all right, and that the only place there was a remote likelihood of my visiting was right next door, the bathroom.

He left, surprisingly unhappy that I hadn't accepted his offer. Anyway, having locked the bedroom door, I settled down to read as I do every night. I had the bedside light on and my pillows propped up.

I had been reading for about half an hour when I was startled by the sound of footsteps at the foot of my bed—only there was no one there! The right side of the bed was against a wall, with the headboard in an alcove. I could hear footsteps travel along the lower length of the bed, up the left side, turn (there was a swish of some heavy material, like silk or velvet) and return to the foot of the bed, inches away from my toes. This went on for about two to three minutes and stopped as suddenly as it had started.

I was more astonished than frightened by what had occurred. I tried to rationalize: Amit's cousins who lived upstairs had probably returned from a party and were walking around in high heels. The sounds may have seemed extraordinarily close owing to the strange acoustics of the vast house and the stillness and silence of the floor.

I went off to sleep, and woke up the next morning with bright sunshine streaming in through the window. The events of the previous night came back to me in all their vividness, and I resolved to clear up the mystery of the footsteps at the earliest by asking Amit to accompany me upstairs to say hello to his cousins, and to enquire casually whether they were out late the previous evening.

Over breakfast I said, 'I am amazed at the way sound carries in the house. I could have sworn that there was someone walking about in the bedroom last night. It must have been your cousins back from a late evening.'

I was taken aback by his reaction. He didn't utter another word, but took me up immediately to his cousins' place. After exchanged pleasantries, he led me through to the part of the house located over his bedroom. This was merely a passage leading to a disused rusting spiral staircase which had earlier been the way up to the roof. It had not been used for several years, since the house had been modernized and a new staircase built.

Amit's cousins had not been up late the previous night, they had not been wearing high-heeled shoes, and no one had come near the staircase—there was no reason for anyone to, especially late at night.

I couldn't believe it. I had never seriously considered the possibility of any other explanation. When we to Amit's place, he launched into the story.

'The house, or at least a part of it, is haunted. I have had similar experiences. I was in the shower one evening, when the power went off. I opened the bathroom door, and could clearly hear footsteps moving between the bathroom door and the bed. I had locked the bedroom door, so it was impossible for anyone else to be in the room. I called out anyway, but received no response. I was frightened, man; I just bolted the bathroom door and waited till the generator was switched on. Then I cautiously opened the bathroom door and confirmed that there was no one in the room. The bedroom door was bolted from the inside, just as I had left it. I swear there was something out there, something evil, something distinctly not nice.

'A few days later I was woken up by footsteps at the foot of the bed. This was followed by a violent shaking of the bed. I thought it was an earthquake, and tried to get out of bed. But I found I was held down, as if by a pair of invisible arms. That was it! I haven't spent another night in the room since then. I decided to move into my grandparents' bedroom, it wasn't their idea.'

He continued after a purse, 'You know I'm deeply interested in anything that is out of the ordinary, so I dug into the history of the house. It was built by an Englishman, a Mr Thomas Throne. He had the reputation of getting rid of people who had either displeased him or came in his way. His wife had died under mysterious circumstances. She complained about her husband to the local magistrate: she said he was a sadist and liked torturing people. She said he frequently tortured her, and she wished to return to England alone. She was granted permission to do so—only she never left. She had apparently gone to the botanical gardens, and was reputedly kidnapped by thugs. She was never returned. Two Indian maids disappeared, as did several other people. Several human bones had been found buried in the garden when the fish pond was being dug.'

'What happened to Mr Thomas?' I asked.

'He was murdered.'

'Where?' I asked.

'In this very house,' he replied, 'and his room was located exactly where . . .'

'Don't tell me,' I said, 'his room was located right in your section.'

'Yes.'

Being the ultimate sceptic or out of sheer bravado, I decided to spend another night in the bedroom, much against the advice of Amit and his family. I assured them that I would leave the room immediately if anything out of the ordinary started to occur.

At 11 p.m., I am in bed, settling down to read P.G. Wodehouse's *The Empress of Blandings*.

At 11:45 p.m., the light suddenly goes off. I presume it's a power cut. The footsteps start. I realize it isn't a power cut. This time, I am scared. I try to get out of bed, I cannot. Something is holding me down. I try to shout, I cannot. The more I resist, the more the pressure increases. I become limp. The pressure eases off. I lie there, literally paralysed with fear. I can feel the cold sweat running down my back.

I do not know how long I lay in this catatonic state. It was finally dawn. I crawled out of bed and sprinted out of the room.

That was the last night I or anyone else spent in that room. The entire section has since been demolished.

KAUSHIK BANERJEE

the Poltergeist

I knew them very well. They were friends; their children studied with ours, we lived in the same colony and we often spent our evenings together. But when this thing hit them, we were all taken completely by surprise. For a long time, we did not even know anything about it because they just stopped talking to us, to everyone in fact. But when the first reports hit the papers, they could keep it a secret no longer.

The Indore Daily

Does Indore have a ghost?

From the shops on MG Road to the corridors of Christian College, in temples and in mosques, people in this city are plagued by just this one question. 'Do we have a ghost in our midst?'

It is being said that a ghost lives in the house of a well-known and highly respected resident of Indore. This alleged ghost has turned the lives of the people in this house into a nightmare.

Although the ghost's presence has been suspected for a while, friends of the family say that its activities have become more frequent since 21 September. Books torn, walls defaced and rat excreta in the dal and rice stored in the kitchen—these are just some of the things that the family is struggling with.

According to sources, many holy men have suggested conducting a big yagna on the banks of the Shipra river and a puja at the Mahakaleswar temple in Ujjain.

That afternoon, she called to confide. I asked her over for a cup of tea. She looked like a ghost herself, dark circles under her eyes, her hair unkempt and her sari all crumpled up. She was sobbing, saying that she could not carry on like this any more. JG was angry all the time, and he was blaming her and the children for much of what was going wrong. I held her hand and promised that I would get Deepak to talk to her husband. A week later, she was back again with the following report in hand:

The Indore Daily

Mysterious mischief-maker hits Indore

Indore is heading for its worst winter ever and the chill is not just in the air but also in the minds of its people.

People are scared by the strange and inexplicable acts of mischief and destruction in the house of Mr G of P Nagar, a respected member of Indore society. Cups and saucers falling off the shelves, fresh groceries ruined, dead rats and insects mixed up with the rice—the family's peace has been ruined by acts like these.

It was initially believed that a young child, Mr G's grand-daughter, was playing mischief-maker. The family even suspected its fifteen-year-old maid of some of these acts of vandalism.

But the family has since changed its opinion and they believe that the acts point to some unknown and unseen force.

Meanwhile, this has triggered off a spate of panic among Indoris. Many have approached this correspondent for confirmation of rumours that ghostly beings are to be seen walking the streets of Indore after midnight.

'Why can't they leave us alone? We are trying to sort things out but these papers just make it worse.' She sat quietly for a while after the initial outburst and then left. I did not ask her anything but my maid came up to me later and said, 'Maji, tell them to go to that Pir Baba. He has solved many cases.' I pretended that I did not follow what she was saying. No point in discussing these things with the servants, they talk too much.

The Indore Daily

The ghost of P Nagar

One of Indore's oldest colonies is at the centre of a huge controversy. The house of Mr G has been turned into a local landmark after a ghost came to live there.

The ghost is not a harmless spirit but one that has been ripping books apart, writing over walls with colour pencils, breaking crockery. Besides, there have been instances of eggs leaping out of the refrigerator, and the yolks and whites separating out on their own. Sometimes a slipper disappears or one of the shoes of a pair is found lying torn. Also, a very important book that the family was keeping under lock and key has gone missing with only its cover left behind in its place.

The house has been under attack from an alleged ghost or 'evil spirit' for quite a few months now.

The Indore Daily

A poltergeist in our midst

The house of seventy-year-old Mr G has an unwanted guest who refuses to go away. The guest is a ghost—an evil one at that—it is noisy and carries out acts of mindless destruction. Trouble has been brewing since September and the family is now close to despair.

A few days ago, an expensive shawl was found soaked in ghee. And then, the family was shocked to see small unintelligible writing scribbled all over the ceiling of the house.

Some observers called upon to study the problem believe that the ghost is using the fifteen-year-old maid Bilasa as a medium. It is important to note that poltergeist activity is usually centred on a person and not a place. There may be exceptions but what can be said with certainty is that poltergeist disturbances begin without any warning and last anywhere between a few days to a few years.

Our friends had little choice but to move out of the house for a while. They moved in with us for a few days. JG and his wife were so jittery all the time that I had to get Deepak to take leave from the office and stay with them all the time. We took them to the Pir Baba who agreed to come and visit the house in a week.

The Indore Daily

Is it Bilasa?

The spirit of P Nagar seems to have found a form—a fifteen-year old maid in the G household. According to friends of the family, the spirit may be using the maid as a medium for its evil deeds. The family is said to be keeping a close watch on her.

Meanwhile, the misdemeanours continue. A few days ago, the daughter-in-law of the house was knitting a sweater when the knitting began to unravel on its own. A few days later she found that the wool had been torn to shreds and trampled upon with muddy feet. It has been seen that the spirit works between seven and eleven o'clock in the morning and between two and three o'clock in the afternoon.

The family is disgusted and exhausted not just by the ghostly activities in the house but also by the intense scrutiny that their lives are under by the people of Indore. It has become impossible to carry on with life normally, they say.

We went over last evening. The house was dirty. It looked as if the rooms had not been swept out in months. But a strange sort of calm seemed to have come over JG and his wife. She told me that the Baba had come and suggested a few changes in the house. He seemed confident that the spirit would be driven out if the family followed his directions.

The Indore Daily

The triangle of peril

A solution seems to be in sight for the household that has been plagued by a poltergeist for the last several months. According to sources, a well-known Pir Baba who visited the house has thrown some light on the happenings of the last few months.

According to him, the house is built on a triangular plot of land and therein lies the trouble. A happy home is one that is built on square, rectangular and even circular plots of land. A triangle traps in unwanted spirits, and homes on such plots of land lend themselves to unhappiness and peril.

The G family has been asked to perform a special puja for the appeasement of the spirit that has ensconced itself in their home. The family has also been asked to make a few changes in the house itself.

JG called. It was early morning and we had just woken up. 'I hope you are coming today. Please come early.' He sounded cheerful. I was happy to go. The house looked so different. Everything was new; there was a new gate, the entrance had been changed and so had the positioning of the rooms. Inside, I could see Mrs JG plying the guests with food. She looked bright and cheerful.

The Indore Daily

Peace returns at Sonali

The New Year has brought good news for the G household in P Nagar.

After a puja in the house where almost the entire city of Indore was invited, members of the family thanked everyone around for the support shown during the troubled times. Various changes have been made to the house and a number of pujas are being performed to keep evil spirits away from its doors, according to the family.

Also, the family's fifteen-year-old maid, Bilasa, has been dismissed. According to some of the people present at the puja, Bilasa was being used as a medium by the poltergeist and the family decided to send her back to her village.

ARUNDHUTI DASGUPTA

✦

Village Stories

Why Women are Witches

A traditional tale from the Santhal Parganas.

Once upon a time our god, Marang Buru, decided that he would teach men witchcraft. In those days there was a place at which men used to assemble to meet Marang Buru and hold council with him; but they only heard his voice and never saw his face. One day at the assembly when they had begun to tell Marang Buru of their troubles he fixed a day and told them to come to him on it, dressed in their cleanest clothes, and he would teach them witchcraft.

So the men all went home and told their wives to wash their clothes and keep them ready for the appointed day, as the god was going to teach them witchcraft. The women of course began to discuss this new plan amongst themselves, and the more they talked of it the less they liked it. It seemed to them that if the men were to get this new strange power it would make them more inclined to despise and bully women than ever; so they made a plot to get the better of their husbands.

They arranged that each woman should brew some rice beer and offer it to her husband as he was starting out to meet Marang Buru and beg him to drink some lest his return should be delayed. They foresaw that the men would not be able to resist the drink, and that having started on the rice beer they would go on till they were dead drunk. It would then be easy for the women to dress themselves like men and go off to Marang Buru and learn witchcraft in place of their husbands. So it was said, so it was done; the women duly made their husbands drunk and then put on turbans and dhotis and stuck goats' beards on their faces and went off to Marang Buru to learn witchcraft. Marang Buru did not detect the deception and, true to his promise, taught them all the incantations of witchcraft.

Some time after the women had come home with their new knowledge, their husbands gradually started sobering up and remembered their appointment with Marang Buru. So they hurried off to the meeting place and asked him to teach them what he had promised.

'Why, I taught it all to you this morning!' answered Marang Buru. 'What do you mean by coming to see me again?'

The men could not understand what he meant and protested that they had not been to him at all in the morning.

'Then you must have told your wives what I was going to do!'

This they could not deny.

'I see,' said Marang Buru. 'Then they must have played a trick on you and learnt the mantras in your place.'

At this the men began to lament and begged that they might be taught also, but Marang Buru said that this was impossible. He could only teach them a very little; their wives had reaped the crop and they could have only the gleanings. So saying, he taught them the art of the ojha, in order that they might have the advantage of their wives in one respect and be able to overcome them. He also taught them the craft of the jaan, and with that they had to be content. This is why only women are witches.

NILANJANA GUPTA

the lemon tree

Baikuntha was returning to home after a long time. For the last two years he had been working in the city and sending whatever money he could save to support his family back in the village. Now he was looking forward to seeing his father and mother and his two younger brothers who still laboured hard at tilling the small plot of land they had been allotted by the zamindar. It was back-breaking work and the *khazna* or rent due to the zamindar left them with very little surplus.

Baikuntha had left the city early in the morning. But he still had some distance to travel as the journey was long and tiring. A bus took him from the city to a junction, which was a good two hours' walk from the village.

As he approached the familiar landmarks, Baikuntha was filled with the sweet pleasure of homecoming. Memories of his relatively carefree childhood came flooding back to him—the huge mango tree which they used to pelt with stones to eat the green sweet-smelling unripe little fruits with a little bit of salt and chilli. How they used to suck the skin till their stomachs would cramp from so much fruit! Then there was the huge pond where they and the village flock of cows and buffaloes would all splash about at the height of summer. How he would swim underwater and trip up his friends so that they would surface gasping for air! As he thought of his past escapades, he wondered where all the young boys were. It was the time of day when he would have thought some of them would be splashing about in the cool greenish water. The pond looked really inviting and Baikuntha would have taken a dip himself except that he was already late and he knew his entire family must be waiting for him eagerly.

Come to think of it, the entire area looked strangely quiet. Where were all the men in the fields? There seemed to be an eerie silence around him. Not even a crow could be heard. Normally any stranger to the area would be greeted by the stray dogs who would bark warningly until a villager came and greeted him. The dogs would then slink away, satisfied that the stranger was a friend.

Baikuntha reached his old neighbourhood. This area too was silent. Not a sparrow chirped, even the air seemed to be still and heavy. As his footsteps thudded in the dusty lane, he could see at last his own house. He saw his mother stand by the door. His heart leapt in joy as he saw her. As the eldest son, he had had to take on family responsibilities even when he was a small boy and he always felt that his mother tried to show her sadness at his truncated childhood by being just that little bit more affectionate towards him. Not that anyone else would have noticed, but he knew that his mother had a special place for him in her heart.

There she stood, just as she had stood and waited for him when he was late returning from the fields, silent, patient, her *anchal* drawn modestly over her head so that no passer-by could gaze on her lovely face. No, that privilege was reserved only for the closest members of her family and a few friends. Baikuntha ran the last few steps and bent low to touch her feet. As usual he could only touch the hem of the coarse red border of her sari. His mother was so modest that she always tried to cover up as much of her body as possible.

'Come, come, Khoka. I have been waiting for you for so long. You must be tired. Come, take your towel down to the well and wash while I prepare your meal. You must be so hungry and hot and tired.'

'Oh, Ma, it's so wonderful to be back and to see you again. But where is everyone? Where are Baba and Chhotu and Bicchu?'

'Oh, they will be here soon. Come and wash your tired feet in the cool water of the well.'

Baikuntha took his towel and went to the backyard and found a bucket of water already drawn. He gratefully doused himself with the cool sweet water and wiped himself dry. He went back into the hut. His mother had already spread a mat for him to sit and heaped his plate with rice and vegetables and bhajis. In separate bowls there were dal and fish. She sat on the floor gently waving the palm-leaf fan in her hand. 'Come, sit and eat. You must be very hungry.'

As he sat down, he realized that his mother had gone to a lot of trouble to prepare such a feast for him. It was true that he was hungry. As he started eating, his mother talked to him. Mealtimes were always when she spoke to him 'Eat, my Khoka. It is so nice to have you home after such a long time. I hope you like the food. Let me go and warm some milk for you. You always liked a bowl of hot milk at the end of the meal. Eat properly. I'm coming.'

She rose and went into the kitchen. Baikuntha happily continued eating. It was true: no one could cook as perfectly as Ma. Everything was just right and tasty, though so simply cooked. This dal would be even better with a little lemon juice. Then it would be heavenly.

'Ma, do you have any lemons? I feel like adding a squeeze of one of our own lemons, from our own tree, to the dal.'

She replied that there were some. 'But wait, Khoka, the milk is about to boil. I'll bring it.'

'Don't bother, Ma. I'll come and get it myself,' said Baikuntha getting up from his mat. He could hear his mother protesting— 'No, no, Khoka, you shouldn't get up in the middle of your meal. It is inauspicious'—just as he knew she would. However, two years in the city had cured him of such stupid superstitions. He walked into the kitchen with a smile on his face.

His mother was sitting in front of the oven, with her feet in it and flames leaping out from them. As he stared uncomprehendingly, she stretched her left arm out of the kitchen window to the lemon tree several yards away, by the side of the well. Her bony fingers plucked a lemon, her long arm wound back and she gave it to him. Struck speechless, he took the lemon in his hand and fled from the hut as fast as he could.

Panic-stricken he ran through the empty streets and empty fields, silent and deserted.

Suddenly he heard a voice: 'Hey! Aren't you Gadadhar's son Baikuntha? Why are you running like that with a lemon in your hand?'

Warily, Baikuntha stopped and asked, 'Who are you?'

'Don't say that two years of city life have erased all your memories! I am Haripada, the grocer's son. I too went to the city to work, like you did. That is why I survived.'

'What do you mean?'

'You know, the epidemic, cholera. The entire village was wiped out. Not a single survivor. Don't tell me you didn't know?'

NILANJANA GUPTA

the Wedding feast

I am Harendranath Das, Village Rajnagar, PO Khaltola, District 24 Parganas North. Really and truly I have eaten a ghost's wedding feast. My friend Kalicharan is an exorcist. He can tell any ghost to exit from the body and the ghost, he must go. All the ghosts in my village and all around are fearing Kalicharan Gunin for he can beat up any ghost very hard, very hard.

One day, Kalicharan and I were having a pull at our hubble bubble when he said 'Haru, do you want to eat a ghost's wedding feast? You like sweets, there will be many kinds of sweets!' Of course I agreed readily, for yes, I love sweets. 'Come, let's go,' said Kalu, and off we went towards the big field where no one goes at night.

'O Kalu bhai, I am afraid,' I said. No one crosses this field, full of not only ghosts but robbers who aim their deadly wooden *phabras* at your legs and then as you fall down, they rob you of all. If you die of fright, then you will join those ghosts who live in the big tamarind trees and tall tal palms.

'Do you like *rosogollas*, *kheer*, *dahi*, *sandesh*, *jilipi*, *darbesh*?' demanded Kalu. I couldn't deny it. I would risk much for that feast. So we went along far into the field and then Kalu picked up a stone and threw it in the air. I didn't see it fall but from all around came shrieks of laughter in high, higher and highest tones.

'Shut up!' said Kalu, 'get the feast ready, can't you see my friend is coming?' And we walked on and on until we came to a big tree. A little way from it was Kalu's stone and under the tree, Madam, was the grandest feast my poor eyes have ever seen. There were pots of dohi, *handis* of rabri, of kheer, of rosogolla, and a great big *changari* full of jilipi, *bondey*, sandesh, *khaja*, *gaja*, the biggest and the best, better than what I have seen in the shops in Calcutta when I went with my uncle to see the city. We ate and ate and ate and we took as much as we could in our *gamchhas* for our families at home who would tell their grandchildren of the ghost's wedding feast.

Now did you like the story, Madam? It is absolutely true, I tell you on my honour.

BUNNY GUPTA

✢

raaghu and the Kudpalbhoota

This is a story from Mangalore. kudpalbhoota *means 'the hairy ghost'. If you can catch it by its long hair and can hold on tight, it can take you to the sky and back, trying to shake you off. If it cannot shake you off it grants whatever you ask for.*

Raaghu was a lively young fellow. He was a great favourite in the fields because he and his friends were agile enough to work the *yeta* or the *pane*, the manual instrument used to irrigate the fields. Once the large wooden *marai* with its 200 litres of water was sunk into the well the three young men had to leap backwards into the ten-foot-deep pit that helped them man the long, strong ropes and the heavy wooden bar that levered the marai in and out of the water to run it into the fields. While Raaghu had an impish sense of humour and a healthy streak of adventurousness, he did lack one virtue: patience.

'You want to get through everything at one go, Raaghu,' his friends would say to him. 'You are so good at doing things you have no patience with slower people! You want everything quickly. How would you ever hold on to the kudpalbhoota if you ever see her?'

'That dirty hairy thing? Yaah! Thhu!' Raaghu would laugh and hawk and spit as if even to say the name of the creature polluted his mouth! But fate plays strange tricks and Raaghu was to find this out very soon.

Raaghu lived with his widowed mother. She wove the strong ropes that were used in the fields, made baskets and dried paddy for the family's single meals.

Raaghu, his mother and sisters were very poor, yet they were not unhappy until Girija, Raaghu's mother, fell ill. Nobody could tell what was wrong with her and no one knew how to cure her.

To make matters worse, Raaghu fell in love with Padmavati. Her father was a rich man who did not think that a poor labourer was a fitting match for his beautiful daughter. He had forgotten that he too was a labourer's son. Padmavati was tall and slim and graceful with long lustrous hair and a smile that lit a thousand lamps. She was also as clever as she was lovely. Of all the boys in the village she liked Raaghu the best, though she said nothing of the sort to her father. She knew that would make him so angry he would not listen to anything she said.

When her father said 'Daughter, it is time that you married,' she said, 'Father, you know that it was I who brought the goddess Lakshmi into your house. Your land and your business prospered after my birth.'

'That is true, my child.'

'Then if you force me to marry against my will, you will drive the goddess out of our home along with me.'

Ramananda looked worried. Then he said, 'Very well, and what is it you would have me do, daughter?'

'I wish to marry a man who has above all courage, determination and patience.'

'These are certainly laudable virtues, my child,' nodded her father sagely.

'Anyone who can catch the kudpalbhoota has all three in good measure, Father,' said Padmavati. 'I will marry the man who can catch the kudpalbhoota and ask for the most sensible boon.'

Now Padmavati often went to the beautiful meadow at the edge of the forest to pick flowers, and Raaghu used to cut across it on his way home from the fields. This is how they met and how they continued to meet.

Padmavati told Raaghu of her conversation with her father.

'Tomorrow morning you must be the first to present yourself at my gate, then Father will have to allow you to try and catch that bhoota first of all.'

Raaghu didn't like the idea much but he knew he needed a few dreams to come true. For one thing, his mother was growing weaker and weaker, they were growing poorer and poorer, and he truly loved Padmavati. He wished desperately to marry her but did not feel that he was worthy of her until he had proved himself.

'One thing though,' said Padmavati. 'Do not ask for riches, do not ask for your mother's good health and do not ask to be able to marry me!'

Raaghu was puzzled and worried. These were the things he desired the most in the world. What else could he possibly demand from the creature?

'These are all impermanent things,' said Padmavati. 'If you truly want everything to happen as you desire, you will know what to ask.'

Raaghu spent the entire night outside the gates of Ramananda's house. As soon as Ramananda announced he would give his daughter's hand in marriage to the first person who could catch the kudpalbhoota, Raaghu made his appearance and went off to hunt the dreadful creature. He knew that it roamed in places where rotting carcasses were thrown by villagers too poor even to burn their dead, and in pits where rubbish piled high. Where the stench was strongest, there the creature would lurk.

He waited and watched, but it was a long time before he noticed any movement. The rats came out first, and then the jackals. Then, just as Raaghu was wondering if he would find the creature at all, there it was, crouching and snuffling in the dirt, its hairy body and long nails scrabbling and scrabbling for he knew not what. He steeled himself to look at it. It was most horribly ugly. It was all he could do to look at it—and now he had to catch it!

The creature raised its head and sniffed the air once or twice as if it knew someone was watching it. Raaghu moved away from the wind and circled round behind the creature and gave the highest leap of his life. His arms were strong with the lifting of the marai, and he could leap high and fast thanks to his daily task of raising the irrigation water, but it was all he could do to hang on tight to the evil-smelling shrieking creature whose long filthy hair he clutched in his fists.

'Aaaiyee, aiyee,' shrieked the spirit. 'Let me go!' It flew, screeching and shaking with rage, high into the sky over the village, with Raaghu on its back.

Raaghu hung on all through the night while the creature desperately writhed and buckled under him. Finally, exhausted, it said in desperation, 'What will you have of me? Health? Wealth? The love of a beautiful woman?'

'Take me back to the ground and I will tell you my heart's desire,' said Raaghu, who had been doing some thinking.

The kudpalbhoota sank to the ground in the middle of the village, groaning and panting. Then Raaghu whispered softly, 'May good luck follow me in everything I wish to do. May everything always go the way I wish.'

'Your wish is granted, now let me go,' hissed the kudpalbhoota and Raaghu gladly let go of its hair. He knew now he need no longer be poor, his mother need no longer be sick and Padmavati would be his for always, for this was what his heart desired.

Padmavati and her father, along with the other villagers, had gathered to watch the struggle in the sky as light dawned. Raaghu went up to Ramananda and said, 'I have kept to my part of the bargain. Now you must keep to yours.'

Ramananda looked at Padmavati and said, 'Is this agreed, my daughter?'

'Yes,' said Padmavati, blushing and averting her eyes, 'but I have one request.'

'What is that?' said Raaghu, puzzled.

'Please bathe immediately!'

Everybody burst out laughing and there was much celebration as Raaghu with a rueful grin went off to bathe before he told his the good news.

SHAIONTONI BOSE

One Summer afternoon

Ye re, Ye re pausa,
Tula deto paisa,
Paisa jhala khota,
Paus aala motha.

Rain, rain,
Come to our mountains and our plains,
We wait for you with open arms
And some silver in our outstretched palms,
The silver turns out to be no good
But the rains have come in a flood.

A Marathi folk song

Summer had covered the countryside in every conceivable shade of brown. The village wells were drying up, the fields looked parched and the trees stood withered and bare. So it was in the village of Khed where the men and women went about tilling their lands and doing their daily chores with less energy than usual. But the children basked in the sun and ran along the dry river beds singing and screaming.

Smita skipped along, her pigtails swinging and her voice raised in song, '*Ye re, ye re pausa . . .*' She was oblivious to the heat and to the stares that she drew from passers-by.

A voice giggled in her ear, 'Your song will only drive the rain away . . .' It was Ushi with her large eyes and thick curls falling all over her face.

'Why so late today?' Smita asked as she grabbed her by her arms.

'Aai asked me to stay at home and look after Bala but I slipped away when she was combing her hair,' Ushi told her friend.

Smita and Ushi had known each other for most of their nine years. And for as long as they could remember, they had spent almost every waking hour together.

'Where shall we go today Ushi?'

Ushi was busy unwrapping an old rag that she had filled with *besan laddoos*. 'Have some, I got them when Aai was not looking. Umm . . . Let's go to the old woman's orchard today. Maybe we can get some *kairis*.' Smita's eyes shone at the prospect of an afternoon spent eating green mangoes.

The orchard known among the locals as Mhatari's orchard was a long way off. Moreover, it was forbidden territory. Their mothers and grandmothers had always warned children about the ruins next to the orchard. 'It is a house of spirits,' Ushi's grandmother had told her. 'If you girls go there, the spirits are going to catch you by the hair and drag you to their homes.' Ushi shuddered as she remembered her grandmother's words. Smita wasn't as worried. After all, she had no intentions of going into the house. All she wanted to do was to eat mangoes.

As the two girls made their way to the orchard, they opened their hearts to each other. Their deepest wishes and worst fears tumbled out. Ushi wished that she did not have to wake up while it was still dark to line up for water near the well. She wished that she did not have to look after her baby brother and that her mother did not look so tired all the time. Smita wished that she could go to school like her brothers and that she did not have to wash their clothes as well as hers. She wished that her father would get her new pink ribbons to tie her hair with and that her mother made besan laddoos like Ushi's mother.

'Ushi, Ushi,' her mother called out far away. Both looked at each other and giggled. Pretending not to hear, they ran ahead until the distance drowned her voice.

The girls spent a lovely afternoon in the shade of the mango trees feasting on kairis and laddoos. They left only when the old woman, whose orchard it was, chased them out with a stick. The girls ran out as fast as they could, their dresses filled with green mangoes, mimicking her and sticking their tongues out at her and laughing as they ran, looking over their shoulders to check on the pursuit. 'Mhatari, old woman, Mhatari,' Ushi yelled. Smita giggled and sprinted as fast as she could.

Panting and sweating, the girls stopped for breath once they were sure that the old lady had stopped following them. They flopped down on the road and found that they had run towards the very ruins that they had been told to steer clear of.

The heat and stillness of the afternoon wrapped itself around the ruins like a cloud, and the dust from the plains swirled all around like a brown mist. As the two girls watched, a soft breeze disentangled itself from the peepal and mango trees and blew across, lifting the mist to reveal circular maze of walls.

'It must have been a fort, Ushi,' Smita said, awestruck.

'Look, that must have been a look-out window.' Ushi pointed to a gaping hole in the wall.

'That there must have been a cannon hole and . . . there must have been a large terrace where soldiers watched their enemies from, but now there is no roof . . . and there from that hill the enemy must have marched,' Smita muttered.

'No, maybe it was a *wada*, one of the Peshwas' houses. Look, those gates probably opened up into rows of neat houses and shops . . .'

The girls sat there dreaming and chatting. The red brick walls with weeds and creepers growing out of their crevices, stared down at Smita and Ushi. A large iron door sealed the walls off from the world outside. A smaller door lay wedged in, slightly open.

Ushi and Smita sat there, letting the breeze dry their sweat, watching the door glisten in the afternoon sun. The girls waited and waited . . . until they could contain their curiosity no longer.

'Should we take a peep, only a peep? We won't go in,' Smita's voice trailed off.

Ushi was afraid, her grandmother's voice rang in her ears. But she too was mesmerized by the half-open door. 'We won't go in, all right? Only from the door . . .' she said, more to herself than to Smita.

The door swung open with a nudge and the girls found themselves standing in a huge courtyard. What lay in front of them was a maze of broken walls, paths and staircases that seemed to lead nowhere. Plants and weeds grew wild, and cats lay curled up in the corners. Birds twittered on a peepal tree that grew out of the middle of the courtyard and the air lay heavy on its leaves and its branches.

Smita and Ushi both saw it together. A large creaky swing swinging in the middle of the courtyard. Sunlight had spread itself around the swing but left the swing itself in darkness. The girls squinted for a clear look at what seemed like shadows stretched across the swing. As they stepped closer, they saw an old lady with her hair over her shoulders rocking back and forth on the swing. Her long fingers held the rusty iron rods on both sides of the swing and her face was covered with tiny lines.

The old lady also seemed to see them at the same time and she smiled. Her red, paan-stained lips drew wide to show a toothless grin. She held out her hand and the girls saw a small silver box filled with tiny green leaves, tied together. She beckoned and the girls involuntarily moved closer. Then Smita spoke, 'No, no, we don't eat paan. My mother will be angry.'

'But don't you want red lips like mine? Come, come, don't be afraid,' she said in a strangely raspy voice. 'And don't you want a red tongue like mine? See . . .'

The old woman stuck her tongue out and then before the girls knew it, they were screaming . . . Her red tongue uncoiled and stretched itself out. For a few seconds that seemed like hours, Smita and Ushi stood rooted to the spot. The tongue slid across the space between them and the old woman reached out . . .

The girls ran. Ushi sped with her eyes tightly shut, muttering prayers to every god that she could remember. And Smita had tears running down her cheeks, her pigtails flying in the wind and the mangoes scattered all over the brown landscape.

For almost a month after that, Smita and Ushi were ill, very ill. The fever refused to come down, the girls could not eat or sleep. They lay staring at the ceiling, wrapped in thick blankets and yet shivering through the hot and humid summer nights.

Their parents tried every doctor and every quack but none had a cure. They despaired until neighbours and friends told them to go and visit an old nurse in the village. The old nurse sat bunched up in a corner of her hut. Tiny black eyes shone out of a thin, parched face. She said, 'Water is the purifier and the cure. Go pay your respects to the river, break a coconut and light a diya and then wait for rain. The first shower will cure them, you'll see.'

ARUNDHUTI DASGUPTA

Silence

In the world of magic, the name of a person, animal or creature has immense significance. To know the name of a person is to have some kind of power over him.

It was during the first few months on my farm, tucked away in a corner of north India, in the low foothills of the Himalayas, that I had first-hand experience of how traditional beliefs (and superstitions too!) are alive and flourishing and very much a part of life even today. Although our farm is in quite a developed zone, it is situated at the edge of a forest and the folk living in the area not only depend on forest products for fodder and fuel but also respect and worship it.

We had planted corn for the first time, just after the first rains, and the crop was coming up well. Tender green shoots sprang up everywhere, and you could see the plants grow and relish the rain.

Girwar and Istaq, two of the labourers, were devoted to the farm and worked on it as if it were their own. Girwar was a Banjara, from a nomadic tribe now settled in a more sedentary existence in hamlets called *tandas* just outside the villages. Most Banjaras have converted to Sikhism but still maintain their old customs. Istaq was a *nai*, a barber who went broke when he tried small-scale dairy farming.

Night on the farm often entailed *rakhwaal*, guarding the crops against wild animals, and all hands were supposed to pitch in. Each of us assigned ourselves a corner of the farm and sat down to wait out the night. It was around two in the morning and we had just chased some chital from the corn, when a crashing in the thicket followed by a loud squeal from Girwar's corner broke the silence and gave me quite a start. 'Elephant!' The most dreaded word for any rakhwaal, for many farmers are killed every year protecting their crops. I feared for Girwar's life.

'Girwar,' I shouted, 'Girwar!' No answer. I started forward, worried that something was amiss. 'Girwar!' Still no answer. I had by this time almost reached Girwar's thatched hut and saw a shadow by the light of the dying embers. Girwar was stoking the fire.

I wondered why he did not answer me! I walked up and asked him if the noise was an elephant, to which he replied that it had actually turned out to be a group of wild pigs and that he had chased them out. He added that they collectively sometimes made more noise than an elephant.

Girwar did not seem to be deaf, and I asked him why he had not replied. I felt he had been insubordinate! He just smiled and lit a bidi from the coals. He said there was an old belief amongst the folk that lived near the forest. Apparently the spirits of the forest are constantly looking to gain some energy from humans, so they regularly fake the voices of persons known to their chosen victims and call out to them. If there is a response within the first two calls the person immediately falls into the grasp of the forest spirit, who then proceeds to drain the hapless soul of its energy. After the third call the spirit vanishes to try elsewhere, so it was important to wait until the third call to confirm that the caller was authentic—an ordinary human being!

I have tried this out many times subsequently, and always receive no response until after the third call. Girwar has left and so has Istaq, but their successors, including Brim Pal and Manoj, even today behave in the same way.

PHOENIX

Kosi

This story is about the power of memory and about how that power can mysteriously reside in a single, key object. The young woman who tells the tale acknowledges that her life is the way it is because of something that has happened in the past—but what it is she does not know.

In our small two-roomed cottage, Kosi's room was always a mess. It was full of books and papers lying in untidy piles all over the floor, the chair, the table, even the bed. But there must have been a method to this madness, for Kosi always knew where to find even the smallest scrap of paper that he needed. He would never allow me to touch anything, much less try to tidy it. 'I can't find anything if you move my stuff around,' he'd complain. 'If you can't handle the mess, stay out of my room.'

His room was far too fascinating to stay out of—so I ignored the chaos, trying not to step on any precious pieces of paper that might be lying on the floor, and grabbed every chance I could to visit his den. Kosi was a writer—I think. At least, he was always busy scribbling away on yellow sheets of ruled paper, and looking up dictionaries and muttering strange lines to himself. Some days, the wastepaper basket in his room would overflow with yellow scraps—those were the days I needed to keep very quiet and not bother him in any way. On other days, he would emerge smiling from his room and perhaps sit and chat with me. I would know that he had managed to finish some work the way he wanted to.

Sometimes the postman would arrive with a large and rather heavy parcel. Kosi would immediately shut himself up in his room for the day. He would appear for dinner looking tired and bleary-eyed and depressed. He never liked any of his books once they were published. Sometimes the postman would arrive with a letter and a cheque. Kosi would then take out his rusty old car from the garage and drive off with a great deal of noise towards the town. He would come back a few hours later laden with books and loads of food, and we would have a party.

Life was peaceful with Kosi. I was allowed to do pretty much as I pleased. My memories of those years are chiefly of long solitary walks over the hills and fields, of shopping expeditions to the village where we would buy bread and butter and eggs and milk, enough to last us a week, of long summer evenings with Kosi telling me stories about the stars. The only thing that Kosi insisted upon was school. He would make sure I left on time, would check my work to see how I was getting on, and would even remember to turn up for the odd parent-teacher meeting, looking neat and clean and as conscientious as any parent could. Kosi cared, I know, but he was different from other dads—and in a secret sort of way I was rather proud of his eccentricities.

One day, the wooden egg arrived, and our lives, Kosi's and mine, changed forever.

I even remember the day: it was Sunday, 12 October, and Kosi and I had planned to pack some sandwiches and go for a walk over the hills. It was a rare treat for me to get Kosi for an entire day, and I was excited. The postman arrived, cheerful as ever, and handed me a small brown-paper parcel. It's too small and light to be books, I remember thinking. I ran in and gave it to Kosi, who was busy cutting the sandwiches. He looked at it for a long time, and then opened it slowly, as though afraid of what he might find. He left it lying on the table and vanished into his room for a day and a half.

The box lay on the table, its brown-paper wrapping half off. Inside the box lay a wooden egg in a nest of cotton wool, smooth and brown and shining. I had never seen anything so beautiful. Its oval surface was criss-crossed with a million lines, glinting gold and amber in the morning sun, whorls marking the wood like fingerprints. I went closer and reached out a hand to touch it. It was warm and smooth—so smooth it felt like silk, though it was hard polished wood. The egg fitted snugly into my palm. I closed my eyes and ran my fingers over its smoothness; a ridge ran down its spine, marring its perfect beauty—like nail varnish that hasn't been applied evenly, I thought. It lay nestled in my hand—brown and lovely. A smell of old lace and talcum powder filled the air around it: a smell that reminded me of elegant clothes, of pots of makeup and face cream. A smell gathered over the years, overlaying perhaps the smell of ancient forests, of grass and leaf and wood, of rain at night and dew in the morning, of fragrant earth and fungus growing, of rising sap, of old leaves dying . . .

Images flashed into my mind, of love and beauty, of passion, dark and burning, of sunshine and laughter, pain and grief and joy, emotions I had hardly experienced and could barely understand. That night, alone and wondering, I slept with the egg on my pillow.

The next day Kosi had taken the egg away from me—sadly, sorrowfully. He had looked at it a long while and then put it away as though saying goodbye forever to someone, something very precious. A part of Kosi seemed to have died.

It was almost as though a cloud had come between us and the sun, a cloud that was here to stay. Kosi became quiet, very quiet. His step lost its bounce and his room was never so untidy again. The postman would still come with parcels, but Kosi would not open them any more. We would still have our parties when the cheques arrived, but soon I would be dancing alone—Kosi would not dance any more.

Kosi would no longer spend the evenings with me; there were no more stories, no more quiet chats, no walks over the hills. Instead he would look at me in that new sad way of his, and shut himself up in his room. Sometimes I would wake at night, convinced I was alone in the cottage, and peering out of the front door I would see Kosi, outlined against the stars, contemplating the night alone. He seemed bowed down with a weight almost too heavy for him to bear, a weight that not even time seemed to lighten.

This carried on for many many months, till it was autumn once again. That year the sun hardly shone. The trees shivered in the sharp winds; the leaves, gold and rust and red, twirled sadly, silently to the ground. Only Kosi seemed to cheer up. He had a bright alert look about him, like a squirrel or other small animal listening for danger. He would sometimes smile at me; sometimes he was almost like the old Kosi again, the Kosi who would laugh and play and ruffle my hair in between books. I would start hoping that life would soon be happy again, when the same lost look would come back and he would wander off across the fields. Sometimes he would stand listening at the door, or even a window; sometimes he would stop whatever it was he was doing and look around as though at a sudden sound—he'd smile and nod and go away.

I was feeling more lost, more confused and more hopeless than ever. Till one evening Kosi called me into his room. I knew then that something was terribly wrong—his room was neat, so neat that I could not recognize it. There were no papers anywhere, no books, no dust, no mess. In fact, it was as though Kosi did not live there any more.

Kosi smiled at me and drew me close. He hugged me, as he had only once before when I had broken my leg falling off a fence. He opened my clenched fist, and put into my hand the egg—the wooden egg upon which I blamed all the changes in our lives. 'We would like you to have this,' he said. 'Remember, we will always love you, no matter what.'

Those were the very last words my father ever spoke to me. He gave me one long last look and walked out of the door—never to be seen again. The neighbours soon arrived and so did Nona; she took me away to live with her in her small cottage by a river where school and friends and lots of loving care chased all dark thoughts away. I may have forgotten my life with Kosi, had it not been for the beautiful wooden egg which lay on a small table in my room. Once, when Nona and I were going through an old family album, I saw a picture of Kosi with a dark and beautiful woman who held in her hand my egg. I never saw that photograph again—and Nona said there never had been any such picture in her album.

The egg still sits in my bedroom on my dressing table. When I look into the mirror, I sometimes see that dark and mysterious woman looking back at me; sometimes I catch a glimpse of Kosi, his fair hair shining like the gold in my own . . . I smile at them, and they smile back, knowing the egg is safe with me and always will be.

ROHINI CHOWDHURY

✦ ┼ ✦

tales from the City

‒I‒

the legend of padmasambhava

This wonderfully syncretic story combines dakinis and djinns, magic and transformations, reincarnations and demons, and figures from all over the Near and Middle East within its religious framework.

Padmasambhava was apparently a native of Udyana, which, like Kashmir, was the home of magic arts, and he appears as a magician *par excellence* who claimed to excel Gotama himself in this dubious accomplishment. The legendary account of his life makes him a spiritual son of Amitabh, produced for the conversion of Tibet, and he is said to have been born from a lotus as the son of the childless, blind king Indrabhati—hence his name, which means 'lotus-born'. Educated as befitted the heir of the monarch, he surpassed all his equals in accomplishments and was married to a princess of Ceylon. However, a supernatural voice urged him to abandon worldly things, and he succeeded in obtaining banishment from the kingdom by killing some of his father's retainers, whose past lives had earned them this punishment. Dakinis and djinns brought him the magic steed Bal~ha, on which he sped away.

After a prolonged period of meditation in cemeteries, whereby he won supernatural powers through the favour of dakinis, he travelled through all lands and despite the fact that he was, as a

Buddha, already omniscient, he acquired each and every science, astrology, alchemy, the Mahayana and the Hinayana, the Tantras and all the languages. He converted the princess Mandarava, the incarnation of a Dakini to Buddhism; she thereafter accompanied him in all his wanderings, now in human form with a cat's head, now in other shapes. Then he set himself to the conversion of India . . .

At last, on the invitation of the King of Tibet, K'ri-sron-Idebtsan, he proceeded there to contend with the demons who hindered the spread of the faith in that land; and though Mava himself sought to frustrate his success, the fiend was defeated, and the evil powers were forced to yield, Padmasambhava's victory being marked by the building of the monastery of Sam-yas, thirty-five miles from Lhasa, the oldest of Tibetan monasteries.

LOUIS HERBERT GRAY

the living dead

Classical Sanskrit literature has numerous ghost stories. This is from the Kathasaritsagar.

Sridarshana was a young man much addicted to gambling. His parents, now both dead, had given him a good education, but all he was interested in was gambling. Soon he was reduced to utter penury, and there came a time when he had had nothing to eat for three days. His clothes were in such tatters that he was ashamed to venture out of the house. He was too proud to ask anyone for help, and so remained indoors. It was in such a state that his friend, Mukharaka, found him.

Mukharaka himself was a seasoned gambler, who as a boy had left home with other gamblers. He advised Sridarshana to leave the city and go somewhere new where no one knew him and make a fresh start in life. Sridarshana agreed to this, and the two friends left their hometown late at night.

On the evening of the second day they reached a village. They sat down to rest by a pond where they drank their fill and washed themselves. Shortly after, a beautiful young girl came to fetch water from the pond. She and Sridarshana fell in love at first sight. She asked the two young men, 'Who are you, sirs? Why have you come here, like moths flying into the flame?' In turn, Mukharaka asked her who she was. From her answer, they realized that she was none other than Mukharaka's own sister, Padmishtha. When Mukharaka had left home, his mother had died of grief, but his father and Padmishtha had gone looking for him. Ultimately they had reached this village which was inhabited solely by thieves and robbers. Their chief had robbed and killed the father and held the daughter prisoner as a prospective bride for his son. Padmishtha urged the two men to escape before the thieves caught them.

Hearing of the fate of his family, Mukharaka burst out wailing and embraced his sister, crying out that he himself was the wretched Mukharaka. Recognizing him as her brother, Padmishtha wept too. But Sridarshana was more pragmatic. 'This is not the time for grief,' he said. 'We must find a way to get away from here.' He advised the brother and sister what to do.

Sridarshana himself was very thin because he had not eaten for so many days. He lay at the edge of the pond, while Mukharaka sat at his feet and wept. On hearing about them, the robber chief came to the pond with his servant and asked Mukharaka why he was weeping.

'This is my elder brother,' said Mukharaka. 'We are brahmins. My brother is dying and I beg you to find a brahmin to perform his last rites, and mine too, for I will also kill myself. I cannot live without my brother. If you get us a brahmin priest, we will give you all our money and jewellery. We no longer need them.'

Then the chief said to his servants, 'Let us kill the two of them and take their valuables.' His servants replied, 'Sir, they will both be dead in the morning anyway. Why should we commit a mortal sin? Let us wait until morning. If they are still alive, we will kill them. If they are already dead, we will merely take their valuables.' The chief agreed to this.

At night, when the thieves slept, Padmishtha quietly crept out and joined her brother and his friend. The three of them escaped to the great city of Malava. In the meantime, Sridarshana had professed his love for Padmishtha and she had agreed to marry him. It was decided that they would marry as soon as an opportunity presented itself.

When they reached Malava, they heard that the king, Srisena, was dying of consumption. A sorcerer had told him that he could cure him, but he needed a brave man to help him. This man would have to come to the burning ghats at the dead of night to rouse the spirits. But although this had been announced all over the kingdom, no brave man had dared to come forward, even to save the king's life.

Then the king said to his ministers, 'Make a fresh announcement. I have had a rest house built for gamblers. Find out if there is one among the visiting gamblers brave enough to go to the burning ghats. Gamblers care nothing for their lives, since they have been given up by their families and friends. So they are naturally fearless, and can go anywhere without fear, like the sages who live under trees and have nothing to lose.'

When Sridarshana heard this announcement, he said, 'I am a gambler. I think I am capable of doing this.' And he went to the palace.

The king was pale and emaciated, terrified of the advent of death. But he cheered up as soon as he saw Sridarshana, as though already on the way to recovery. He called the sorcerer and said, 'Sir, this brave man will help you.' The sorcerer looked Sridarshana over, and said, 'Good man, if you fancy yourself brave enough to help me summon the spirits, then this is what you must do. This is the fourteenth night since the full moon. You must come to the burning ghat tonight, and await my instructions.'

Sridarshana left his fiancée and his friend at the rest house for gamblers, and went that night to the burning ghats alone, armed with his sword.

The night was pitch dark. Ghosts and evil spirits darted around on all sides. Not a human soul could be seen anywhere, only jackals howling for the dead. Into this terrifying spot walked Sridarshana, looking for the sorcerer. Soon he came to the middle of the ghat and saw him making preparations to rouse the spirits. He was clad in black clothes, his body smeared with ashes from the funeral pyres. His sacred thread was made out of corpses' hair. Even his turban was fashioned out of the clothes of corpses. He was a ghastly sight indeed! But Sridarshana strode fearlessly up to him with folded hands and said, 'Sir, here I am. Tell me what to do.'

'Go west,' said the sorcerer, 'and you will soon come upon a simsapa tree, its leaves scorched by fire, with a corpse lying under it. Fetch the corpse here, undamaged.'

'As you say, so it shall be,' replied Sridarshana and hurried away. Soon he reached the tree, but to his astonishment he saw another man carrying off the corpse. Sridarshana ran after him and seized the corpse. 'Give it to me,' he shouted. 'This is the body of a friend of mine. Where are you taking it? I have to cremate it!'

'I will not give it to you,' said the other. 'This is my friend. Who are you?'

Both men tugged at the corpse, arguing over it. Evil spirits hovered all around, watching closely and enjoying the scene. One of them chose this moment to enter into the corpse, which then turned into a *vetala* or 'living dead'.

As soon as the ghost had entered the corpse, it stirred and let out a most horribly weird cry. Sridarshana's rival was terrified. His heart gave a tremendous lurch and he dropped down, dead. Sridarshana at once slung the first corpse over his shoulder and hastened back towards the sorcerer.

In the meanwhile, another ghost entered into the second corpse, which now stood up and ran after Sridarshana. The second vetala called out, 'Stop! Stop! Give me back my friend!'

Sridarshana realized that this was another of the living dead. He answered calmly, 'What proof can you produce, that this is your friend?'

Then the first vetala, slung over Sridarshana's shoulder, spoke. He said, 'I will be the judge. I am hungry. Whoever gives me food is my friend. I will go with him.'

The second vetala said, 'I have no means of feeding you. Let him find food for you if he is your friend.'

'Certainly,' said Sridarshana. He raised his sword and struck at the second vetala.

Taken unawares, the ghost speedily vanished, leaving Sridarshana with the first vetala which again said, 'I am still hungry. Give me some food.'

'Wait a minute,' said Sridarshana, and with his sword cut off a chunk of his own flesh.

'I am pleased with you,' said the corpse to Sridarshana. 'Your body will become as it was before, as if it had not been cut. Take me with you. But that wretch of a sorcerer is going to perish.'

Sridarshana saw with astonishment that his body showed no wound. He carried the corpse to the sorcerer.

'You are very brave,' said the sorcerer. 'Now I must do my part of the work. Wait a while, for I may need you.'

Sridarshana stood to one side, and watched the sorcerer as he laid the corpse out on the ground. He adorned it with garlands of red hibiscus flowers and red sandalwood paste. He ground human bones and traced a circle around the corpse with this powder. He placed a pitcher of human blood inside this circle. He lit some lamps with human fat and placed them too inside the circle. Finally, he sat astride the corpse's chest, and from a human skull, poured blood into the corpse's open mouth.

The next moment, this mouth widened in a dreadful yawn and flames rushed forth from it. The terrified sorcerer dropped the skull and jumped up. Slowly the corpse rose from the ground, but the sorcerer seemed rooted to the spot, and could only stare at it in horrified fascination. Before Sridarshana's very eyes, the sorcerer disappeared gradually into the creature's hideous gape.

When the sorcerer had vanished entirely into the vetala's maw, Sridarshana seemed to wake out of his nightmare and rushed forth with his sword. The vetala spoke, stopping Sridarshana in his tracks. 'I am pleased with your bravery. Do not try to save this sorcerer. He had planned to kill both you and the king, and to imprison me forever. Now he is dead, and cannot harm anybody. Take these mustard seeds and ask your king to tie them to his head and hands. That will cure his disease.' And the vetala spat out a handful of mustard seeds.

'But how can I go back alone?' asked Sridarshana. 'Who will believe me when I tell them what happened to the sorcerer? They might easily think I killed him!'

'Fear not!' said the vetala. 'I will vacate this corpse I am inhabiting now. You can cut open its belly and show them the sorcerer's body inside.' The next moment the corpse fell forward, inert. The ghost had gone.

Sridarshana returned to the city with the mustard seeds. The next morning, he brought the king's minister to see the sorcerer's body, so that nobody suspected him of killing the sorcerer. The mustard seeds cured the king, who was endlessly grateful to his benefactor. Since the king was childless, he adopted Sridarshana with much pomp and ceremony. Sridarshana married his Padmishtha, and they all lived happily ever after, as they always do in fairy tales.

Retold from the Sanskrit by BIJOYA GOSWAMI

✦┼✦

aida

The stage was simply set. Warm circles of light bathed each player, and in its magical glow the individual performer looked one with the instrument he or she played. The music soared, and the audience soared with it, breathless, expectant, transformed from their everyday concerns into celebrating Alpha and Omega, the joy of being.

The ensemble was originally a quintet but one of the players had died, leaving a gap the group did not even try to fill. Today was the first time they were playing together after Aida had died.

Rahul stood up and faced the audience. 'The next piece was composed for the violin. Aida used to play the sax with it. It was an unusual and haunting combination. I would like to play it in its original form in memory of her.'

The sound man sat at the side and fiddled with the knobs and wires. The quartet got ready to play. There was an expectant hush. The tuning of strings, the scrape of bows, the adjusting of chairs and coat-tails, the twiddling of keys and the clearing of throats—all added to the feeling that something momentous was about to happen.

Rita, recording the concert in the shadows, raised her head. There was a kind of buzz—a kind of hum that didn't seem quite to belong. She adjusted her headphones, puzzled. There was a crackle she couldn't account for. She turned to her assistant and said, 'Check this out fast. They are going to begin.'

The bow of the violin hovered, quivering. With a slight tilt of the head, Rahul's arm and elbow swung in one smooth flowing movement, his long sensitive fingers and his ascetic face intensely focussed on rendering the perfect C.

There was no time for Rita to do very much else but record. 'We'll have to do something about the electrical disturbances later,' she hissed to her assistant. He nodded and they put on their headphones. Suddenly they stared at each other in amazement. They looked back at the stage. Their bewildered eyes met again. Rita shook her head and almost got up.

When the piece was over, Raoul stood with his head bowed. He whispered, 'I felt she was here.'

The audience was completely spellbound. No one wanted to break the silence that was their tribute to Aida.

Rita played the cassette over and over again. Tarang nodded, his head cocked. 'There's no mistake,' he said. 'We both heard it. We both know what we heard.'

'Here,' said Rita. 'Listen to this part.'

Their intent faces puzzled Raoul who had just walked into the studio. 'What . . .' he began and stopped, staring in amazement, as very faintly the sound rose to meet and flirt with the tragic, sweet highs of Rahul's violin—the mellow, sunlit tones of the saxophone.

SHAIONTONI BOSE

the auto ride

Jagdish's auto-rickshaw was parked at its usual place. The lights from the Lighthouse twinkled as he sipped his second cup of tea that night.

'Jaggubhai, I am off. Still waiting for your first customer?' It was the concierge who stood outside the Lighthouse, a well-known nightclub in a Mumbai suburb, packing up for the day. Jagdish waved back. He decided that he would wait another half-hour outside the club and then move off elsewhere to look for customers.

But he was in luck. A young woman in her late twenties walked up to him asking to be taken to Andheri, a suburb in western Mumbai. A flick of his head to indicate a yes and Jagdish was ready to roll. He had barely started when he saw another woman, around the same age as his passenger, waving her arms at him.

'What luck, two together!' Jagdish heard the beggar sprawled across the pavement mutter. He glared at him as he ran his fingers through his hair to fluff it up like a hero in a Hindi movie. 'Do you mind, miss, if I am taking another customer too?' Jagdish said in a language that he hoped to master some day. The passenger did not object to sharing the journey and soon Jagdish was off, chugging into the night across the roads that he had grown up on.

'I am asking full fare. No halfing, madam,' Jagdish told the two of them.

'That is cheating. You should have told us before,' one of the women objected.

But Jagdish's swagger won him the argument and the women agreed to pay him what he wanted. In about fifteen minutes, Jagdish screeched his auto to a halt in front of Bandra Lake. This was where one of his passengers was to get off. 'Rs 52.50,' Jagdish told her. The woman argued a bit. But when she saw that Jagdish was not about to relent, she took out her wallet.

And then, strangely, without waiting for the money, Jagdish started his auto and fled into the night. His hair standing on end and his face a shade of white, Jagdish kept muttering, 'Hai Ganaraya! Hai Vithal! Hai Deva!'

'What happened? You did not take any money from her. And what are you muttering?' asked the passenger who was still with him.

'*Baap re*! You not seeing what I see. God, save me, that is no woman. Her feet are not like ours,' Jagdish stammered and stuttered. Fear had clamped its hand on Jagdish's throat and his words came out in a whisper. He stopped his auto at the side of the road to drink some water. 'Her feet. All wrong. *Ulta* like a *bhootni*,' he told her between gasps and gulps of water.

'You mean something like this?' said she with a smile.

ARUNDHUTI DASGUPTA

the dharavi murder Case

The story takes place in Mumbai's largest slum.

The rain was creating quite a din on the tin roof of the police *chowki*. Inspector Anil Kamble sat smoking his cigarette, his eyes red and stinging. He had gone two nights without sleep and then spent the entire day chasing half-baked leads. He was sleepy and extremely irritated at having to spend one more night awake. But he had promised his friend that he would stand in for him tonight and a promise was a promise. He had to keep his word.

The rain lashed down filling up the gutters, blocking up the streets and setting the entire city to its music. Monsoons, traffic jams, *lafdas,* houses falling down—such unpleasant thoughts raced through the mind of Inspector Kamble as he smoked one cigarette after another.

Suddenly through the blackness of the night, a man came rushing in. 'Saheb, saheb,' he shouted, his breath coming in short spurts. 'I have been murdered!' The man's face seemed blacker than the night itself and his yellowish-red eyes popped out of his head.

'How much have you had to drink tonight, haan? One night in your *sasural* [in-laws' house, slang term for prison] and you'll stop talking about murder and all such nonsense.' Inspector Kamble stood up, his stick raised menacingly.

The man exhibited no fear. He stared at the inspector without flinching and said, 'Saheb, please listen to what I am saying. I am

Shankar. I live in a *jhopdi* in Ramabai Nagar. I have a wife who is there. You can go and check with her, saheb.'

Compelled by the pain in the man's eyes, Inspector Kamble heard him out. 'My body is lying in the Dharavi swamp. Come with me now and I will show you. Come soon, don't delay otherwise that murdering rascal, that Vijay . . . he wanted to run away with my wretched unfaithful wife. Please saheb, please, put them in jail for what they have done to me.'

Disbelieving and yet unsure, Inspector Kamble decided to follow the man. He ordered two constables to come with him and set off behind the man who called himself Shankar. Shankar walked at an amazing pace. The policemen had to run to keep up with him. The distance between the police station and the swamp, which was usually a walk of thirty minutes, was covered in ten minutes flat.

The dim yellow light of the street bulbs flickered on the road. Dharavi looked like a bombed-out battlefield, with huge potholes and overflowing gutters. There were people sleeping along the sides of the drains and the ditches, and the men had to step carefully to avoid the bodies.

The three policemen stepped into the slush, their raincoats flapping in the strong breeze. 'There, there, saheb. Just a few steps to your left,' Shankar directed. His voice seemed fainter. Maybe it was the rain, but Inspector Kamble could not see him too clearly. He peered at him but Shankar seemed a blur in the darkness.

The constables did not have to dig for long. Soon, they unearthed a body that was completely covered in waste and mud. Upon looking closely, one constable ran away, shrieking and flailing his arms, while the other collapsed in a faint.

Inspector Kamble's face turned white. He dragged the body out of the swamp and let the rain wash the muck away. He peered closely to check, to verify once more that it was not a trick that his eyes were playing on him. It wasn't. The dead man lying belly up on the road on this dark rainy night was the same man who had stormed into his station an hour ago.

Kamble sat down on the road, head in hands, to steady himself.

The constable had come round and was throwing up by the side of the road. Kamble knew he had to hurry—he had no time to waste wondering about what exactly had happened in the last hour.

He tracked Vijay down to Ramabai Nagar where he and Shankar's wife were getting ready to escape. The two confessed to the killing. Shankar had discovered that his wife and his friend were lovers. In his rage, he threatened to kill both of them. But his wife pleaded and swore that she would never be unfaithful again. Vijay fell at his feet and then took Shankar out for a drink. On the way back home, he knifed him.

Inspector Kamble's successful handling of the murder case won him a promotion and a transfer to Mumbai police headquarters.

ARUNDHUTI DASGUPTA

Shah Mat

They were the best of friends, Naveen and Somesh, and the greatest of rivals. Their friendship flourished over books and music and even the women they pretended to vie for. Their rivalry flourished over chess. Every morning they would sit down with the dailies in their respective homes, sipping tea and working out the best moves in the chess columns of the newspapers.

Naveen and Somesh met every weekend with their chessboard and the beautiful wooden pieces that Somesh had made for Naveen, or the exquisite jade pieces that were a legacy of more flourishing times in Somesh's gently fading family.

Somesh's spectacles would shine with an earnest light as he reminisced during their tea break, 'You know, that raga was better played by Hari Prasad Chaurasia in the year . . .' and Naveen's eyes would dance with mischief as, thin and small, he would chuckle and jolly his friend through life.

As they grew older and family responsibilities claimed time, their meetings were reduced to once a month. Naveen had switched jobs. Somesh now lived elsewhere, but their friendship and their chess survived the trials of time.

Somesh's thick lenses glittered as he leaned forward over the chessboard. They had been at it for three hours now, Somesh pondering every move, breathing heavily.

'Arrh!' he groaned once as Naveen made a lightning move and crowed, '*Shah mat*!'

'This time I will win the game, Naveen,' said Somesh as he pondered his way out of his predicament.

Children clattered in and out. Tea cups clinked and rattled. Wives bustled around but the two men, united as one in their concentration though divided in their objectives, noticed nothing but the moves and countermoves they must make.

Here a bishop slashed his diagonal way to claim a knight, and there a cornered ruler stepped and shuffled around, behind castles and queen, in a strange mimicry of reality.

The battlefield was almost emptied of all but its key pieces when Somesh reached out, his eyes glittering feverishly. 'Naveen,' he chuckled. 'I shall have the last laugh after all. Shah mat, my friend!'

Naveen, having worried like a terrier over his friend's final move, at last admitted defeat. He laughed ruefully and raised his head. 'Yes, you've won this one,' he began, but the words froze on his lips. Somesh was staring, his eyes unblinking, at the chessboard, a chess piece between his stiff, cold fingers, a small smile playing about his lips.

The doctor was called immediately. 'He has been dead for over two hours! How can it be no one noticed?'

'They often sat for hours on end,' wept Somesh's bereaved wife. 'We left them undisturbed and went about our work. They had tea at four o'clock and that's the last we saw them.' She sniffed and dried her tears with a corner of her sari. 'Sometimes they would not talk and would stare at the board for hours on end. They wouldn't have noticed even a bomb go off.'

She turned to Naveen who was staring still at the chessboard, unmoving. He turned his head slightly and muttered, 'Shah mat!'

SHAIONTONI BOSE

the Piano

'I hear the piano playing
Just as a ghost might play.'
O, but what are you saying?
There's no piano today;
Their old one was old and broken;
Years past it went amiss.'
'I heard it or shouldn't have spoken;
A strange house this!'

Thomas Hardy, 'The Strange House'

'When you told me about your friend and her hired piano, the bad luck it brought, and the appearance of the malevolent woman, the story was so like the tale I heard all those years ago. I still shiver when I hear the Moonlight Sonata and remember the garden where we sat on a wooden garden seat.' My friend, who was not the quietest of people, spoke in a hushed whisper, as if what she was about to tell me was secret even from the trees . . .

'Sixty or seventy years ago, when my *pishi thakurma*, my great-aunt, was a young girl, this was a grand mansion humming with activity and the *jalshaghar* was hung with red velvet curtains and there were mirrors on the walls. The ceilings were moulded rococo and the Minton-tiled floor was carpeted with Persian carpets where the great musicians of the day played the sitar, the veena and the khol. Thakurma's family were great exponents of the khol. At the far end of the room stood a grand piano which no one touched and no one went near. Karuna thakurma, for that was her name, was a tomboy and very self-willed. She slept in the room we shared last night. She had been told never to leave the room by herself at night, but always to call for her favourite maid, Mokshada. But of course she didn't listen, and what happened to her will make your hair stand on end.'

Another sleepless night. Those same notes played over and over again, the same painful melody, deep into the night, crying of an untold sadness. Crying into the darkness from where there is no light. And yet, each time she had taken courage and gone into the music room, all she had seen was the light of her candle flickering in the mirrors which covered the walls. The piano had stood silent, waiting for the player to come back and play that haunting message of despair. She covered her ears and tried to sleep, but the sound came through, penetrating her very being.

'Mokshada,' she called, 'oh Mokhshada!' Then she remembered her old maid had been told not to sleep in her room because she wanted her peace, her privacy.

Through the slight parting of the curtains, she could see the clear winter sky aglow in soft moonlight. Of course! Those were the notes of the Moonlight Sonata, played jerkily, a note at a time, as if to dull unbearable pain or to pass unending hours.

She thought back to the day the piano had arrived. What excitement there had been in the house, how she had watched it being carried up the marble staircase by the eight men who had brought it all the way from Beadon Street in north Calcutta. It had fitted into the side of the jalshaghar, complete with its stool which opened to accommodate music sheets. Miss Mabert had been appointed to give music lessons to the girls, but she had yet to make her appearance. And so the piano stood silent by day, waiting for the phantom player to touch it to life at night.

She got out of bed, unwillingly, but was drawn to the sounds of the notes. As she came to her door, the handle seemed to turn by itself. Imagination, she thought, and pushed open the heavy teak door and walked into the passage which led from her room past all those empty rooms, to the jalshaghar. She dared not switch on the lights, although electricity had been installed in this part of the house, for her mother the Maharani had a habit of walking around the house at night just to see if all was well.

The doors of the great hall were of painted glass, framed in teak. The artist had used images of woodland scenes with sylphs and wood-nymphs and the great god Pan playing his pipes. In the moonlight they cast strange shadows on the passage wall. Gently she opened the door, feeling the red velvet of the curtains which draped the doors as she entered.

The moon had thrown its light on the piano in a silvery mist. As she stood there half frightened, staring at the beauty, the mist slowly took the shape of a woman, fluorescent in the moonlight, featureless, with no identity. And the piano, hitherto silent, played and she knew it was Chopin, his Nocturne in E Flat, surely one of the saddest of his compositions. The music was not jerky any more but flowed like waves of emotion. The woman played as if her heart would break.

Some unknown urge made her look to the far end of the room. Something dressed in a coarse white sari with a red border, long black hair thrown forward to cover the face, arms outstretched, eager for a victim, came towards the piano, stumbling in haste, as if it could not get there soon enough. As the creature neared, the music stopped.

The hatred, fear and terrible rotting stench that filled the room were too much for Karuna. 'Ma!' she screamed and shut her eyes tightly.

The next thing she knew was that she was in her mother's high bed, covered with a finely embroidered *kantha* quilt. Bottles of red medicine stood on the marble-topped table by the bedside—dosages clearly marked with a warning to shake the bottle before use. The faithful Mokshada sat by her, gently pressing her forehead.

'Didimoni,' she said, 'I warned you not to go wandering about the house at night, but would you listen? Bini mashi from Beadon

Street told us all about that new musical instrument. It's a cursed one, it is.' And then the simple woman bit her tongue, having said too much.

But her charge was an obstinate, headstrong girl and bullied the story out of her.

'Don't tell Ma, Didimoni, or she will have my head. You see the young son of Kedar Ghosh, you know who I am talking about, married this beautiful young girl who had been to the convent school and learnt to be a memsahib. She brought with her this instrument which she played night and day. Can you do that when you are newly married, tell me? Now did she know that her man had a mistress? That wicked Narmada had seduced him soon after she came to the house. Yes, I knew that wanton; whenever she came to our village, she caused trouble. She was not even pretty! When she saw the young master so enamoured of his new bride, her jealousy knew no bounds and she tried all sorts of black magic until the poor dear faded away and died. And she? Why, she went home to her village and was drowned in the pond while bathing. They found her floating in the water with her hair covering her face.'

When Karuna recovered from her shock, the jalshaghar was once again a peaceful room, its mirrored walls reflecting sitars and tablas, veenas and esrajes, sedate in their cloth covers. The piano had been sent away to Mackenzie Lyall, the auctioneers, to be sold.

BUNNY GUPTA

advice to motorists

There is a legend in Pune about a bridge near Wanawadi Bazaar.

Stray not by that bridge at night,
For there a lady clad in white
Sits and weeps.

Tho' her wails may rent the air,
Take care you do not linger there,
Nor trysting keep.

Steel your heart and move on by,
Pay no heed to tear or sigh,
Or sorrows deep.

For if you do then you will be
Doomed for all eternity
And evil reap.

Tho' she will vanish like a cloud,
Her presence fell your days will shroud,
And steal your sleep,

Till wandering in witless woe,
Knowing neither friend nor foe,
Beyond the pale you leap.

SHAIONTONI BOSE

a Spirituous interlude

When I was having a tubewell bored, there were innumerable difficulties. Three contractors had already given up. An old villager told me of a spirit who had to be propitiated. Twenty rupees had to be first set aside and when the boring was successful a white chicken had to be provided.

The fourth try was difficult but ended in success. The chicken was brought, the money was spent on buying some country liquor, and a puja was performed. The fowl was released, and we were told that when it was taken, it was the sign that the spirit was pleased.

The bird moved about the farmland for two days, and then was seen no more.

I had had a long, hot day, cycling back and forth in town, shopping, finishing several chores and meeting people. I was tired out, mentally as well as physically. Returning home, I headed straight for a bath.

The cool water playing lovingly over my skin, removing fatigue and irritation, was an almost voluptuous pleasure; I indulged in this as long as I could. Finally, clean and cool, I got into a comfortable old T-shirt and track pants. I thought I would further improve the evening by having a drink before dinner, and I got out a bottle of rum brought by a retired army friend, and a large bottle of Coke.

I did not really like the idea of drinking altogether alone, so I decided to invent a friend, and accordingly picked up two glasses and went downstairs to sit on the porch. I placed a small table and an empty chair facing me. Pouring myself a very small rum, I filled the tumbler with Coke, and gave the friend of my fantasy a largish shot. About to top his glass up with Coke, I was stopped by a deep, hoarse but not unpleasant voice, telling me in Urdu to forget the Coke and top the glass up with neat rum.

I did so and looking up was, funnily enough, not surprised to see a stranger sitting in the chair opposite.

The evening had grown quite dark and the moon not yet risen but it was still light enough to see that the stranger was lean and dark with black beady eyes which were slightly bloodshot. Taking the glass which I had filled for him, he drained it in one long swallow and held it out for more. I duly obliged.

The conversation that followed was in pure Urdu on his side, and broken Hindustani from mine, which I loosely translate into English:

'That was a nice plump fowl that you left out for me,' he said.

'I thought,' I replied, 'that a jungle cat had got it.'

'Hmm!' he said, smiling a little, 'yes, yes, of course.' He continued, still in the voice that appeared to come up from his navel, 'The liquor wasn't bad either, for country-made stuff, hardly to be compared with this (looking at his glass appreciatively) but one must do with what one can get these days.' There was a pause, as he applied himself to the glass and replenished it from the bottle. Then he said, 'I see that you struck a good stratum of water finally. I was hoping you would. You were trying so hard. Water, like gold, is where you find it, and I have seen instances where sinking a bore only two feet away from a prolific tube well has proved dry.'

'I had the place carefully studied scientifically,' said I, 'and the professor said I would find water in this belt at 140 feet, and this stratum would continue for several hundred feet more.'

'Yes, yes,' he replied, 'but your contractor encountered rock too, did he not? In fact he was about to give up, I understand, until you thought of me and it was that that encouraged him to persist.'

I could not deny this.

Meanwhile, I had been sipping at my drink from time to time, and a warm relaxed glow pervaded my being. My companion also fell silent and we sat contentedly, enjoying each other's company.

After a while he said, 'I was visiting my cousin, the Pir, at Dholkhand some years ago, when you came up with a group of guests.' I nodded agreement.

'My cousin is quite a shy, retiring type,' he went on, 'and while normally he takes a stroll in the evening, that day a man— incidentally, he resembled you—

'My brother,' I interposed.

He continued, 'started to walk up and down the terrace, just when the Pir would have done so. The latter, being so shy, went back into hiding in a hollow tree. Normally his official residence is his grave, but that is so cold and damp, he prefers the tree.'

I stifled a desire to ask my companion where he lived, as much out of politeness as out of fear he would tell me. Instead, I remarked that my brother's pacing had alarmed the others.

'I don't wonder!' he remarked. 'He was striding up and down that roof like a soldier! My cousin wouldn't have frightened them half as much. When he walks all you can hear is an intermittent soft shuffle, and maybe a muffled thump or so. Not so his father, my uncle, who lives out in the Harnol Gujjar settlements on the banks of the Harnol Rao, in the foothills. He is a creature of sudden whims.

'For forty years, he allowed Shamsher Ali's family to live peacefully in their hamlet near his home. Then one day, he decided he wanted that area all to himself. Members of Shamsher's family began to fall ill with various ailments. His children started to talk in their sleep with alien voices. The message they gave was clear. Let the family move out to a fresh site which the old Pir would show them, and all would be well. Shamsher heeded the warning and moved to a new place.

'However, soon afterwards, a new and brash Gujjar family occupied Shamsher's abandoned huts, which put the old Pir's nose out of joint. He was on the point of starting some fresh trouble, but the Forest Department preempted him, and forcibly moved the family to a resettlement colony.'

I murmured noncommitally and then stated that I was hungry and asked him if he would care to share my chilli con carne and rotis with me.

'No,' he said. 'Thanks, but I'd rather stick to this.' He held up his glass. 'However, please put my share at the foot of that large siris tree there and somebody will come for it.'

So while I ate, enjoying the hot chili and chapatis, a perfect complement to my drink, he helped himself to what was left in the bottle.

'This,' he remarked, 'is very much like me, warm, dark, strong and as sweet a spirit as I have seen.'

'What do I call you?' I asked.

'Sayyad,' he replied.

When I looked up again, the chair opposite me was empty.

I placed a dish of meat and beans at the foot of the tall, dark siris tree and went to bed. Later that night, I was awakened by the frantic barking and howling of my dogs. Looking out in the pale light of the new-risen moon, I saw a jackal nosing into the food.

SUGATO CHAUDHURI

What's in a name?

There are many tales revolving around the calling of a name, the most popular being those of nishi dak *(night call).*

When we were little, our lives were supervised almost as much by the servants in the house as by the family. There was much that was passed down to us via these channels that was very different from the knowledge we acquired at school or from our own family. The horror channels on TV today pale in comparison to the kind of entertainment we received from these trusted retainers. It cost us much in terms of sleep but, strangely, perhaps our lives were enriched by our illicit gains.

We ask her her name just to hear her say it in her own unique way. 'What's your name, ayah?' we ask.

She cackles good-naturedly, announcing proudly, 'Mary Pphanchis.'

'What are your daughter's names?' we ask and hold our breaths to stifle our wicked giggles.

'Alpphoose and Pilmone,' she says. We are ecstatic.

I don't suppose the Church or the nuns who named these respectable ladies could have dreamt that Mary Francis, Alphonse or Philomena could be so gloriously corrupted.

Mary Francis is a repository of stories ghoulish and ghastly. She is a classic amalgam of Christian ritual and pagan belief. She sits and rolls her eyes and shrieks, 'Baby, *udhar mat jao*! Don't go there!' The smallest and wickedest of us all glares defiantly.

'*Kiyon nahin*?' asks P, older and always curious, 'why not?' and holds his breath.

She nods sagely. 'She waits outside. You will see, if you look at her feet, they are turned round the other way, and you may not see it, but there is sure to be a hollow at the back of her neck . . .'

Delicious shivers run up and down our backs. Appalled, 'Baby' scurries to her lap, biddable once more.

Mary Francis goes with us everywhere. She takes an annual break to return to her home in Kharagpur, though her family is from Tamil Nadu, and comes back armed with NP chewing gum for her 'babalog'. I am not strictly in her charge, but she brings me up, roughly but kindly, along with the rest. I get NP chewing gum too.

Mary Francis is full of warnings. We live outdoor lives, running in and out of gardens all the time. If at dinner we discuss a snake we saw while at play it is not cause for alarm, but if we happen to mention the creature by name, Mary Francis will lean forward, her kindly face creased in disapproval, the twinkle gone from her eyes. 'Never say that word after dark,' she will hiss, looking around in alarm. You can say rope, we are told, but never 's __ e'. It is as if by naming the creature we will call it to us and tempt fate.

An epidemic breaks out. Cholera? Small pox? Typhoid? We are vaccinated in horrible ways, and the dread names of these diseases fall on our ears with an ominous ring. They claim thousands of people, we hear. We must be careful about what we eat, and where we eat. 'No roadside rubbish,' we are told firmly by the powers that be.

There is something else we must be careful about.

'There are sorcerers, I am told, wandering around at night, until cockcrow, till about the stroke of four,' says Mary Francis, lowering her voice. 'They carry a green coconut. They cut off the top and hold it like a lid in one hand. The other hand holds the coconut. They can learn all about you. They can call evil spirits to imitate the voice of someone you know. They will call your name and, wherever you are, you will be able to hear it. If you answer before the third call, they will clap the lid on to that coconut and your *jaan*—your soul—is trapped inside it. At night if you hear your name called, always make sure you don't reply till your name has been said three times.'

'But why?' we ask, in horrified fascination.

'Sometimes they use the energy they collect like this to make someone else well. They charge money. Just now many people are falling ill.

'Sometimes they do it because they need a soul for all the magic they do, for their own work. You may be left alive but your body is a shell. You will lie there,' she glares at us between chews of betel nut, 'and no one will be able to tell whether you are alive or dead!'

We swallow this exceedingly indigestible bit of information along with our food. It affects each of us in different ways. No one thinks of disbelieving a word.

That night, I wake stiff with terror, in the darkest hour before dawn, unable even to blink my eyes. I can hear a soft gentle voice calling my name, breathing it softly—once, then a long gap . . .

Then again . . .

My ears strain, listening for either the clock to strike, or the cock to crow, or for the third call that means deliverance. The third time I hear it, I begin to breathe again, but I still do not reply. I will never reply. Why tempt fate? I dive under the covers, now able at least to tremble. Waiting, waiting for dawn to break. All at once the sound of the aazan greets the new day from a mosque nearby. The birds begin to twitter. I find my voice and call my grandmother. It is her voice I thought I had heard.

'Did you call me early this morning?' I ask her.

She looks at me in surprise as she shakes her head. 'No,' she says and looks at me, smiling. 'You must have been dreaming.'

'It felt like I was awake,' I said. 'I thought my eyes were open. I saw the day break. I heard the clock strike four. Then it stopped. I was scared.'

She gazes at me thoughtfully and doesn't say a word, but that night as I go to bed, she gives me her keys to put under my pillow.

'They are made of iron. These will keep you safe,' she says as she sends me off to bed. 'Good night.'

Perhaps she doesn't believe a word of it, but she certainly knows enough not to try and rationalize. I have never been afraid of the nishi dak again, but to this day if I hear my name called in the dead of night, I check to see if there is really anyone there before I reply—after the third call, of course!

NILANJANA GUPTA

ticketless travellers

Folklore in Kerala is full of stories about Kuttichathan, a mischievous spirit who stirs up trouble in people's lives. Sometimes demonic and sometimes harmlessly wicked, his life seems to be devoted to the pursuit of fun at the expense of others. According to one legend, Kuttichathan is Shiva's son, created to destroy the evil demon, Bhringasura. In this form, he is worshipped as a god, with a temple dedicated to him in Kerala. Popular all over Kerala, tales about him have also been made into films: Kuttichathan *in Tamil and Malayalam and* Chhota Chetan *in Hindi.*

The platform was waking up to the noise of trains pulling out, hawkers shouting and families chattering away. Young men selling idlis and appams with egg curry walked up and down offering their wares to hungry travellers and cries of 'coffee, chai' rent the air as the sun made its way lazily across people sleeping on the benches, coolies dressed in red and white uniforms, and stacks of luggage.

Apar Desai stood with his rucksack clumsily strapped onto his back. He waited, cigarette in hand, blowing smoke rings into the air. The 6.05 to Kottayam was late and he contemplated stretching out on one of the empty benches. He had spent all of the previous fortnight chilling out on sunny beaches and sailing on Kerala's famous palm-fringed backwaters, and now he was off to see a friend in Kottayam.

By the time the train finally pulled in, the station had filled up. Young men in sarong-like *mundus* and shirts, armed with briefcases and umbrellas, and women in bright synthetic saris with wet hair tied loosely around their shoulders were milling around. Apar patted his pocket to check if his ticket was safe and then hauled himself onto the train.

The sickly sweet smell of coconut oil filled the compartment. Men and women scrambled to find a place to sit, pushing their bags under their feet. One old woman sat with her feet up drawing angry glares from some of the other passengers, but that did not get her to budge. A group of young girls sat with their books on their laps, studying furiously.

Venkata Menon found himself a window seat. His white shirt sparkled in the sunlight and he took out his prayer book in preparation for the journey ahead. He was late again today. But the bank manager was a nice fellow, he never said anything. Besides, Venkata Menon knew his boss's weakness for prawn curry and he was carrying some especially for him in his tiffin carrier.

Mary sat with her brown sari draped tightly over her thin frame. Her hair was held up in a neat bun, unlike that of the other women in the compartment. Her years of working as a nurse had forced her into the habit of keeping her long hair always tightly knotted or plaited. Frankly, she found the *sanjipinnal,* the hairstyle that most women in Kerala adopted, quite distasteful and untidy.

The train lurched out of the platform and rolled gently through languorous green fields. Apar gazed out of the window, taking in the dewy-fresh greenery outside. Most of the passengers sat quietly, reading the papers or their books. Watching them all was a young boy of about fourteen or fifteen. He looked small for his age and his ears stuck out of his rather small head. His eyes sparkled and danced, and a goofy grin seemed to be pasted on his face.

He stood staring silently. He saw Mary's hair prise itself out of the bun while she dozed. He could barely hide his grin as the pages of Venkata Menon's prayer book turned faster than he could read. Mr Menon blamed the breeze but the boy knew better. He giggled softly at the sight of Apar's colourful underwear, a packet of glucose biscuits and a red mug—all peeking out of his rucksack that had mysteriously snapped open.

And then, in walked the ticket checker, a small man with a large stomach. His shirt was stretched over his paunch so that its buttons bulged and wobbled every time he moved. To the boy, he looked like an oversized toad gasping for breath.

Before the boy knew it, the ticket checker was by his side. 'Ticket!' The boy ignored the voice that boomed so close to his ears. He looked out of the window. '*Edo*, you dwarf, where is your ticket?'

'Sir, ticket. Yes, just a minute.' The boy set up an elaborate search. He emptied his pockets, looked under his shirtsleeves and every place possible. By now, other passengers had collected near the duo. An old woman who had dozed off sat up straight, several men from other compartments edged closer. Everyone was glued to the drama that they anticipated would unfold before them when the ticket checker collared this ticketless good-for-nothing.

'So, you take me for a fool, or what? Even your father won't get away without a ticket, do you know? That is how sharp these eyes—the eyes of Chandramohan Pillai—are. Now stop putting on a show; you'd better come with me to the station at the next stop.'

The boy smiled but did not budge. 'Sir, please excuse. First time. I always buy ticket, this is the first time, sir.'

But Chandramohan Pillai wasn't listening to his pleas. He had his first offender of the day and he was not letting him go without at least a night in jail or a sizeable bribe.

Suddenly the boy changed his tune. 'All right. I'll come with you but only if you find me one person in this entire compartment who is travelling with a ticket!' A snigger ran through the crowd. The ticket checker was not quite sure what to make of this, but he too smirked at the foolish bravado of the adolescent.

So Chandramohan Pillai went around, from one passenger to the other. Apar's pockets were empty. He fumbled and fidgeted but, do what he might, he could not find his ticket. 'I had it, I swear I had it here,' he said repeatedly to the ticket checker who gave him a dismissive look. 'You city slickers, you think you can come from the big city and take us innocent people for a ride. Wait till you spend a night in jail with that other good-for-nothing.'

Mary turned red. She stood up, shook her sari to see if the ticket had lost itself in its folds and foraged around in her bag but there was no ticket. 'Sorry, sorry. I had it, I bought it, I don't know what's happened.' Tears welled up and she could say no more. Chandramohan Pillai moved ahead with a disgusted look on his face.

Venkata Menon found himself staring goggle-eyed at his prayer book, turning its pages over and over again. He was sure he had put the ticket in there but then where had it disappeared? '*Ayyo* saar. But this is very strange. Please believe me, a trick is being played, somebody has stolen my ticket.'

Mysteriously, the same thing had happened to all the thirty-odd people in the compartment. As for the boy, he was nowhere to be found. A pool of clear yellow sunlight was all that was left on the spot where he had stood.

ARUNDHUTI DASGUPTA

the 11.43 to nowhere

The old man on platform 4 was closing down his tea stall. In a corner of the same platform, the girl who sold newspapers, flowers and peanuts depending on the hour, was counting her earnings for the day. And, oblivious to the goings-on around them, four men stood sipping tea and waiting for the 11:43 to Thane.

Tonight seemed no different from any other night.

Old Mr Murthy, who always sat on his newspaper, was there and so was the old lady who hawked chips and *chevda* during the day. A couple of young urchins who were too tired to beg any more lay sprawled out on the benches. And the four men, who took this train back home every night, were getting ready for an hour of gossip and cards.

Tonight seemed no different from any other night. Yet the darkness carried a chill edge that was uncharacteristic for a warm April night.

The train arrived and left as it usually did, two minutes after 11:43. The men settled in by the window. Mr Murthy made himself comfortable on his paper and the old lady spread herself out on one of the empty seats.

The wind rattled as the train pierced the darkness of the night. Shankar, Vincent, Animesh and Prakash began their card game. 'Hey Shankar, your deal,' said Vincent, and placed his black bag in the centre as a table for the cards.

Shankar worked in a multinational company as a junior

accountant. Vincent, the youngest, was a student and worked as a bartender in a five-star hotel after college. Animesh, who always wore an expression of unspeakable sadness, was a programmer in a software company and Prakash, the quietest of the lot, was his colleague.

They were strange friends, the four of them. They knew very little about their lives away from the train. They had never visited each other in their homes or their offices. Yet they shared the deepest confidences, and were worried when any of them went missing for a few days on the 11:43.

'It's chilly,' Vincent said as he looked at his cards. It was a strange comment given that this was the middle of summer. But they noticed that the compartment seemed enveloped in a cold breeze, which would have been quite pleasant, had it not tingled their spines so.

The darkness whistled as the train cut through its stillness. Inside coach 5, the card game began.

'It's getting very boring, this game of ours. Every day, we play the same thing. Time to change, don't you think?' Prakash said, startling the rest of the group.

But, before anybody could answer, they saw her.

She was wearing a lemon-green sari and sitting on the edge of the seat. Nobody had seen her climb on. They stared at her out of the corners of their eyes as she shifted uncomfortably on her seat and clutched her bag tight.

'*Phataka*,' Shankar said with a sneer. Vincent threw him a disgusted look. 'What else, *yaar*! What kind of a woman would be out so late at night?' Shankar retorted.

'A person like you,' Vincent snapped back, 'someone who happens to be working very hard and very late.'

'Please, please—why are we spoiling our game for the sake of someone we don't know! Let's continue,' Animesh whispered.

The men went on with their game. But it was not the same. The night had soured. The banter was missing and so was the sense of camaraderie that they usually shared. And the compartment seemed to grow colder. The men drew close.

'Excuse me. I am sorry to intrude but you see, I am very scared. Where are you going?' The softness of the voice startled the men. It was the girl in the green sari. Her face seemed paler, close up. She was now sitting beside Prakash and none of them really knew when she had moved.

Prakash stuttered since it was he that she spoke to. Shankar spoke. 'Thane. And yeah, you can sit here.'

'Hey, I am Vincent. What's your name?'

The girl did not take the extended hand, merely smiled and replied, 'Preeti. I stay in Mulund. I don't usually work this late.' She clutched her bag tighter and said, 'Today it just got so late.'

Animesh felt uncomfortable. His sad face turned a shade of grey. And he could not dismiss the awful feeling at the pit of his stomach as the usual case of the blues.

Vincent spoke up. 'We are going right up to Thane. Nothing to worry about. We are here. And this city is very safe.'

For the first night, ever since any of them could remember, their card game had been interrupted. Although the men tried to keep it going by occasionally muttering about the rotten hand that they had been dealt or otherwise, it was obvious to all of them that their hearts were not in it. They were merely going through the motions and the game was going nowhere.

Tonight was turning out to be a truly unusual night.

Shankar tried to get everybody to focus on the game by speaking very loudly about how they needed a new pack of cards. 'These cards have your oily fingerprints all over them,' he nudged Animesh. 'Stop eating so many chips, Animeshbhai!' Animesh blushed as he crumpled an empty packet and threw it out of the window.

Prakash turned to the girl. 'Where in Mulund are you from?'

'I live a little way away from the station. Takes about ten minutes to walk it. Are you familiar with the place?' she said. Without waiting for an answer, she went on, 'Rajmohan Lane, Chawl 10,' she smiled. Prakash quietly withdrew into his shell, overcome by this uncharacteristic burst of conversation.

To Shankar, it seemed that the girl's face grew paler as her destination grew closer. He kept the game going and stole a look at his companions to see if they had noticed.

The station before Mulund, the girl got up and walked towards the door. She waved goodbye to the men who huddled close to each other—the breeze in the compartment seemed to have got colder. 'Shimla in Bombay or what?' Vincent shivered as he muttered. 'One last game and then it's time to pack up.'

As the train chugged over the Mulund creek, Animesh looked up for one last goodbye to the girl. He stared as fear rose from the pit of his stomach and collected at his throat. He gaped and grasped Shankar with a cold hand.

The girl had disappeared.

The men stumbled out when the train stopped at Mulund, a station before theirs, because . . . well, because they just could not let a girl, who they had shared a conversation and a journey with, disappear, could they? They had to do something.

A quaking Animesh sat down on the platform saying, 'You think she may have jumped, don't you?'

They decided to walk along the tracks to check if she had fallen off the platform or jumped off the train. But their search came to naught.

'There's nothing else to do but go there, I guess,' Vincent said shakily. 'I know the road but I haven't ever seen the chawl.'

'We'll find it. Let's go,' Shankar said firmly.

'But—but, look at the time,' Animesh tried to protest but he was ignored.

The men walked through the dark lanes of Mulund. It was well past midnight. The night had suddenly turned still and hot. Their shirts stuck to their backs, and they wondered whether it was just a few minutes ago that the cold night air had pushed them into a huddle.

Chawl 10 was dark and silent. Except for a dim light that showed them the number on the building, everybody seemed to have turned in for the night. Vincent nudged a sleeping watchman awake and asked for one Miss Preeti. 'No one here, sir,' the watchman replied.

Shankar was not willing to give up so fast. He described the girl to the watchman and said that it was of utmost importance that they speak to her family as she may have met with an accident.

Reluctantly, the watchman pointed to the light on the first floor. 'Ask Aunty. She has lived here a long time. She will know,' he said.

Aunty knew. She had seen them through her window and had the door open by the time they walked up to her flat. All of them started speaking at once. But before they could say anything, Aunty herded them in and offered them a glass of cold water.

'I know. You are all my Baby's friends . . . but Baby is dead. Baby is not coming back. Poor Baby.' She cried and rocked herself back and forth as the four men stared blankly at her. 'Baby worked late many nights. But those men, that night . . .' Aunty closed her eyes in pain.

Animesh fainted and the rest sat slumped on the sofa. On the wall was a framed and garlanded photograph of the girl they had just met.

ARUNDHUTI DASGUPTA

✛

possession and reincarnation

Nikhil

'Dear Diary,

'I got four—f-o-u-r—demerits today. One was because I forgot my badge, another because I'd left my workbook at home, another because I couldn't remember my tables and was told I hadn't learnt them when I'd spent half the night reciting them and the other half dreaming about them, and the fourth . . . I've even forgotten what that was for!

'My class teacher called me irresponsible, lazy and careless, and rapped me one. Then people call me a dork and laugh when I ask what that means. Bet they don't know themselves, just pick it up from TV and try it out because it sounds as if it could mean uncool!

'I hate school. I hate maths. I hate homework. I hate tests.

'Wish I could stay home and draw all day. I'd draw the earth and the stars and the animals around the house and draw how the sea feels around my toes, and my black mood on the way to school . . . and the blacker one on my way back!'

'Nikhil!' his mother shouted from the kitchen. She had been making hot pakoras for his after-school snack.

Nikhil left his diary on the table. His pen rolled off to the floor but he didn't notice. He was starving.

'You haven't changed out of your uniform, Nikhil.' She unknotted his limp, grubby tie. 'How do you get your tie in this mess! Get your uniform off, you're sure to drop tomato sauce on it.'

Nikhil went back to his room, shuffling his feet and swinging his tie. He threw it on the bed, hurriedly put on his shorts, spent five minutes hunting for his T-shirt, found it under the bed, and pulled it on back to front.

He hadn't noticed that the pen that had rolled off was back on his desk, neatly placed between the pages so it wouldn't roll again.

He dashed off to play with his friends in the building, glad of the hour he had to do his own thing.

When he got home it was time to have a bath, do homework, eat dinner, and go to bed, the same old, same old . . .

His room was surprisingly neat. His clothes were hanging in the cupboard. His shoes were all lined up in a corner. His socks were in the laundry basket. Nikhil naturally assumed his mother had cleaned up, as she often did without mentioning it, but in fact she had been busy with bossy Mrs Parekh who had dropped in and could talk the hind legs off a donkey.

Mrs Dutt usually left her housework for later when Mrs Parekh trundled over because this nosy neighbour had the unfortunate habit of following one around commenting on every room and pulling things out of cupboards to inspect them. If I go in now I'll have her breathing down my neck clacking about how clean *her* kitchen is and how she manages so beautifully and then she'll cadge something or the other off me saying I have so much I won't miss a little, she thought.

Nikhil's mother suffered from an overdose of politeness and was usually unable to deal with such inroads on her privacy, but she was beginning to learn to be firm with Mrs P.

She had been warm and friendly when the old couple had moved in next door because they were even newer than she was, but there had to be a limit.

'Here's Nikhil,' she exclaimed brightly. 'I must see to his dinner. Mrs P, you'll have to see to Mr P too now, I'm sure.' She looked pointedly at the door.

'Oh but Mr P can wait a little longer, I'm sure I could help with the cooking. My puris are the best in town, I always make them fresh so they can be eaten hot and puffy,' said Mrs P.

'That would be wonderful, Mrs P, but it's pizza for Nikhil today. You know these youngsters, and since I'd rather he ate home-cooked pizzas, I've kept one ready, but I must heat the veggies and make a salad.'

Nikhil looked in amazement at his mother. She had distinctly said it was puri-sabzi tonight. He remembered he'd been really pleased. She avoided his eyes as she pushed him out of the room saying loudly, 'Your hands are filthy, Nikhil. Wash them pronto.'

He looked down at his hands which weren't filthy at all, but caught his mother's grin and trundled off to lay the table. He took the thalis out and dropped one with a clatter.

Mrs P got up heavily and said, 'Well then, I must be off and fry our puris for Mr P, mustn't I? He certainly won't put up with junk food!'

Mrs P hadn't the faintest idea how to make a pizza and was quite miffed that Nikhil's mother had. Mrs Dutt had figured out that the only way to get rid of Mrs P was to mention something she couldn't do.

When Mrs P left, she chuckled as she bustled about frying the puris, 'Mr and Mrs P will soon have to change their names if they eat too many of Mrs P's puris, don't you think? Mr and Mrs Puri, hot and round, newly fried, filled with gas!'

'Ma,' said Nikhil, disapprovingly, 'just chill!' But he couldn't resist a chuckle.

'Don't forget to pack your bag as soon as you go up. I'm not going to the school to hear complaints about you again. Next time I'll send your father,' said Mrs Dutt.

'Yeah, yeah Ma,' said Nikhil, as this went in one ear and out through the other.

After dinner, Nikhil stood looking a little puzzled at his desk. His books were in his bag, neatly packed according to the timetable in his diary. Nikhil scratched his head. He certainly didn't remember doing it.

Ma must have done it, he thought, or maybe I did and don't remember! This was so common he shrugged and got engrossed in choosing the book he would read that night. After he fell asleep with the light on as usual, it switched itself off.

When his mother came in later that night, she was amazed to find the room neat and tidy and the light off. Ever since they had moved into their new flat Nikhil had slept with the light on. He said the dark in his room breathed at him! Really, his imagination!

'Don't tell me he's growing up at last!' she exclaimed to herself, but she knew how erratic her son could be and thought she would wait a while before she mentioned it. She hoped this attack of tidiness would last. Her daughter Nisha would be home from college for a short while soon, and hated sharing a room with Nikhil's mess.

The next morning, in the rush, Nikhil forgot to thank his mother for tidying up. He was thoughtful and appreciative, though scatty, but he did remember to hug his mother as she pushed the hair off her worried forehead. Her husband had been away for a while and there had been no news for quite some time. Since this was unusual, she couldn't help a niggling little worry. Nikhil always knew when she was worried.

'Don't worry Ma, he'll be back soon. Maybe he couldn't get to a phone. You know I can feel it in my tummy.' Nikhil patted his ample middle and shouldered his school bag. He gave his mother an extra hug as he raced off to the lift.

'Nikhil, your water bottle!' shouted his mother just as the lift came. She shook her head at him, smiling as she handed him the bottle. His reassuring words had left a glow of relief. 'Vikram will be all right,' she murmured. 'Nikhil knows these things. Nothing wrong with my boy that I can't handle. His heart's in the right place.'

She went into Nikhil's room to dust and make the bed, but found the bed was already made. 'Well, this is a pleasant surprise!' she said as she stooped to pick up the book she had seen lying on the floor beneath Nikhil's desk just as he was leaving. It wasn't there. 'Funny,' she thought, 'I could have sworn . . .' She pulled down the blinds so that the room would stay cool, and shut the door. It closed with a little click—as if the key had been turned in the lock inside.

She frowned. She should be pleased by all this effort on Nikhil's part. But she was strangely disturbed by it. There was no chill in the house, in fact it was hot and still, too still, but somehow . . . She shivered as she pulled down all the blinds. 'A storm in the air?' she wondered. But the day went by as usual, with no storm. There was a gentle balmy breeze blowing outside which was strangely at odds with the stillness inside the house. She kept the louvres of the blinds open, hoping to let in some air.

When Nikhil came home, she sat him down at the table for his snack and said, 'Chhota, you tidied your room very nicely today. Do you think this will last?'

Nikhil looked up from the comic he was devouring along with his sandwich. 'Hmm?' he said, then looked puzzled. He was about to say something when the doorbell rang and the dhobi arrived with his huge bundle of laundered clothes.

'Memsaheb,' he said as he put down the bundle, 'you told me to remove the ink stains from this sheet from baba's room, but there were no stains. I have just washed it and brought it back.'

The strange feeling at the back of Nikhil's mind grew more persistent and niggling, but he decided not to say anything.

'Take your bag to your room, Nikhil,' said his mother distractedly. 'I must be growing old! I could have sworn there were ink stains on that bedsheet.' The funny thing was, so could Nikhil.

When Nisha came home during the weekend she was all geared for conflict on many counts with her noisy, cheerful, untidy brother.

'Ma,' she said, 'is Nikhil sick or something? He's very quiet these days, barely goes down to play, spends most of his time studying, hardly talks, and the music he listens to: shenai, sitar . . . Not even the lively pieces we listen to but the kind that drones and moans and goes through your soul. Very depressing really. Hardly a smile or a laugh, no jokes, no pillow fights . . .'

Worst of all, the child whose grades were always middling suddenly began to come at the top of his class consistently. Now why was this so disturbing? 'I should be delighted,' Mrs Dutt wondered. Delight was very far from her mind though.

Nikhil's friends hardly ever came over now; he had stopped playing games; he was beginning to lose weight at an alarming rate and seemed completely disinterested in food.

The doctor checked him out and gave him a resoundingly healthy chit, but said, 'He seems to be developing quickly, he is more like a fourteen-year-old.'

'I don't know what to do about Nikhil, Nisha,' said Mrs Dutt. 'You know how he always rushes out and throws himself at Papa and wants to be swung around even though he's grown so much? And how he peppers Papa with questions . . . He hasn't done any of that, and when Papa praised him for his school report, you should have seen the look Nikhil gave him!'

That look had shaken both Mr and Mrs Dutt to the core. The expression of contempt coupled with smug satisfaction on the child's face was not one familiar to either parent. They were used to a child who whooped with joy at good results and bothered very little about bad ones.

'The little fellow got any new friends lately?' asked Mr Dutt that night. 'He's changed quite a bit, suddenly. And he's taken to walking about silently so that you don't know when he's going to come up behind you! Those squirrels he used to feed don't seem to come around any more either.'

'He's started waking up very early these days,' Mrs Dutt looked at her husband, trying to place what was bothering her more and more. 'Now that you mention it, he used to play with the dogs in the compound, take a ball down for them whenever he could . . . He doesn't do that these days and now they seem to avoid him— slink off with their tail between their legs whenever he passes them by—though I haven't noticed him throwing anything at them or shooing them away. He doesn't even look at them!'

Just then the door opened and Nikhil himself came in. He hardly looked at his parents, just spoke in a cold precise way, 'I will be leaving early for school tomorrow morning. Please see that my lunch box is packed by seven.'

'Come and sit here for five minutes, Nikhil. I've hardly seen you since I came back,' said Mr Dutt. Nikhil looked at the father he used to worship with a look that reduced the man to nothing. 'I don't have all the time in the world,' he said coldly. 'Goodnight.' He walked out of the room silently and swiftly. Mr and Mrs Dutt looked at each other.

'Even his voice doesn't seem the same,' said Mr Dutt.

That night Mrs Dutt had a nightmare. She dreamt that Nikhil was hammering at the window screaming, 'Let me in, let me in.' She woke up in a cold sweat and sat up in bed. It was two o'clock. She got out of bed to look in on her son, crept into his room and turned on the light to see him lying asleep. She missed the innocent angelic chubbiness she knew to be her son. What had happened to that twinkle? Where were they going wrong? Neither parent had pushed him beyond his limits. They were firmly aware that he would shine when he was ready to, and steadily supported his love for life.

She looked around the room which was now a model of clean efficiency: a cold calculating room. All the posters on the wall were gone. The desk had books neatly stacked on it. The school bag was packed and ready for the next day. 'This is not my son!' she murmured, her heart lurching inside her.

Her skin prickled as she turned round to face the boy who lay in her son's bed—who sat up in her son's bed, his black eyes glittering with rage. 'Don't touch my books,' he said as he stared at her in cold fury. Mrs Dutt went cold with shock. Nikhil's eyes were a soft deep brown, not a glittering black.

She stared back and hissed, 'Where is Nikhil? I want Nikhil back. Who are you?'

'Why, Nikhil of course, your beloved son,' he sneered. 'Look, Ma, are you mad?'

'What do you want?' she whispered. 'What must I do to get my son back?'

The boy on the bed sniggered. 'What does anyone want?' he said. 'Money. Fame. Success. Whatever everybody else wants . . . more of it.'

'My son is not the one to give that to you,' said Mrs Dutt, trembling. 'He only wants to be a little boy.'

'But I am your son, Ma, look at me. Who do you suppose I

could possibly be?' He got up and reached his hand out to her. His smile was not pleasant.

'Get away from me,' said Mrs Dutt, stumbling out of the room. 'I will get my son back.' A soft laugh followed her as the door swung shut firmly.

'What is it?' whispered Mr Dutt who had heard noises.

She shook her head, hardly trusting herself to speak.

The next morning as she went out to fetch the milk she noticed her sari hanging on the line. It was in shreds, ripped and slashed. She could almost hear a sibilant whisper: 'Don't try to mess with me!'

Some days later, the Parekhs invited Mr and Mrs Dutt to meet Mr Readymoney, an old friend of theirs. Nikhil was in the house, just back from school. As they were leaving, Mr Readymoney remarked, 'Your boy—I saw him go into your flat as I arrived here . . .'

'Yes,' said Mrs Dutt nervously.

'Er, this is really strange, but he looked so much like another boy I knew! I stayed in this flat opposite before the Parekhs, you see,' said Mr Readymoney.

Mrs Dutt stiffened. She had a feeling she knew what was coming and hastily began to say goodbye, but Mr Readymoney was so puzzled that he didn't notice her reaction as he mused on the strange resemblance.

'I could almost have sworn . . .' he mused and paused as he pursued the elusive idea. 'Strange boy he was, though,' he said and added hastily, 'I'm sure your boy won't be like him! Looked down on his parents, thought he was too good for them. Controlled them as if they were puppets. They spoiled him dreadfully, so proud of having an intelligent boy like him, pampered him terribly, but it backfired of course!' Mr Readymoney carried on as if he had to get it out of his system. 'Bright boy, no doubt, but warped, goodly apple rotten at the core and all that . . . Did very well in school but I don't think he was particularly liked somehow. They say he specialized in torturing his parents creatively! Certainly they went about looking more and more like the empty shells of insects sucked dry, though they hardly ever really spoke to anyone!

'Everybody avoided him if they could, strange for a youngster like that. Tall he was too, and around fourteen. Came to a bad end. It was the mother finally cracked. They found her collapsed at the old mandir weeping and beating her forehead, begging forgiveness, saying he would have killed them all if she hadn't taken preventive action! She died soon after, in an asylum, screaming in agony. They found her skin in shreds, just the skin. Auto-suggestion, I suppose.'

He shuddered but collected himself, saying, 'I'm sorry, my apologies if I have upset you. I didn't mean . . .'

'My son is ten,' said Mrs Dutt coldly, but with a lurch of her heart as she said her goodbyes and quickly fumbled for her key. It was dark and she took a while. Mr Readymoney fished out a torch he had in his pocket and shone it for her, but before she could turn the key the door opened and the long thin figure of the boy stood framed against the evening grey that filled the living room. Mr Readymoney gasped and Mrs Dutt hastily thanked him and bustled in, twittering, 'Why haven't you switched on the lights?'

'That's the way I like it,' said the boy in a voice that brooked no argument.

But there was no distracting Mr Readymoney who came forward and peered at the boy and said, 'Don't I know you? What's your name?'

'Nikhil to you,' said the boy rudely and slammed the door.

'Very odd ten-year-old, I must say,' said Mr Readymoney to himself, shaking his head. 'I have never seen such a strange likeness . . . If the boy had not died I would have said there was something really fishy! Besides, he would not be a boy any more, he would have grown up by now.'

'Do at least try and be more polite while you are in this house,' said Mrs Dutt to the boy. 'You'd do better in the world with some manners.'

He bent over to her ear, put out his hand in a loving, Nikhil kind of way, moved the lock of greying hair away from her cheek, and said in a gentle whisper, 'I'd do better in this world without *you*! Now what would be the best thing to do, hmm? Lock you up?'

He laughed softly as she spat back, 'Never! I'll get you first.'

'Remember Nikhil,' he said and slid in to the bedroom, turning round with engaging grin for a last cheery twinkling word in a childish voice: 'Just chill, Ma.'

SHAIONTONI BOSE

the homecoming

It was many years since they had had guests staying over, Lakshmi thought as she walked to the cupboard for some clean bedsheets and linen. 'Chhotu!' she yelled, 'you still haven't finished putting up the new curtains in the room. What are the guests going to think?'

Chhotu hobbled into the room, muttering under his breath. He had come to this house as a boy, when Mataji was still alive. In those days, she managed a much bigger family and there were so many children . . . She had never shouted at him, he thought, as he hurried to put up the curtains with his old fingers.

Lakshmi sat on the bed, holding the white damask tablecloth which had been with the family ever since she could remember. It had turned yellow around the corners and was even tearing at the folds, she noticed, as she opened it out. 'No, this won't do,' she said to herself, already nervous at the thought of the guests arriving before she had finished laying out the linen.

Kumud's letter from Bareilly had come almost a week ago. 'Bhabhi,' it said, 'your son-in-law's cousin, Sarita, who lives in Moradabad, and her bhabhi Preeti are travelling to Agra. Preeti's daughter, who is only four years old, will also be going with them. Sarita has to come to Agra to take her honours exams in history. I know you will look after them.'

The only daughter in a family of five sons, Kumud was everybody's favourite. According to the letter, Kumud's cousins-in-law would be arriving by the morning train today, and would be staying for a week. Lakshmi remembered Sarita as a shy and skinny eleven-year-old with bangles running up to her elbows at Kumud's wedding. Preeti and her daughter would be coming to the haveli and, as the letter said, to Agra for the first time.

The haveli was spinning with activity. All five bahus ran about, getting the house ready. The courtyard and the garden were swept clean, the steps leading up to the two-storeyed white haveli were scrubbed, as were the huge iron gates that led into the garden. Chhotu had cleaned up the temple at the end of the garden and the well near it that had been closed up many years ago.

Lakshmi, finally done with the guest room, went to arrange the flowers on the table at the head of the staircase. The eldest bahu of the house, she had married Giridhar when she was sixteen. Babuji was then the collector of Agra, and Kumud was still studying at the university. The haveli was under Mataji's care at the time and she used to worry a lot about Kumud. 'Beti, she is already nineteen and there are no marriage proposals that your Babuji has approved of. And then there are only two more years for his collectorship. What will we do after that? How will we marry our daughter?'

Within a year of Lakshmi's coming, however, Kumud was married off into a wealthy business house. Her husband, the youngest in a family of four sons, was considered to be a good match and Mataji, Lakshmi remembered, would always say, 'Beti, it was all your doing. You are truly the Lakshmi of our house for you have brought us luck.'

More luck came their way when Babuji managed to keep the haveli after he retired. They had been fortunate that the government did not own the house and that it belonged to an old Muslim family who were quite happy to rent it out to Babuji after he had retired. The house, close to Agra University, was away from the bustle of the city, on a road lined with trees and red brick houses, known as *chhili eent* houses. Mataji was happiest at the the thought of being able to keep the house and they had had a special puja to thank the gods who had made this possible.

'Meera, oh Meera, is the cooking done?' Lakshmi shouted out.

Meera was married to the second brother, Rameswar. She was in the kitchen which was at the other end of the house. The kitchen opened out into the courtyard which was being scrubbed clean by Sarla, wife of the third brother, Gopinath. The other two bahus, Vidyadhar's wife, Vinita, and Hariprasad's wife, Manasi, were supervising the sweeping and weeding in the garden.

It was a large house but Lakshmi's voice carried right across. 'Haan haan, Jiji,' Meera shouted back. 'Kamli is making the chapatis. Everything else is on the table.' Meera had come to the house only a year after Lakshmi. Soon after Rameswar, Gopinath and then Vidyadhar brought their brides home.

Vidyadhar's wedding was the last that Mataji attended. Lakshmi still envied the ease with which she ran such a large house. An extremely soft-spoken lady, she had died quietly one morning in her puja room. Sarla had found her bunched up over the Ramayana. Sarla said that she had taken one look at her and knew that it was all over.

Mataji's death came as a shock to everyone. Although she had grown old and frail, none of the sons could imagine the huge house being run without her. Every morning, she would sweep the courtyard clean of its cover of neem leaves. She would then clean the corner where Babuji sat with his morning cup of tea and newspaper, while she went about praying to her gods. Next, she would wash the steps that led up to the house, which was a level higher than the courtyard and the rest of the compound.

The neem tree should never have been cut down, Lakshmi thought as she changed the covers on the divan cushions. But Sarla had insisted, saying that it was impossible to keep the courtyard clean otherwise. One has to move on, Lakshmi reflected as she went to the window for the hundredth time that morning to check if the guests had arrived.

Babuji had taken Mataji's death very badly, worse than anybody else. He did not eat for days. All he would have was a glass of orange juice in the morning. 'Beta, I can't bear to live without her,' he would tell anyone who asked him to get back to his usual routine.

Unable to let her go, he kept a small urn with her ashes. Some months later, he built a small temple where he kept the urn.

The temple was built within the gates of the haveli, but outside the courtyard. Babuji had chosen a spot near the well that touched the haveli's boundary walls. Flanked by a fence on one side and trees on the rest, the well had its own eerie history. Old-timers in Agra referred to it as the mystery well. Many people were known to have drowned in this well, which was believed to draw people to their death. Its waters were said to rise mysteriously every time anyone fell in. Mataji too had lost her firstborn, a daughter, to the well. She had been just a little girl when she was found floating in its waters. The family had the well covered up soon after.

Soon after Mataji's death, Babuji passed away and the haveli passed on to the next generation. After that, Kumud did try and come once a year but her visits grew less and less frequent. She was busy bringing up her children while the bahus, at the haveli, were raising their own. It was a huge family at the haveli but it was a long time since they had had guests over. Everybody was excited, but a bit nervous too. After all, it was Kumud's in-laws that they were entertaining.

The train was almost two hours late. Sarita stepped out of the train with two bags, bhabhi and four-year-old Lali in tow. She scanned the platform until her eyes spotted the middle-aged man in black trousers and a white shirt that had not been tucked in. 'Hari bhaiyya,' she yelled.

Once they had loaded their luggage onto the tonga, Hari asked, 'How did you recognize me after all these years?'

'Simple,' Sarita smiled. 'Kumud Didi showed us a picture of the haveli and all of you taken during your daughter's *naamkaran*. I am carrying it with me. How is everybody?'

'Bua,' Lali piped in, pointing to the horses pulling the tonga, 'where do they sleep?' Everybody laughed.

'Children,' Hari said laughing, 'they think of the weirdest things!' The tonga slowly weaved its way out of the crowded streets of Agra towards the university.

'It is such a relief to get away from the crowds. Oh, this is so beautiful, but I don't remember it at all,' said Sarita, shaking her head.

'Well, how could you? You were only a little bit older than Lali here,' said Hari, grinning at the three guests.

The tonga pulled up at the haveli where Hari's children were swinging on the iron gates. They let out a shout, 'Ma! Chhotima! Barima! They have come, they have come!' Manasi ran down the steps to help the guests out of the tonga. She held out a hand to help Lali climb up to the house.

But Lali shrugged it away and straight up the front steps without anybody's help. She stood at the door of the long front room. 'Mummy,' she yelled, 'there was a table here!' She stood pointing accusingly at an empty corner of the room which had a staircase running through it to the first floor. In the other corner were a divan and some chairs.

Nobody paid any attention to Lali except for her mother, Preeti. 'What table, beti?' she said, gently leading her towards the rest of the family. 'How can you say such things?'

Lali plonked herself next to Giridhar. 'Who is that?' she asked, pointing to Manasi.

'She is my wife,' Hari said with an amused look. 'The way you talk, it is as if you know everyone here, except for Manasi,' he said.

Lali did not say anything but jumped off the sofa and walked around the room, peering under tables and out of windows. She then went and climbed onto Rameswar's lap—to his great surprise, as most children did not take to him at first sight.

'When do your exams begin?' Rameswar asked Sarita.

'Monday,' Sarita smiled back.

'Well, that means you only have tomorrow free. We shall have to take you to the Taj after you finish your papers. You can't really go without seeing the Taj,' he said.

Sarita nodded. 'No no, I want to see the Taj and on a full-moon night, Rameswar bhaiyya. I think the day after my exams will be the perfect day as it is Purnima. Oh, and Kumud Didi has sent gifts for all of you,' she said. 'Bhabhi, where is the bag?'

'All that can be done later,' Lakshmi said, guiding the guests up the stairs to their room. Chhotu had finished putting up the curtains and was now waiting outside the room. Lali skipped up the stairs and ran towards Chhotu who instinctively picked her up.

'You have a very friendly child,' said Lakshmi. 'You would hardly think she just met us.'

Her mother smiled. She was a bit surprised at Lali's familiarity with the family. She was a shy child and rarely spoke to outsiders but today . . .

'Mummy, what has happened to this room? It was much bigger,' Lali said, stepping inside. Chhotu and Lakshmi stared at each other.

'Please don't pay any attention to her,' Preeti said, taking her daughter into the folds of her sari. 'She says these things which don't mean anything. She was also mentioning something about a table in the room below . . .'

Chhotu started to say something but Lakshmi interrupted him saying, 'Table! No, there was no table but this room used to be a bigger one. We split it into two but that was a long time ago. How did you know, beti?'

Lali said nothing, only smiled at Chhotu.

Chhotu's face had gone white. How did this girl know so much? And, he thought to himself, Lakshmiji was wrong. There used to be a table at the corner of the room downstairs where Mataji would keep her *paandaan*. But how did this girl know that?

'The toilets are in the courtyard, if you need to go,' Lakshmi said as she left the guests to unpack.

'I want to go,' said Lali, walking out of the room.

'Come, I will take you,' Lakshmi held out her hand.

But Lali refused help. She ran down and found her way out of the kitchen into the courtyard. The toilets, five in a row, were at the end of the courtyard. Lali walked past some of the children who were playing in the courtyard and started to unlock the door on the extreme right.

'No, don't go there, that is not used,' shouted one of the kids. But Lali did not listen. She unlatched the door and walked right in.

Once she came out, she walked round the courtyard and then came to the centre where the kids were playing.

'There was a tree here,' she said.

The kids giggled. Sarla, who had been hanging out some clothes, smiled and took her by her hand. 'Tree! We never had a tree here,' she said.

Giridhar, who was sitting in a corner, came up to the girl. He got down on his haunches and very softly asked her, 'Where was the tree?'

'Here,' Lali said, jumping on a square that was right in the centre of the courtyard. Giridhar's face paled and he yelled for his wife. 'Lakshmi!'

She came as fast as she could at the sound of her husband's voice. Hari and Vidya who were in the living room also heard their brother's shout and came out. 'Lakshmi, where was the neem tree?'

The look on her husband's face set Lakshmi's heart pounding. 'Why? Right where Lali is.'

'Dada, what is the matter?' Hari asked Giridhar.

Giridhar turned to all of them and said, 'I have been watching this girl right from the time she asked about Manasi. She seems to know everything about us and the house. First, she walks out and heads right for Maji's toilet which has not been used for years. Then she surveys the courtyard and asks about the neem tree which was cut down years ago. I think it must be at least six or seven years ago.'

Lakshmi told them about the room at the top of the stairs, her voice trembling with an unknown fear.

Lali had wandered away. When Giridhar and the rest of the family came looking for her, they found her standing near the well, sobbing. Lakshmi could bear it no more. 'Who is she? Why is she crying at this spot?' Giridhar and Vidya ran towards her.

'What is this? This temple was not there!' Lali asked between her sobs.

By this time the children had called the entire household outside into the garden. Chhotu too had joined the group. Hari turned around to face Preeti, who was completely bewildered about her daughter's behaviour, 'Bhabhi, please ask her why she is crying?'

But Lali refused to reply and continued to weep.

Giridhar was the first to pick her up. 'Maji, you have come back!'

It was clear to all of them that this could be the only explanation. She knew things about the house that only Mataji would have, she recognized everyone but Manasi, the only bahu who Mataji had not brought into the house, and she sobbed near the well where she had lost her firstborn.

There was no stopping the family after that. Chhotu fell at her feet, crying, 'Mataji! Mataji!' Hari and Rameswar rushed to the market to bring home her favourite sweets. Meera ran to the kitchen to cook rajma, a dish that Mataji loved. Lakshmi didn't quite know what to do so she took her to Manasi, the only bahu that she had not seen, and asked her to bless her.

Lali's mother grew restless and grave. She did not want to lose her normal four-year-old daughter to this strange new-found identity. After a couple of days, during which Lali was feted and feasted, her mother took her back home. She apologized to the family but said that she had to do this for the sake of her daughter.

Lali is now a grown woman with her own children. She does not remember much about her past life—but she does remember visiting the haveli.

ARUNDHUTI DASGUPTA

her grandfather's Voice

There is a thin line that divides reverence for the dead from an unhealthy clinging to their presence, often seen in the way the dear departed's possessions are preserved till they virtually become a shrine.

Everybody knew the Haldars. In fact, in a town like Jabalpur, everybody knew everybody. They also knew everything about everybody. So naturally, the entire town knew about the evening ritual at the Haldar home.

And it was this evening ritual that Ajay Haldar was hurrying home for. With one end of his crisp white dhoti tucked into the pocket of his kurta, he marched briskly down the narrow streets of Jabalpur. He stopped at the Galgala Bazaar to buy a fresh garland of flowers. Rows and rows of women sat with baskets of vegetables, fruits and flowers, and shopkeepers sprinkled water in front of their shops. The sizzle of water on dry earth and its unique fragrance filled the market.

At home, Ajay's wife Purnima and eight-year-old daughter Piali too were preparing for the evening ceremony. The special offering for the day had been cooked and a bunch of incense sticks was kept ready for Baba.

Baba was eighty-year-old Debendranath Haldar who in death, as in life, ruled over his son's life. Dead for almost four years now, his photograph had taken his place in the Haldar household. And every evening, the family of three gathered to garland him with bright orange marigolds, burn some incense sticks and offer him the day's special delicacy cooked by Purnima.

The photograph occupied the most important spot in the Haldar household. Large and grim, it sat on an old teak table that was once used as a study table. With its carved legs and a border etched with tiny tribal dancing men and women, the table was almost as imposing as the photograph itself. And the two seemed to take up more than just the corner that they occupied in the large Haldar drawing room.

Ajay washed his feet under the tap in the courtyard before entering the house. He bowed low before the photograph and yelled, 'Purnima, Piali, where is everybody? Baba can't keep waiting, you know.'

They hurried in with a gleaming bowl of hot *payesh* and a plate of rasgollas. The three of them bowed low before the photograph. Hands folded, they began their daily conversation with the photograph. Ajay Haldar narrated a couple of incidents from the office and Purnima told her father-in-law's photograph about her trip to the Marble Rocks on the outskirts of Jabalpur. Piali was quiet.

A slight breeze blew through the room. The February breeze always carried a bit of chill with it. Piali shivered and yawned.

'The fish yesterday was very bad. Go and tell Karim Fishwala that we will not buy from him if he gives us such bad fish,' a booming voice thundered.

Ajay and Purnima Haldar went pale. 'Baba!' they shrieked together, tripping over to touch his feet in the photograph. 'Piali, touch his feet!' Purnima whispered.

But Piali was doing no such thing. Her parents watched aghast as their daughter spoke to them in her grandfather's voice. 'So Ajay, why do you let that rogue Ghosal Babu order you around so much? And I am tired of these flowers—make a garland of the white and orange *shiuli* flowers that cover our courtyard at this time of the year—and why don't you keep the radio on all through the day, like I used to?' Piali drummed her fingers on the large armchair that she sat on as she spoke.

Ajay Haldar did not know what to do. That his daughter should address him so was scandalous. But then, was that his daughter or was that his father? He turned to his wife for guidance.

Purnima Haldar had sat down on the floor. 'Baba,' she said covering her head and touching her daughter's feet, 'Baba, we are indeed very lucky to have you back.' Nudging her husband, she whispered, 'Go, go, touch his feet.' A bewildered Ajay Haldar fell at his daughter's feet as directed by his wife.

Piali's transformation was complete. She hobbled around the house like her grandfather. She walked to the cupboard behind the door where his walking stick was usually kept and then leaned on it to move around the house. She asked for a cup of tea and then spat it out, furious, 'Who has made this tea? Have you forgotten I don't take sugar? Take this sugar syrup away and bring me another cup!'

This continued day after day, evening after evening. And it always started with a yawn. Piali would stretch and yawn and then speak, walk and behave like her grandfather. This lasted a couple of hours, after which Piali would yawn once again and drop into deep sleep. When she awoke, she had no memory of all that had happened and went about her eight-year-old life as usual.

Once a close friend dropped by. She did not know about Piali's evening changeover and was shocked to hear the girl reprimand her, 'Speak to me with the respect that is due to my age.' The friend advised the family to wean their daughter out of this evening trance as it could be dangerous, but the family paid no heed.

Why should they? They were ecstatic.

The entire Haldar clan poured in from all over the city for a chat with the great and late Debendranath Haldar. And soon old friends, acquaintances and even complete strangers from all over Jabalpur began dropping by to see the old man. However, Piali's health began to suffer.

A few months later Piali fell very ill. Several doctors were consulted but they failed to diagnose what it was that kept her so unwell. Matters got to such a state that Purnima Haldar could take it no more. Tears in her eyes and a plate of steaming hot mutton samosas in her hand, she appealed to her father-in-law one evening. 'Please tell us what to do. I don't need to tell you but still, your granddaughter is becoming so weak and so ill. Show us what to do.'

'You have to let me go. As long as all of you hold me back, Piali won't get well,' Piali said firmly in her grandfather's voice. Purnima Haldar was mystified. She could not comprehend why her father-in-law, dead for four years, needed to be set free.

'All of you have never really let me die in peace. I have been consulted with, complained to and fed with delicacies every day. I must say that I enjoyed it but this has trapped my spirit in the world of the living. It lives in that shallow, dirty pond behind the house. I started coming into Piali's body because she, poor child, is very weak. She will not get any stronger and nor will her health improve as long as I continue visiting you through her.'

'Tell us, Baba, what must we do? We want our daughter well. We will do anything you say,' Purnima said between her sobs.

The prescription as set out by her father-in-law was simple. Clean the pond, stop seeking him out for everything and set out a feast for the people of Jabalpur. He also specified a couple of things that he would like to eat before he left. That done, he left as quietly as he had come.

ARUNDHUTI DASGUPTA

the greedy imp

A noble Raja, great and good
And mostly very wise,
Often shed his courtly clothes
And walked in simple guise.

Once upon a sunny day
When he had walked some miles,
He laid himself beneath a tree
To rest himself awhile.

As he slept, a wicked imp
Who lived up in the tree
Said, 'Here's a chance to have some fun!
Free passage, just for me!'

He rose up in a grey-black cloud
And stretched up to the sky,
Then made himself a tiny gnat
Invisible to the eye.

The King, asleep beneath the tree,
Did not stir or sigh,
As through his nose the creature flew
Within the man to hide.

Now in the kingly abdomen,
Residing in full state,
The imp began to feast upon
All the Raja ate.

So while the imp grew sated quite,
The King grew weak and ill.
The doctors could not cure him
Though they tried with herb and pill.

The Minister was a clever man,
And guessed there may be more
To this than meets the mind or eye,
Than anybody saw.

He called a priest, who chanted twice
And spake both loud and clear,
'A wicked imp doth plague our lord
But there's no need to fear.

'The imp is greedy, and can be
Removed within a trice.
Give him the choicest morsels
Of what he thinks is nice.'

The Minister observed the King,
And saw he ate a vat
Of little yellow bananas
In half a minute flat.

He had this vat filled up again
With tempting yellow fruit.
The imp could smell them all the way,
He knew it tasted good.

'Bring that here,' the Raja roared,
But he was not obeyed,
For the Minister in his wisdom
Had this order stayed.

'The vat,' he said, 'remains out here
In the palace grounds.
Our royal lord must stay inside,
The doors are locked all round.'

The Raja in his hunger raved,
He roared and wept and begged.
He stumbled to the window pane,
His face was strained and red.

The imp, unable to resist,
Restrained and locked and barred,
Flew out again into the vat
And all the fruit devoured.

The palace guards, they seized the chance
And slammed the lid on tight.
The Raja's troubles were duly cured
And all was put to right.

SHAIONTONI BOSE

the first Wife

This story was told to me by my *jathaima*, my father's older brother's wife. When she came to our home as a young bride, she knew nothing of her husband's first wife, or her attachment to her home and her possessions.

The first wife had been a beautiful woman who spent hours in front of her mirror. Her hobby was to have jewellery reset and remodelled, a common pastime among affluent Bengali women of the nineteenth century. Unfortunately she had a harsh voice which did not match her good looks, so she rarely spoke above a whisper. She had been a very spoilt child, used to getting her own way, and found life in our family—which was not poor, but not royally rich either—rather constricting. She died a rather sad death, having been infected with typhoid, a dreaded killer in those days. Her last words were 'My jewellery . . .'

When my jathaima sat all decked out in her bridal finery, she felt a hard push and a pull at her *shaatnori,* the seven rows of pearls which had been her husband's gift to her. Shy and frightened, she said nothing, and the blessing of the bride by the family elders proceeded. As her mother-in-law came forward to put the thick gold bangles on her, they flew out of her hand and landed on the floor. They were quickly changed for another pair for it was, of course, considered inauspicious to pick them up and use them.

Then came the family photograph, a novelty in those days. The photographer hid behind his black hood, and took an age to focus while the subjects kept their faces in stiff smiles. My poor jathaima managed a tearful smile, but again she felt a cold breath behind her. She had been told to be absolutely still so she made no movement but sat in frozen terror. There was great excitement when the pictures were delivered; they were the first photographs in that family. But who was the extra person in the photograph? Behind the bride and groom stood a shadowy figure with no features but seven rows of pearls around the spectral throat.

Months passed by. My jathaima became accustomed to the sudden tugs at her sari, the milk spilling over while she boiled it, the fish burning to cinders within minutes of being put into the pan—and then one day, while she was cutting the vegetables, a huge bell-metal platter got stuck to her back. The poor girl could hardly move, and no amount of pulling and tugging could move it a fraction.

The oldest and sagest member of the family suggested the help of an ojha or exorcist. This exorcist lived in a village near Calcutta and came the next day. Meanwhile my gentle and soft-spoken jathaima was shrieking the most filthy obscenities in a loud harsh voice, accusing the family of robbing her, of torturing her, and anything else that would bring them dishonour.

Enter the ojha with his paraphernalia. He intoned his magic formulae and commanded, 'Now lift this bucket up with your teeth.' Sure enough, the delicate young woman took an iron bucket, ran a few paces and fell down. As she fell, the metal platter rolled off her back with a terrific clatter.

'How will we know you have gone?' asked the ojha, and a huge branch of a sturdy full-grown tree fell with a giant crack. 'Now she is free!' said the ojha, and jathaima crumpled down in a dead faint. She remembered nothing of what had happened in the two days when she bore the platter on her back, and from that day on, she was never haunted any more.

BUNNY GUPTA

Strong ties

*This story was told by my great-grandmother, Didimoni.
It is part of the tradition of ghost stories where a mother's
love for her child is seen as harmful.*

I am an old woman now. I have forgotten what it is to walk briskly down to the bazaar for vegetables or wake up in the morning without an ache in some part of my body. But I am not bitter. I can walk, read, eat and do most of my daily chores myself and my mind, despite my ninety-odd years, is still active and alert.

Any time I feel the burden of my old bones weighing me down I think of Monideepa Chatterjee. My daughter-in-law's mother. She is younger than I am but look at her!—she can't even go to the toilet on her own. *Baba re baba*, I am very scared of falling into such a state. Hai Gopal, I hope I don't live to see such bad days.

'Gobindor ma, o Gobindor ma.'

I know she is there in that small courtyard behind the kitchen washing the pots and pans. But that wretched woman won't answer. She thinks I am going to pile more work on her. All of them are the same, they don't want to do any work but they want to take home the money.

Where has she kept my supari cracker? I can't have my paan and that wretch thinks I am just another old woman raving and ranting. These people. *Oof!* Who would have thought that I, Karunabati Sen, would have to suffer like this?

When I came to this house as a young bride, the stairs were never silent. Servants ran up and down doing our bidding. Whatever we wanted, we had only to ask and it would be done for us. Sejo was such a shy one, she was too scared to shout out loud for Khushi, that little girl who oiled and tied up our hair. I was shy too but only for a few months. Once I got to know my mother-in-law, Sasuri Ma, better, I was running about this house as I did in my father's house.

And there was such a lot of work to do in those days. Lighting the lamps once the sun set, getting the coals ready for the incense, cleaning the puja room every morning and evening, and then getting the meals ready. My Sasuri Ma would not touch her food if it had been cooked by anybody but me. I was young then and I could do all this without any help but look at me today, I am at the mercy of people who don't care.

'Gobindor ma, o Gobindor ma.' Still no answer. I shall have to get up. My leg is all swollen up but why should that wretch care? She only wants her money at the end of the month. I can shout myself hoarse but why should she care?

There was a time when our word was considered to be the last word. No arguing, no talking back, nothing. They listened to us. . . . Where is that supari cracker?

Karuna, what are you rambling on and on about! Have you forgotten? You say they listened, they did not always. If they did, today, Sejo Bou's son would have been alive.

Thakur thakur! What am I saying? My mind seems to lose itself nowadays. Sejo Bou. How could I forget: Those nights were as if they would never end and how scared we all were. And then within a fortnight, that tiny child too. It still sends shivers down my spine.

It had been a hard winter, I remember. First, Ma lost her hearing due to some wrong medicines that had been given her for her arthiritis, and then Baba took to his bed with paralysis. And I had just had Moni, my firstborn, whom we called Charulata. Ma was disappointed that my firstborn wasn't a boy but Moni's father would have none of that. He was very proud of his little daughter and said that she was his *chokher moni*: the pearl of his eyes.

A month after Moni came Sejo's son. What was his name?

Look at me! Age has eaten away my memories. I can't even remember the name of the boy I nursed at my breast.

Sona, of course. That's it, that is what we called him, the poor fellow did not even get a *bhalo naam*. If he were here today, he would have been as old as my Moni and probably as happy.

Moni's father would have been so happy to see his daughter today, married to a husband who has brought fame to his entire family, and her children are all doing so well. One has even become a doctor, what more could we want?

There I go again. No wonder Ranjana and Purnima, my daughters-in-law, don't want to come and sit with me. My mind keeps wandering and if there is someone to listen to me, my mouth doesn't stop chattering. Now, it does not even matter if there is no one, I seem to be very happy talking to myself! These people probably think I am going senile. But then, I know better.

I loved Sona like my own. Poor fellow, lost his mother before he could even know what a mother meant to a child. He looked so much like Sejo, her eyes seemed to shine through his tiny face. I remember the night he was born. Sejo was too weak to be taken into the room kept aside for such purposes so we got the midwife to come to the bedroom. That bedroom at the far end of the balcony on the top floor which is now used by Amar and Ranjana. If I told them all that has gone on there, I wonder whether they would be able to spend another night there . . . But who am I to tell them?

Anyway, I remember that was a noisy night. The wind shrieked and howled through our windows, the doors kept slamming shut and Sasuri Ma was particularly angry that day and was shouting herself to tears in the room next to where Sejo lay. I don't remember now why Ma was so angry but I do remember the fear on Sejo's face. Her small face was white and her eyes seemed to be dropping out of her head.

She clasped my hand tighter and tighter as her pain grew worse through the night. She was also running a fever, poor thing. She was so frail and little, always melting into the shadows. We would often hunt the house for her while she would be sitting in a corner in the same room. Some days, she would sit in the dark without bothering to light the lamp in the room and Sasuri Ma would be furious. 'It brings evil into the house, this sitting in the dark with your hair untied! Hasn't your mother taught you anything at all?' she would shriek at Sejo who rarely said a word. Head down and covered with her aanchal, she would stand in front of Ma listening to every word being hurled at her. She never argued, never glared back and, unlike me and Mejo, never once complained about Sasuri Ma and her ways.

The only time I heard her speak out aloud was when she was going to have Sona. She died two days after Sona was born and the poor fellow was left motherless without anyone to nurse him. I took him to my breast the same night as his mother died. The house mourned for his mother but, frankly, I was more worried about him.

The thirteen days were not over yet and I told that little tramp, Khushi, never to leave the child alone for even a minute. I remember my mother used to say that a motherless child has the most to fear from its own mother. Especially one as small and helpless as Sona. 'A mother's soul does not get *mukti* easily. If she dies in childbirth, her soul is torn with torment until it can gather the child unto itself. You see, we mothers think that no one can love and care for our children as we can,' my mother would tell me.

Ask any old woman like me in this city and she will tell you the same. A mother cannot let go of her child, worried as she always is about his well-being, especially if she dies in childbirth. But who wants to talk to old people nowadays! Everyone is happy to do what he or she thinks best and makes faces when I try and give them any advice.

Karuna, you are letting yourself get too bitter now. You were not like this. Get a hold on yourself.

Yes, yes. I must not let myself feel sad. Whatever years I have left, I must not let them get blurred by anger or bitterness. I read the Gita every day, pray and sing to my Gods every day, yet why do I get this way?

Anyway as I was saying, a mother who dies in childbirth is

unwilling to go without the child she has left behind. I knew that
and everybody else knew that and still . . . That entire day is framed
in my mind like a picture. I can't seem to erase it and neither can
I hold back the tears any more.

Poor boy, just ten days old. I had nursed him throughout the
day and he was still hungry. He was running a low fever and had
been crying incessantly. Such a quiet child otherwise, but that day
he would not stop wailing.

Maybe he knew.

I was sitting by him all day but then Moni's father came and
said he wanted to hold his child for a while before sitting down
for dinner. So I had to go.

I did not like leaving the boy alone. I would have taken him
along but he had just quietened down and seemed to be sleeping
peacefully. So I called Khushi, that irresponsible wretch . . . 'Don't
worry, Didi, I won't move from here. What else do I have to do? I
will sit here and watch Sona,' she said.

I still remember everything very clearly. I must have been gone
ten minutes. I left Moni with her father and then went to the
bathroom. When I came out, I felt an inexplicable fear clamping
my throat and my chest. I rushed down the stairs, my sari and my
hair flying, to the room where Sona lay sleeping.

The room was just as I had left it, only it looked darker than
usual, as if someone had put out one of the lamps in the room.
Khushi was not there but Sona was sleeping quite peacefully. I felt
a little foolish at having rushed back like this. I was about to pull
my hair back into a knot before Sasuri Ma saw me in this state
when . . . I don't why but I suddenly turned to the extreme corner
of the room.

There she was. With her arms hugging her knees, she was
huddled into the edge of the wall where it met the door. The red
border of her aanchal was glowing and she, with her big eyes, was
staring at me.

My voice stuck in my throat and my hands seemed paralysed,
when she just got up and walked. As silently as she had been sitting
there, she stepped out of the door, leaving its curtains flapping in

the wind. Her back to me, she stepped out into the courtyard and within no time at all was one with the darkness of the night.

I knew then that we had lost Sona. And sure enough, the next morning he was gone. The doctors did say it was something terribly complicated but I did not believe them. I knew then as I know now that Sejo had taken him away. She did not trust any of us with her child and so she took him with her.

I cried, I shouted at Khushi and cursed myself for not having been more careful. But in the end it was all in vain. Khushi apologized and continued to work in the house until she was married off, and the rest of us just went on with our lives, our husbands and our children. Only Sejo and her son were not with us.

ARUNDHUTI DASGUPTA

afterword

The Weretiger contains only a fraction of stories we discovered once we started looking around for tales of the fantastic, the unreal, of things that just could not have happened. We talked to people about folktales and folk beliefs, asked others for their stories, consulted old *Gazettes*—a veritable goldmine—and collections of ancient myths and other books, and dug into history ourselves. What we came up with was much richer, more diverse than we had ever expected.

At the beginning, our goal was imprecisely defined: we merely set out to collect some Indian ghost stories. Our unconscious model was, perhaps, the innumerable collections of ghost stories that we read in English—all about haunted mansions and clanking chains and ghosts who carried their heads under their arms. We were soon to learn some home truths about our homespun tales.

First, we found that everybody ad a story, or knew someone who had a story.

Second, unlike the ghost typical to the western, or perhaps more accurately, the Christian world, we discovered that in the orders of the Indian supernatural, ghosts—the soul of a deceased individual which hung around close to his place of existence as a person—were merely one of several diverse kinds. Parashuram, the author of some hilarious ghost stories in Bengali, explained the difference of 'Hindu ghosts' and 'Christian ghosts' in relation to the two different concepts of heaven and hell. Atheists of both kinds, of course, have no soul and so when they die, become 'oxygen, hydrogen, nitrogen and other gases'.

> Sahebs . . . do not have rebirth . . . they become ghosts and congregate in a huge waiting room. After waiting for an eternity, they face the Last Judgement . . . some of the ghosts gain the shelter of an everlasting heaven and the rest go to hell. Though the sahebs enjoy a great deal of freedom when they are alive, it is greatly curbed when they are ghosts . . .

As Hindus believe in 'rebirth, heaven, hell, karma, nirvana, everything', when they die, they first becomes ghosts, and are free to live wherever they choose and keep their connections with the human world. This state lasts until they are reborn, which may be anywhere between two days later to three centuries later. Sometimes ghosts are sent to heaven (to enjoy themselves) and hell (to lighten the burden of their sins), just for a change of scene and to meet other people.

It is widely believed that those who have been unable to extricate themselves from the entwining lures of life—perhaps a house, a child, a loved one or ever the taste of good food—become ghosts. They seem to be materialistic to their insubstantial core. Perhaps because its inhabitants are so deeply connected to the *samsar*, the ghost world seems to carry over the features of the 'real'. Ambrose Bierce, author of several spooky tales, suggests that the supernatural 'are the outward and visible sign of an inward fear'. This seems only partially true: Ghosts and spirits are of various kinds, and not all are necessarily frightful or frightening.

The spirits of the departed like to keep in touch with the living, to communicate messages or fulfil desires. One popular method is through possession, as seen in 'Her Grandfather's Voice', and in many actual incidents. According to the psychoanalyst Sudhir Kakkar, while the hysterical personality is frequently the same worldwide, manifestations of spirits during the period of possession is usually culture-specific. According to Kakkar, 'The rich mythological world, peopled by many gods, goddesses and other supernatural beings, in which the Indian child grows up, his early experiences of multiple caretakers, all contribute to the imagery of possessing spirits.' As a result, the hysteric personality is perhaps uniquely aligns itself with 'the prevailing "myth of passivity" of its culture. I am the "passive" vehicle of gods, or of the devil . . . which make me do these things, not my own desires.'

In the nineteenth century, Reverend Lal Behari De wrote a remarkable 'brief account of the different classes of Bengali ghosts, their habits and modes of appearance, or strictly speaking, of Bengali-Hindu ghosts, for of Muhammadan ghosts, usually called *mamdos*, who are regarded as infinitely more mischievous than Hindu ghosts, I do not at present enquire':

> Of Bengali ghosts, that is the spirits of Bengali men and women, there is a great variety; but there are five classes which generally make their appearance, if not in cities and towns—for they seem altogether to have left the seats of enlightenment and civilization—at least in the villages of Bengal. The first and most honourable class of ghosts and those which pass by the name of bramhadaityas, or the spirits of departed Brahmans. They generally take up their abode in the branches of the *gaya asvatha*, the most sacred species of the *ficus religiosa*, and also in the branches of the holy *sriphal*. Unlike other ghosts, they do not eat all sorts of food, but only those which are considered religiously clean, They never appear, like other ghosts, to frighten men, such an object being beneath their dignity. They are for the most part inoffensive, never doing harm to benighted travellers, nor entering into the bodies of living men or woemn; but should their dignity be contemned, or their *sanctum sanatorium* be invaded or desecrated, their rage knows no bounds, and the neck of the offender is ruthlessly wrung and broken—a species of vengeance to which they are somewhat partial. Hence a Hindu will hardly ever climb up the *ficus cordifolia* except in dire necessity.
>
> Another class of ghosts, and they are by far the most numerous class, are simply called bhutas, that is, spirits. They are the spirits of departed Kshatriyas, Vaishyas, and Sudras. They are tall as palmyra trees, generally thin, and very black. They usually live on trees of every description, excepting those, of course, on which the Brahmanical ghosts have taken up their abode. At night,

especially at midnight—the hour and power of darkness—they go about in villages and fields, frightening night-walkers and belated travellers. They prefer dirty places to clean, and have never been seen in the precincts of the temples of the gods. They are always stark naked. They are rather fond of women, whom they usually possess. They eat rice and all sorts of human food, but their favourite dish is fish. Their partiality for fish is so well known, that a large bribe is necessary to induce a Bengali peasant to go at night from one place to another with some quantity of fish in his hand. The best way to defend one's self from the attack of a bhuta, is to repeat the names of the gods and goddesses, especially of Kali, Durga and Shiva, the last one being named *bhutanath*, or the lord of ghosts. Another mode of preventing the attack of a ghost is to carry with you a stick or rod of iron, a metal of which spirits are, somehow or other, greatly afraid. Hence Hindu peasants, who require in some seasons of the year to go out to the fields at night, carry with them rods of iron. All ghosts, owing to the peculiar conformation of their mouth, speak through the nose.

The bhutas are all male ghosts; but there are two classes of female ghosts, called petnis and *sankhchihnis*. Of the petnis not much is known, except that they are terribly dirty—the stench of their bodies when near producing violent nausea in human beings; that they are very lascivious, trying to waylay benighted passengers for the gratification of their lusts; and that intercourse with them is sure to end in the destruction of both the body and the soul. Sankhchihnis or *sankhachurnis*, so called, in the opinion of some demonologists, because they put on clothes as white as *sankha* (conch shell), and in that of others, because they are fond of breaking conch shells to pieces, are female ghosts, not so filthy as petnis, but equally dangerous. They usually stand at the dead of night at the food of trees, and look like sheets of cloth as white as any fuller can make them.

Another class of ghosts are the *skandhahatas*, so called from the circumstance that their heads have been cut off from above their shoulders. These headless ghosts are probably the most terrible of the whole set, as they have never been known to spare any human being with whom they have come in contact. They generally dwell in low moist lands, outside a village, in bogs and fens, and go about in the dark, rolling on the ground, with their huge arms stretched out. Certain death awaits the peasant who falls within the folds of those gigantic arms.

The carryover of the caste system and religious affiliations into the next world is particularly fascinating. Because of their close ties with the world of the living, these spirits interfere in the affairs of men and women quite cheerfully, and not with malignancy, as the stories like 'The Helpful Spirit' reveal.

In *The Folklore of Bombay* (1924) R.E. Enthoven writes that there are three classes of churails: *poshi*, *soshi* and *toshi*. Those women 'who have enjoyed before death the pleasures of this world to their satisfaction' become poshi churails, and take care of the children and 'render good service to their widowed husbands'. Women who were 'persecuted beyond endurance by the members of their families' become soshi churails. 'They dry up the blood of men and prove very troublesome to the members of the family.' Those women who were strongly attached to their husbands become toshi churails and 'bring great pleasure to their husbands in this life'. As such stories were usually narrated by the women in the community, it is possible to see them as an effective way of intimidating dominating mothers-in-law and overbearing husbands!

Yet there are other spirits that coexist with ghosts—the jungle spirits of the forests in remote Nagaland or Assam, the kudpalbhoot of Mangalore, the yakshis and gandharas of Kerala, and the rakshasas found almost everywhere in India. Some of these have special names and have evolved into Hindu deities, like Mumbadevi in 'Yeo Ka?'. Others have remained part of folklore and tribal superstitions, like the Bongas of Santhal traditions. Many of these stories live on in oral tales which communicate the chill of fear on a dark moonless night, when the air is still and the world seems to be breathless in anticipation of the unnameable. Then, just to name something can make it appear. Some of these older spirits seem to be jealous of their territories and warn off trespassers into their territory. The Gurkha Hill Council, the autonomous government of the Darjeeling district, is an example of an official body which is aware of that the spirits of nature can make their wrath felt in landslides and other disasters. Therefore, the Council conducts a puja to propitiate one such spirit—all with full government sanction and audits done in triplicate! Similar practices are found in the Himalayan foothills of Himachal Pradesh.

In many stories, men and women are transformed into tigers, bears, snakes and even the ferocious wild jungle dogs of the south. Though traditions vary from region to region, these stories reflect the power these animals have over the human population, and the fear they cause.

In some areas, trees and even inanimate objects are host to human souls. Young girls were married to trees, rather than remain unmarried. If a man wished to marry after the death of his wife, he was advised to wed a tree before marrying a new wife so that the dead wife's jealous wrath would be directed at the tree, not the woman. There are stories that describe the painful and lingering deaths of the tree-wives. It seems that as far as the supernatural is concerned, there is little or no distinction between animate and inanimate, human and non-human, the spirit and the flesh. There is an inclusiveness in these stories which does not recognize boundaries, exclusions, the superiority of human over non-human in these notions of the supernatural forces.

Men and women seemed to need the supernatural for various uses. Ghosts make death seem a continuation of life, and thus, just that little bit less terrifying to us mortals, but supernatural stories also seem to be a process of remembering the past. Thus stories abound of the cruel indigo planter, the vicious landlord who comes back to haunt the villagers, or the victim of wrong come back to claim some form of justice. Thus wrongs are righted through the agency of the supernatural, or wrongs are remembered in tales that are told in communities who had suffered unbearable pain. We read and collected a number of stories from the times of indigo plantations and the 1857 War of Independence, a few of which are included in the collection. All of them show a consistent pattern wherein the nationality of the narrator determines who is portrayed as the villain: the cruel treatment of the rulers by the mutineers, or the cruel and unjust judges and army sahibs who hunted down the poor sepoy. Ghost stories, like history itself often is, seem to be constructed to fit the ideology of the teller.

Ghost stories also function as a narration of community memory. 'Why Women Are Witches' may be read as a tale of the shift in the Santhal society from a matriarchal society to a patriarchal one. This does not always apply only to the past—stories like 'The 11.43 to Nowhere' show how contemporary memory reinvents the ghastly death of woman commuter on the infamous Mumbai local trains.

The supernatural can be held responsible for the problems that one is beset by, a spirit may be disgruntled and so create mischief in one's life as in 'The Temple Spirits.' A proper propitiation of the spirit is needed and things will be better as they do in 'The Legend of the Leaping Dolphins.' Similarly, the supernatural can make possible the unthinkable—Raaghu can marry the girl he loves, thanks to the kudpalbhoot, there may be unlimited supplies of food, or your most secret wishes can come true.

The supernatural can also provide more mundane security for one. In the inexhaustible store of knowledge, the *Gazetteer*, we learned that in what is now the Bihar-Uttar Pradesh belt, one could buy ghosts in bottles made of bamboo stems in the marketplace. If you had, for example, a plot of land and your crops were being stolen, and you wanted a security guard, then you could buy such a ghost. Then you would have to call the local purohit or priest to perform some rituals and let the ghost out of the bottle and take its residence in a tree. It would then guard your crops from thieves. Of course, you had to be sure to invite all your neighbours to the ceremony, so that word would soon spread about the ghostly watchman in the tree. Apparently, the watchmen were very efficient!

But these beliefs are not confined only to the past. An article in a leading national magazines documents the creation of the AIDS Amma temple. Young people and newlyweds from the area come here to receive education about AIDS, and after performing certain common rituals are given condoms instead of *prasad*—to ward off the AIDS 'demon'.

Oral histories and folklore also reveal the processes of fusions of social beliefs. Djinns, for example, are found in local stories on the west coast of India and probably were imported by the early sea merchants from west Asia, along with sugar, gems and other goods. According to the Koran, djinns are a separate order of being, also created by God—'He created man from potter's clay and the djinn from smokeless fire . . .' Yet in Indian folklore, they are seen as no different from other forms of the supernatural: the British researcher R.E. Enthoven classifies the djinn as a minor evil spirit at the same level as *prets*, churails and *pishachas*, seemingly oblivious to the differences.

Islam does not believe in ghosts, as we were admonished very severely by the caretaker of a beautiful Imambara on the banks of the Ganges, which seemed to be a wonderful place for spirits to reside. But the strange, the eerie and the unexplained are not circumscribed by religious strictures, as the narrator admits in 'The Song of the Hunter'. Djinns begin to act like indigenous spirits and take possession of innocent men and women and need to be driven out by ojhas, who may be Hindu or Muslim. Similarly, ancient customs found in tribal times have not been erased by the advent of modernity. In the northeast, anthropomorphic beliefs coexist with the anthropocentric beliefs of Christianity.

In Tripura, it is still common for people to gather and participate in *bhut chalaan*, that is calling on the spirits—just for a chat.

We hope that this collection was successful in reflecting some of the great variety and inventiveness that the supernatural holds in a society like ours where the past mingles and merges with the future, where superstitions and cyber-crimes coexist, where the heterogeneity of cultures make our time and place in history unique.